MARILYN

R. S. GARDNER

This is a work of fiction. Names, characters, places, and incidents are products of the author's imagination or are used fictitiously and are not to be construed as real. Any resemblance to actual events, locations, organizations, or person, living or dead, is entirely coincidental.

WCP

World Castle Publishing, LLC
Pensacola, Florida

Copyright © R. S. Gardner 2014
Print ISBN: 9781629891460
eBook ISBN: 9781629891477
First Edition World Castle Publishing, LLC, October 1, 2014
http://www.worldcastlepublishing.com

Licensing Notes

Cover: Karen Fuller
Editor: Maxine Bringenberg

CHAPTER ONE

I suspect most people would think it was kind of weird how I chose to spend my time working in the small dingy office above Club Luna. It was boring, smelled funny, and I didn't even get paid for it. But it was a novelty to be there, which meant that I liked it for the meantime.

It was a regular Friday night so I was cramped up, perched precariously on the desk and scribbling out the accounts on a coffee-stained notepad, surrounded by piles of storage and paperwork. Mr. Piotrowicz, who owned the club and several other small businesses in town, had been delighted to realize I was good with numbers, and I, always happy to find a new way to keep my mind occupied, had instantly agreed to help him with the accounting and cash handling. I also blamed my instinctive need to please people.

My friend Adam would accompany me most evenings, chain-smoking out the cracked window and playing crappy indie-rock music on his iPhone whilst I pretended to appreciate the noise, and luxuriated in the novelty of being useful and gainfully employed. Today, however, there was no music as Adam had found a new passionate interest; he had recently discovered a cultural phenomenon called the newspaper. Now he insisted on reading aloud and ranting about various politically relevant topics, whilst his cigarette fumes drifted off into the bromine-stained atmosphere. Me being me, I kept quiet and let him interrupt my work every few minutes with some exclamation about the terrible, and quite frankly, *disgraceful*, state our government was in. My own interest in politics and the government was minimal at best, but it wasn't my nature to admit it to him, so I tended to agree with things.

"The House of Lords failed to pass the genetic technology bill," he told me as I nodded politely and pretended to care.

"Ah yes. That's good," I said.

"Not really. Everybody knows the only reason the Lords refused to agree to genetic technology is because a bunch of rich American religious organizations paid them enough money to fund a small African country. It's sickening, and the CBI are furious about it."

I nodded sympathetically, even though I had no idea who the CBI were, or what the bill was, or what "genetic technology" even meant. And I was too busy double-checking all the figures to ask.

"It's sickening!" repeated Adam, flicking the fag end out onto the concrete streets, satisfied with the contempt in his voice. "I mean, the government is supposed to proportionally represent and protect us people, and all it does is let the needs of those big scientific and business organizations run the country whilst they live inside their Westminster microcosm and make up laws to suit themselves. Don't you agree, Lina?"

"Yes, I agree," I said easily, still not entirely sure what I was agreeing to. "But more importantly, Adam, I think there is something wrong with the club's revenue figures your dad gave me. You should take a look."

Adam snorted and lit up another smoke, the smell of his Mayfairs wafting across the electrical wiring over the top of the stale smell of pollution and alcohol coming from the open window. It was the same smell that permeated the entirety of the small industrial town of Leading Well. We got used to it.

"Double-check it," he replied airily. "I wouldn't have a clue if it's right or not; there's a reason my dad employs you to do that sort of number stuff. It all looks like Sudoku to me."

I laughed at him, but added, "Yeah, but I'm kind of serious, Adam. I've pretty much quadruple-checked the accounts, and I've been keeping an eye on them for a while now, and there is definitely something wrong this month. The gross profit margin is...odd." I made sure to shrug and grin. "Then again, maybe I'm just shit at adding up."

Of course, I knew I wasn't.

Adam yawned. "Ask Dad about it," he said. "Maybe he's been making mistakes; he's been really stressed lately, with the new drinking regulations and that new club guy who is trying to buy everything up downtown."

He clearly didn't want to discuss the matter any further, so I smiled and nodded.

But I now knew that his father was clearly trying to hide some source of money inside the Luna accounts. I'd only ever seen money laundering explained on TV and Wikipedia, but I wasn't an idiot. I just wasn't sure what to do with this information yet — if I did anything.

"Where's your dad now?" I asked, and smiled when Adam pulled a face at me.

"He'll be down behind the bar," he replied, "but don't you dare ask for more work or something. He's already been exploiting you like a Thai orphan in a Nestle factory. Seriously, it worries me, Lina; you need to stop being so damned nice and perfectly behaved all the time. Slack off more, pinch stationary like the rest of us. Or pinch one of the

Polski bartenders instead; we have more than enough of them at the minute."

I laughed, stretching out my cramped limbs. "I would, but I don't have any free cages to keep them in. And you need to stop worrying about my well-being all the time; it just freaks me out. It's like we're an old married couple or something."

He rolled his eyes. "I don't worry about you. Hell, I don't know enough about you to know what there is to worry about. We've been hanging out together for months now and I still don't know anything about you outside of school and Club Luna. Except that you seem to be some sort of nauseatingly nice pinnacle of achievement and excellence."

"The aim of my existence is to inspire and astound. And look at us, always bickering like an old married couple. I think we need counselling, dear."

"You need some domestic abuse." He blew me a kiss to show he was kidding, and I grinned and headed down the stairs to the club.

In the narrow corridor I could see through the window that the dusk had already filtered down into flat night and people were already crowding into the various pubs, bars, and neon-lit cafes of the concrete high street. It was the ritual for people here, getting wasted to oblivion at every opportunity. Mostly to escape the monotony.

I expected Mr. Piotrowicz to be on the ground floor checking that everything was ready before the front doors opened to the drunken masses. It was all part of the routine I had managed to ingratiate myself into. In fact, it had been disappointingly easy to become an established part of Club Luna. Of course, I had been fitting myself into other people's patterns all my life, but there was always a little part of me that expected people to oppose me, to refuse my entrance into their lives because they saw it was all a pretense, a ruse for my own benefit. Adam and I had met on the first day of school's year Thirteen, and I was working at his dad's club by the end of the week. It was a knack I had.

However, Mr. Piotrowicz wasn't in his normal position behind the bar today, so I checked with the bouncers and then in the toilets, where Feliks told me yet another story about him and his girlfriend's tumultuous relationship. I also checked the storage cupboards, and finally thought to look in the back exit, where the supplies were loaded in and out. But it looked deserted. I was just turning back when I recognized Mr. Piotrowicz's low voice coming from outside the exit door, so I instantly put a smile on my face. Ever since I'd first met him I wanted him to like me...I wasn't even sure why. He wasn't the nicest dad I'd ever met, he always wore a bad fitting suit, and he told rubbish jokes. But there was this clear pride and love that he and Adam had for each other, and I could always sense it there. I could stare at the two of them all day. Truth be told, I didn't work at Luna for the money, and I didn't technically "need" any job. But whatever it was that Mr. Piotrowicz could so easily give to Adam and deny everyone else — including me, with all my helpfulness and charm — I wanted it. I wanted someone to give it to me, too. I was quite aware of how screwed up that sounded, and I would never have admitted the feeling to anyone. But no one could ever accuse me of lacking self-awareness, at least.

I was standing in front of the closed exit door when I heard a second male voice just outside. "And if it all works out, we can wire the money directly into the account." The voice was soft, male, undistinguished.

"And you're sure she won't know about any of it?" replied Mr. Piotrowicz. "She's a good girl. I don't want her in trouble…I don't want any trouble for anyone. I'm just looking out for my own, you know?"

"Of course," replied the man. "No one will ever know, and she will be fine. Hasn't she been fine so far?"

I was still hesitating by the door when it was yanked open. I leapt back as Mr. Piotrowicz walked into me. Beyond him, a slender man with a briefcase was already walking away into the dark backstreets.

"Lina, what are you doing here?" Mr. Piotrowicz exclaimed, hurriedly closing the door behind him. There was a nervous ring to his voice that I recognized instantly.

"Just trying to find Feliks," I said in an innocently surprised voice. "I think you left the new order of orange juice outside."

"Oh — oh yes, right." He reopened the door and heaved in the box. I stared out beyond the garbage bins into the small graffitied car park opposite. A clean, sleek, dark blue Porsche was now parked beside the wiring, alongside my own Skoda Fabia — an eighteenth birthday present from my father. In this part of town, no one drove cars, let alone Porsche's; they had nowhere to go. It was all factory workers, bored teenagers, and office drones, and they normally took the bus.

"Why are you looking at that car?" asked Mr. Piotrowicz, shutting the door quickly behind us.

"No reason," I commented. "Just curiosity. I've seen that car waiting around an awful lot lately, both here and around town." I was rewarded by a slightly frozen look in his eyes as I helped him carry the boxes to the bar.

"Probably belongs to someone uptown," he said in the same stilted voice. "I wouldn't worry about it; trust me."

"Of course," I said. "You'll know better than me."

I didn't miss his hesitation, nor the watchful anxiety in his eyes as I sweetly unpacked the boxes of orange juice. He was about to say something else when Adam barged down and into the conversation, pausing briefly to check his dark blond curls in the mirror behind the drink shelves.

"Lina, your phone has been ringing for like, the last ten minutes. Oh, did you see the Porsche is back outside – ?"

"Forget about the Porsche!" snapped Mr. Piotrowicz as I interrupted.

"You didn't answer it?"

"What? Oh, your phone? Of course not."

I made my excuses and headed back to the office to grab my mobile. It was already ringing again as I grabbed it out of my abandoned school bag and locked myself into the small staff bathroom. Without checking the caller ID, I pressed "answer."

"Hey Mum," I said, turning to face the sink mirror.

Normally I liked looking in mirrors. I was good with makeup and hairstyling, and I liked seeing myself when I was looking different, or had new clothes or whatever. However, I'd forgotten that I recently dyed my stylishly kinked mop of hair a horrific radioactive green color. It drained away what little coloring I had in my face, and turned my already horribly pale eyes to a jarring shade of washed-out, colorless grey-blue. Very attractive. My dad had the same eyes, but with his tan and older, more masculine features, they just looked striking and graceful on him. Some people got all the luck.

"What's wrong, Mum?"

"Hey babe, where are you?"

"I told you, I'm at Club Luna." Just talking to her, I saw in the mirror how my facial features had automatically shifted into the docile, warmly open expression I adopted around most people. I thought of it as my "twinkle power," and it was pretty good at neutralizing threats and making people trust me at my word. Even at the moment, with the hideous green hair, tight blue velvet trousers, faded *Karma Chameleon* t-shirt, glittery jewelry, and over-sized ratty leather jacket, my twinkle power was still fully functional on most adults I came across. I looked like a nice, sweet-natured if somewhat superficial girl going through a pseudo-rebellious phase. And that suited me just fine.

Mum asked, "When are you coming home?"

"Why? Are you okay?" I smiled at my reflection, cheering up at how kind and genuinely concerned I sounded. I had mad skills, even if I did say so myself. (And I often did.)

"No, I'm not okay, babe! You haven't come home *again* and...." At the other end of the phone there was a silence as my mother tried to force herself into tears. "And it's been one of those days, you know?"

"Oh dear, Mum. I'm so sorry; I didn't know."

I waited for her to force the tears fully out so I could comfort her, as was our routine. However, for once she appeared to give up on the crying before she'd even started, and instead said, "It's just that something feels wrong today."

"Don't get upset, Mum. Just tell me what's wrong."

"It's...oh, I can't explain over the phone, babe. You know what I'm like. It's just been a bad day, you know?"

"I know."

"Though sometimes it seems like every day is a bad one nowadays. It's so hard just to...and I don't even know where you are half the time!"

"I'm working at Luna, like I told you."

Her voice went high again. "Don't take that tone with me! I know exactly what you're doing, what everyone is thinking! Before Luna there was that band you were in, and that Christian volunteering thing, and that maths society, and.... Oh my god, what kind of mother am I, when I never know where my only child is? When my only daughter, my *baby*, can't stand to be in my company, when she hates me? What's wrong with me? I don't deserve to be a mother."

I admired how her voice was perfectly pitched for maximum effect; it apparently ran in the family.

"You're a good mother, I promise. And it's not that I don't want to be with you. I love being with you. I'm just working tonight."

"Can't you take a break for a little bit? I never normally ask, but...come home and talk to me for a *little* bit tonight? Not very long, I promise. I'm just...I'm lonely, babe. I want to see your face before you grow too old, go to university or whatever, and leave me forever."

Although I pretended, I never felt guilty anymore when talking to my mother. I refused to. It was just the sick feeling of resentment that now churned in my empty stomach, kept out of sight as I replied in a sad voice, "I'm so sorry Mum, but I don't think I can leave here. It's really too busy and they need me. I'm so sorry!" I smiled tightly at the mirror. I had to practice keeping my jaw looser.

"Please baby, you don't understand. Something is different today, I can feel it. And I tried to call your dad, but he won't pick up his mobile, and I'm not calling his home with *her* there. Besides, he doesn't love me, not like you do. No one does. And something's happening...I don't know what to do. Who else do I have to talk to? You're all I've got baby, and I just need to talk to someone. You don't understand what a life I've had; sometimes it's so hard to cope."

The speech would have been more effective if it hadn't been so routine. Judging from her voice, it was the normal lows, not like the one time it was more extreme lows. That time she hadn't bothered letting me know in advance, or cared much about my involvement at all.

"It's not my fault, Mum. I'm sorry, but I can't."

There was a long pause before she added, "There was this expensive dark blue car parked outside the window all day, and I think...I think I saw a man inside watching me. For hours, just watching me."

"Was the car a Porsche?"

"I think so."

"I'm coming home," I said abruptly. "See you in about fifteen minutes."

"Only if you're sure, babe," she sniffed. I assured her and hung up, a new sense of unease uncoiling through my veins as I headed back downstairs. Why would Mr. Piotrowicz's "business associate" be outside my mother's house? Something was going on—more than I'd realized—and I was starting to suspect I was going to be involved in it.

***

Mr. Piotrowicz was juicing limes behind the empty bar as Adam sat next to him speaking animatedly. Both went silent as I walked up to them, that uncharacteristic wariness back in Mr. Piotrowicz's eyes.

Why?

"I'm sorry, but I need to nip back home," I said. "I forgot some stuff, but I'll be back in about half an hour."

"Oh, I don't know if that's a good idea, love," said Mr. Piotrowicz quickly. "I don't know if we can spare you tonight."

"Nah Dad, it's fine if Lina goes for a bit," said Adam. "Didn't you say tonight is definitely going to be another slow night? That new Sugar Club is doing their '2 for £2' deal."

Mr. Piotrowicz paused, and then said "I suppose so." Then he added, in a strangely meaningful voice, his eyes on me, "Sugar got bought up by one of the chains; it can afford discount nights. Luna can't, because it's a family business. We struggle because we refuse to sell out." He was looking at me significantly, so I looked back understandingly, though I was feeling slightly alarmed. "It means us decent family businessmen have to do things we don't want to in order to stay in the business, to keep up with the game. You understand me, Lina?"

"Er...," said Adam oddly.

"Well, I really have to g—" I started, but Mr. Piotrowicz was still talking in the same insistent, almost pleading tone.

"I make sure it's known you're a good girl, Lina, but I know you'll always be fine. You're clearly a smart girl, a survivor. It's hard to be a survivor around here."

"Er...," said Adam again,

"You're up-to-date with your school work at the minute, aren't you? A smart girl like you should be applying to a good university, getting away from this dead-end town."

"I'm applying to study economics at Warwick...but I really have to go, Mr. Piotrowicz."

"Don't go to university," said Adam, leaning over to kiss me goodbye. "There would be no point. I'm all you need and I'm here. I'd miss you too much if you went!"

My shudder remained purely internal.

As I hurried back to the car park, still wondering at Mr. Piotrowicz's words, I wondered what it would be like if my own dad ever took such an interest in my life as Mr. Piotrowicz had just shown. Realistically speaking, it would probably be stifling. I wouldn't get my own way as much, I wouldn't be able to do whatever I wanted. Plus, my parents would be forced to communicate more, which wouldn't make either of them happy.

As I got into my car, I took care to memorize the generic number plate of the empty Porsche still parked next to it. Already the sounds of the Friday night crowds could be heard as on the main streets around me, people flooded through the tarmac and brick mesh world, a collective mass of hair spray, glitter, sweat, and cologne. The thudding pulse of club music began to pump through the concrete of Luna as I checked my colorful makeup in the car mirror before pulling out of the parking space. As I left the car park, something made me glance back to the Porsche in time to see the red flash of something — a camera? — go off inside the car, for a brief second illuminating the silhouette of a slender male standing behind the car, before darkness once again swallowed him up.

I sped all the way home. Too restless and disconcerted to listen to my comfort compilations of '80s and electronica music, I obsessed over the Luna accounts instead. It didn't take long before I'd reached the nicer edge of town where I lived with my mum. I'd been pretty young when I figured out why we always lived in such nice houses when my mum was technically on the dole. My dad had paid for this brick terraced house and everything in it — as well as our previous homes and all other possessions. My mum hadn't worked since the day she'd met my dad, although she'd once been an acclaimed professional coloratura soprano. I sometimes felt sorry for my dad, still having to financially support us as well as supporting his other, more proper family in London, especially now with the shit economy and all. The guy hadn't visited our home in twelve years, yet still had to pay through the nose for it, all because of a whirlwind marriage to the beautiful Haley Aske in his youth. Did he regret it? His wallet certainly did; but he'd always been painfully careful never to talk of such things to me. Regardless of his private feelings,

Dad liked to consider himself a good, moral man, and he made sure Mum and I were never lacking for anything. The house even had a cello shop next to it, for my mum to visit when she missed her old world too much.

As I cut the car engine outside the front door, I could already predict the state I'd find my mum in. Not that it took special talent to do so. The lights were on in every window, and the TV and various radios were blaring out from all over the house, yet the curtains were still tightly shut to keep people from looking at her. I sighed, stalling for time. I knew I'd have to deal with her before I could find out exactly what sort of mess Luna was in with the Porsche-driving men. Especially now that these guys were also apparently interested in Mr. Pietrowicz's employees and their families, as well as whatever he was involved in.

Hmm. Marilyn to the rescue. I quite liked the idea of that; I was very good at playing the good girl. Marilyn the superhero. That could be fun.

I kicked the wall as hard as I could, smiled brightly, and walked inside.

"Mum?"

"I'm in the kitchen, baby."

Ignoring the urge to flee, I crossed through the narrow hallway into the harsh, artificial kitchen lights. She was sitting in the corner, huddled on the floor like a guilty child, with her back pressed against the wall and knees up against her chest. She looked up as I walked in and her bottle green eyes were dull and sad and pitiful. Her face looked bloated, her lips swollen and greasy, and her long, dyed golden hair was lank and unwashed. Smile glued in place, I crouched down beside her, pushing aside the empty crisp packets around my feet. I could smell the sour tang of vomit in the stale heated air.

"Told you I'd be back soon, didn't I, Mum?" I said, swallowing before smiling coaxingly into her eyes. "Now let's get you into bed, yeah?"

Her lips twisted downwards. "My tummy hurts," she said. "I won't be able to sleep."

"We'll get you some stomach settlers: a nice cuppa and you'll be fine," I replied, looking up at the mess around us. The kitchen surfaces were heaped with food leftovers and rubbish. Half-eaten cake mixture was strewn around, along with empty packets of biscuits, chocolate wrappers, microwave meal packaging, drained greasy food cans, and spilt cans of condensed milk. I mentally equated the current image with the image of that morning…me leaving for school as fast as possible as she happily baked cakes. I had figured something like this was coming, of course.

"Come on, let's get you upstairs," I said, and slid my hands under her shoulders to lift her. She started to cry and I pushed my lips tightly together, keeping my facial muscles relaxed. If the man in the Porsche had been there watching her earlier, what had he thought?

"I want to be sick again," she told me. "I *need* to be. I can't stop myself. I can't help it." Her voice changed suddenly, now beseeching, even more pathetic. "I just want to be happy, baby, I do, but my tummy hurts so much!"

"It's okay, Mum, just help me and stand up, yeah? Once you're in bed with a nice hot water bottle and one of the mix CDs I made you playing, you'll feel much better."

She snuffled into her palms, ignoring me. "I just want to be happy. Why am I like this? I am the worst person in the world. My own daughter hates me; *I* hate me!"

It always got repetitive. Give me credit…I didn't even roll my eyes, just continued to look like I was the embodiment of eternal concern and consideration.

"It's just the blues talking, Mum. You were so happy this morning; remember?"

I gave up on trying to stand her up and stepped back. She was taller than me; I couldn't make her do anything she didn't want to do...had never been able to do that. "Do you want green tea or chamomile?"

Working around her, I boiled the kettle, got a hot water bottle, and found her usual supply of pills. She revived at one point to reveal she'd bought yet another new type of those herbal teas she liked, and could I use that? I did, sniffing the new mixture distastefully as I popped the teabag into the water, ripping off the strange label. It smelled horrible, but she loved all this homeopathic, alternate stuff.

Finally, I was allowed to help her to her feet, careful not to touch her anywhere except on her shoulders. She couldn't stand to be touched when in one of her moods. It was possibly one of the few things we seemed to have in common, a dislike of personal invasion. And it was the only thing about her I had always immediately understood without trial and error. Besides, I had no more desire to touch her in those scenarios than she did to let me.

Once I'd led her up to her bed, she lay there obediently as I tucked up the covers around her, and I watched her drink the herbal tea meekly.

"The man who sold it to me said it has special healing properties," she murmured to me. "Because of the ginseng, marigolds, and forget-me-nots."

"He certainly sounds like a medical expert," I agreed, sticking the CD in the player. I'd burnt the CD full of her favorite soft songs, aiming for a sort of hypnosis effect. Perhaps it was working, because before I'd even pressed *play* her eyes were already flickering shut, her breath slowing down.

"Mum, you remember you said you saw a dark blue Porsche outside? Did you see the man inside? Or the number plate?"

It was no good and she didn't reply. I breathed into the silence a few times before getting up and closing the curtains, dimming the lights. As I stepped back out onto the landing, she suddenly stirred and said in her most childish, sleepy voice, "He said the herbal tea would bring my loved ones to me. You'll tell your father that I'm not very well?"

"Yes, don't worry."

"You're a good girl."

"Sure, Mum."

She was silent again, and when I glanced back, she was staring up at the ceiling. Guilt or resentment — sometimes I couldn't tell anymore — surged anew in the pit of my stomach. I left. As usual, I hadn't been honest with her. I suspected I was pathologically incapable of it. I was not a good girl. But as far as I could tell, being "good" just meant always doing what people wanted you to do. If I acted in the manner that somebody wished me to act, it would be a clear sign of excellent moral fiber. People thought I was good because they thought I was doing and believing what they told me to do and believe, because I didn't argue, or make my own opinion known...I just agreed with everyone. It was all passive projection; that's all that goodness was.

I cleaned up the kitchen, amusing myself by pretending to be in one of those '50s style soap and detergent adverts, all singing, dancing, and artificial Julie Andrews voices. Scribbled phone messages from the last few days were on a notepad hidden under the piles of congealing food. Someone had called four times yesterday, asking for me but refusing to give a name. Another person had called asking to speak to

Dad, and Dad himself had called, demanding to speak with me, but I'd been out. Typical.

As I stuffed all the mess into garbage bags and kicked them down into the bin, I dialed Dad's home number on my mobile. As a young boy's voice answered down the other end, I had the strangest sensation of being overheard, being watched again. I looked around me.

"Hello?" It was my dad's second eldest son, nine year old Cole.

"Why hello, my beautiful darling, what a gorgeous night it is now I hear your voice," I said, still using the '50s style voice whilst checking out the window. Cole immediately started giggling.

"Mary! I've missed you lots and lots—I was going to call you, but Dad forgot the number again! Why didn't you come over at Christmas? You promised you would and you never did and me, Johan, and Matthias haven't seen you for ages and *ages.*"

"I'm sorry, love! But it's your birthday party soon, right? I'll be there, for sure."

"With a present?" His voice was hopeful, and I laughed down the phone, crossing over to peer out the front window.

Nothing outside on the streets.

"I'll bring you the most beautiful lump of coal that ever existed in all the worlds," I said, scanning for anything slightly suspicious. "A namesake, the best coal for the best Cole."

"What? No, please don't! That's silly...they are spelled differently, anyway!"

"Really? Oh...okay, fine, I won't get you coal for your birthday."

"Good, because I want a new Nintendo Wii, after Jo broke the last one. But you promise you'll come down this time? Dad says the party can be massive, so you need to be there."

"Of course I'll be there. Don't you know how much I love parties?"

He giggled. "Yes, course I do! Um, do you want to talk to Jo? He's with me." I heard the rustling sounds and whining as Johan tried to make his presence known. I felt a rush of affection and longing to see the three of them again. I wanted to have three brothers. I wanted to be a proper big sister. However.

"I can't talk to him at the minute...tell Johan I'll call back later and talk to him especially, but first I need a quick word with Dad. Tell him it's kind of urgent or I wouldn't call."

Instead the phone got passed to Fiona, Dad's wife.

"I'm sorry, Marilyn, he is working late tonight. As usual."

"Oh, right. Well, will you just tell him—?"

"Your mother wants him to know she is not feeling so well, yes?"

Silent for a second, I said at last, "I'm just returning his call, actually."

"I'll tell him. I doubt he will have time to call back though; he's been so stressed with work lately. He is working nonstop. It makes us all very anxious, and I tell you, the last thing he needs right now is your mother and her ways."

"Right. I'll make sure not to do anything that will cause stress...or require excessive thought of any kind."

I never did. I never complained about anything, or said anything to Dad except the stuff a perfect daughter would say. Having nothing else to say to Fiona, I was making my airy goodbyes when she added, "Brendan really *was* sorry he was not able to visit you over the Christmas holidays again, Marilyn. You got the money, though, yes? Directly deposited?

I was worried because you can never trust these technological advances, but they are everywhere!"

"I did. It's fine; tell him not to worry about me."

"You're a good girl."

Through the window, I saw a tall slender man cross the road and walk away down the pavement. As I stared at him in shock, he turned to where I stood in the window, slowly raised one hand, and then turned away, walking, disappearing around the corner. I hung up the phone and ran out the front door after him, down the empty street and further out, the night drizzling around me. However, the man was nowhere to be seen. Just as I was considering turning back, I suddenly saw something from the corner of my eye...the Porsche, quietly gleaming in the leafy shelter of a small side road.

A feeling of sick fear curled in the bottom of my stomach as I approached the car. It was the same number plate as the car outside Luna. The car was empty, and the insides were eerily clean...it could've been a rental car. I peered through the windows into the backseat. Something glinted there, snagging my attention, and I strained closer against the glass. There was something metal poking out, half hidden by the dark blanket covering the backseat. As recognition dawned, I started to swear. I'd only ever seen guns in films. Swearing still, I backed up, looking distractedly around me. This was the UK, not America! We didn't have guns here. We had passive-aggression! We had knife-crime and drunken head-butting.

Adrenaline in my veins, I started to back away when I saw the final thing waiting to be seen, carefully Sellotaped across the front window mirror...an herbal tea bag with a distinctive label.

Why on earth would someone so clearly position a teabag...? But then I recognized the label.

Healing properties—ginseng, marigold, and forget-me-nots.

And I was running back to the house as fast as I could.

In hindsight, perhaps I should've called someone else for help. The police or Adam, maybe. But I never gave it a second thought. I just ran.

As I reached the house, it took only a few seconds to realize something was badly wrong. The front door was now locked and I had no key. There was a dark hopelessness already forming in the atmosphere as I savagely kicked at the door before darting around to the back. The lights were all off and the windows all tightly fastened, as was the back door. I ran back to the front living room windows and battered my fists against the window. A slight crack appeared on the pane. As I paused, trying to think, I realized I could hear something from within the house...the distant sound of the CD player. The Mama's and the Papa's "Dream a Little Dream of Me" drifted through darkness and a second story window to my ears, the melody cocooned in static.

"Say nighty-night and kiss me; just hold me tight and tell me you'll miss me."

"Mum!" I screamed, and punched the front window again. It cracked some more, and I twisted round to kick it repeatedly, ignoring the pain spiraling up through my legs and arms. It wasn't breaking fast enough, so I grabbed a flowerpot from outside the cello shop and threw it at the window. As the window finally smashed, I rammed myself through the broken glass and it cracked and crumbled apart around my shoulders.

"Mum," I yelled again, running up the stairs to fling open her bedroom door. And there she was. Relief spilled through me as I sagged against the doorframe. She lay still in the bed, eyes looking up to the ceiling, dirty hair spread out over the clean white pillows.

"Mum, we need to get out of here," I said breathlessly. "Something bad is going on at Luna and now we're being followed! We need to go *now*."

She didn't move, just kept her eyes fixed on the ceiling above.

"*Mum*, this is no time for your sulking!"

Still, she didn't move. Her eyes were wide and unmoving. Blank, like marble. I stared down at her, thoughts unable to process. She was too still. She wasn't moving. Why wasn't she moving?

"Mum?" I stepped closer. "Mum?" Fearfully, numbly, I reached out and lay my fingers on her hand. It was already cold.

Slowly, so slowly, I turned to the empty mug of herbal tea I'd made her, still on the bedside table. There was a new small note written next to it, in my handwriting.

I am sorry for poisoning you, Mum. But I couldn't take any more. It will be easier this way, for both of us. I will always love you, Mara.

Someone was whimpering, a pathetic whining sound from far off. Was it me? I didn't dare look away from the note. Stupidly, all I could think was how my mum had never called me Mara…she had hated it back when Dad had called me that. She called me her baby. I was her baby.

"What are you doing?" I suddenly yelled at myself. "Stop doing nothing!"

I leapt onto the bed beside Mum and forced her cooling limbs into the recovery position. I pushed down on her ribs, tilted her head back, all my rudimentary first aid knowledge coming back as I forced her ribs in and out and tried to force breath into her still mouth. I was positive that with every push and breath I could feel her recovering. I pushed down, harder and harder. She lay unmoving. I pushed harder and harder, breathed harder. Behind us the CD player crooned.

"Sweet dreams till sunbeams find you. Sweet dreams that leave all worries behind you."

"She's dead, girlie. No CPR will change that; she needs a coffin."

My head shot up. A neat man dressed in an oddly dramatic black suit stood in the doorway, framed by the hall lights. He began to pull on latex gloves, watching me with bright eyes as I struggled to process his presence. He was waiting. And then, finally, I recognized him from the back entrance of Luna, and he smiled at my dawning expression.

"That's more like it," he said.

Flee, my mind screamed at me, flee. But he was blocking the only exit. I was trapped. I stumbled backwards, and he took a step forward. I lunged towards the door, trying to get around him, but he was too quick, easily twisting and kicking me in the ribs. I was slammed backwards without any effort. He flexed his hands and I leapt forward again, trying to run for the door.

"Not much of a fighter, are you?" he commented, kicking my knees out from under me. As I hit the ground he fastened his iron-like fingers around my neck and punched twice on each side of my head. Dizzy, I gasped for air, my vision spinning as he lifted me back up and threw me sideways into the wall. I only heard the noise as I collided into the shelves and fell down to the floor amid the broken shelving and wood. The world was painted in sickening red and black colors, and I could see the man watching me as I struggled to stand back up. Eventually, I fell back down and remained still.

"You're not tryin' to play dead, are you?" he asked as I suppressed my breathing and lay like a statue among the mess. "That is such a cliché."

The CD player halted for a second, then rewound and started the same song again. I listened to the man move over to the bed and bend over my mother, checking her pulse and straightening up, turning towards me. He sighed.

"You *are* playing dead," he said. "That's been done to death, if you don't mind the pun. But y'know, I'm a Showman; I can appreciate what you're trying to do here. I can work with this." I remained motionless as my fingers scrambled in the rubble under my back, trying to reach at whatever the hard metal thing digging into my spine was.

"They said you were special," said the man, inspecting me from a distance. "I don't see nothing special...I was expecting more of a fight." He moved slightly closer. "I mean, from all they said, they spent months planning for tonight, you know. And I'm talkin' every single detail." He bent over me. "They even told me you was going to come chargin' in halfway through your mum dying. They knew everything. Impressive, innit?" I heard the snap of a second pair of latex gloves being put into place. "Too bad you're letting the game down. Now to the instructed message: I am the Showman and my job tonight is to make sure both your mum and you are dead without any trace of suspicion, or external interference. I am to make sure your mum dies first, and that you, the daughter, witness the death. Then I am to kill you."

He paused, and I thought for a second he could hear my fingers working like crazy trying to tug loose what had to be a metal book-end. But then he continued, his accent sounding overly careful now, like a man desperate to sound more educated and detached than he was. "I think I want to make this a real tragic story. A murder suicide; the daughter poisons her mum then slits her wrists out of grief. I'm a real Showman, me."

He paused again, sounding less patient. "My monologue's over now, and playin' dead only works in films, you know. Don't treat me like I'm stupid; get the hell up."

Change of plan. I forced a feeble cry up into my throat, still keeping my posture limp as my fingers finally grasped around the metal bookend. "Please no," I whispered weakly. "Please don't kill me. I swear I won't tell anyone if you just let me go. I think I've broken my arm. Please don't do this."

I started to weep as he crouched even closer over me, his white face now inches away from mine.

"Well, that's too bad, innit?" He said, placing hard fingers around my neck again.

"I don't want to die," I cried hysterically, and shifted the bookend to a better position to attack. Immediately his eyes switched to where my hand was, and as his own hand snatched up my wrist I slammed both my knees up into his exposed throat. His head snapped back and he staggered, and with more speed than I knew I possessed I pushed myself into him. We both smacked into the floorboards, me on top, and as his hands leapt around my throat I brought the metal bookend down into his face as hard as I could. His nose crunched and blood spurted up into my face. I threw the book end away and punched him in the face again, the bones splintering against my wet fist. He screamed with pain, his grip tightening around my neck as he bucked and struggled.

But red panic was giving me a new strength and I punched down again and again, battering his face, his throat, his chest, anywhere I could reach. His hands continued to push my throat in, so I couldn't breathe and I couldn't see or hear anything, but I kept on hitting and hitting, unable to stop as the bone and flesh of his face disappeared under the dark bloody crimson and pulp.

And then I realized his hands had fallen away.

Breath ragged, I sat back. Waited. Time had stopped and I was the only one there. Slowly, I lifted up my shining wet hands. They were dark, the knuckles cut open. I looked at the man, and knew he was dead. I'd killed him. He'd killed my mum, and I'd killed him.

I rolled off his body and vomited all over the floor. I was still retching uncontrollably, cradling my hands to my chest, as the police sirens surrounded the house, the shrieking garish red and blue lights piercing through the closed curtains and chopping up the darkness of the bedroom. I stumbled to my feet, and as the front door below me burst open, I ran into the bathroom, locking the door against the police swarming into the house. It was easy, like a surreal dream, to climb out of the window and haul myself up onto the slanted roof via the piping. Once I was balanced on the steep roof, the cold, damp night air shocked me back to my body, and my mind was panicking, racing, as I crawled along the chilled tiles. Leaning on the chimney, I dug out my mobile phone from my pocket and dialed the buttons, fingers swollen and slippery with blood.

"Luna Club, how may I help?" Mr. Piotrowicz answered.

"What did you do to my mum and me?" I choked in reply. In the road below I could hear the radio transmitters going crazy as the police and paramedics searched the house.

A crowd was gathering on the street around us, faces agog. "Why did that man come after us?"

"Lina? Lina, is that you? Oh my god, what happened?"

"What did you do?"

"I swear...I swear had no choice, Lina. He knew about the debt and the fraud. He offered me a business deal, said he was the only one who could save Club Luna. He knew all about my...past. He said if I cooperated with him he could...all he wanted was to know your whereabouts, what you were doing, and asked me to keep an eye on you. Wanted me to phone up when you left...oh my god, that's all, I swear! He didn't tell me anything else, and he said he knew your dad! What's happened? Oh my god, are the police there?"

I hung up and began to crawl towards the cello shop roof.

"STOP THERE!"

I glanced back; a policeman was clambering up onto the roof.

Time to switch my role again.

"Is he gone?" I cried out pathetically. "Did you get the man who broke in and killed my mum and her boyfriend? I've been hiding from him for hours!"

"Put your hands on your head and stand up slowly," the policeman yelled. Behind him, other policemen were lifting themselves up onto the roof and fanning out around me. I raised myself to my knees, hands on my head. It was a mistake; the policeman's eyes widened when he saw the blood all over me, staining my clothes and skin.

"I tried to save them but they died anyway," I cried out, but his horrified eyes showed he didn't believe me. He took another step closer and I was already on my feet, running away from him. He yelled and I launched myself over the gap onto the cello shop roof. I hit it awkwardly, landing on my hip and knee, and before I could recover I was being tackled by the policeman, followed by another, and another.

"No!" I snarled, but there were too many of them, all around me, crushing me underneath them. I scratched and punched and bit and struggled uncontrollably. I was almost grateful when finally one of the policemen hit me back, scrambling my senses into unconsciousness.

The last thing I remembered hearing wasn't the policemen, or the crowd gathering below, but instead the refrain of a distant song on the CD player.

"Sweet dreams till sunbeams find you. Sweet dreams that leave all worries far behind you."

CHAPTER TWO

When I woke up, it was in a lone, sterile hell. There was a bitter metallic taste in my mouth…an anesthetic. My head hurt and my ribs hurt, and my throat, my hands…all of me hurt. I was trapped in a bare rectangular room with painted pale blue walls, and I hurt. I got out of the narrow bed with its ironed white sheets and tried to open the small window, but the crisp white bars were too close together. There was also a foam flower on the window sill. The only other objects in the room were a small plastic chair beside the fastened bed, and two locked doors without door handles.

I lay back down; it hurt too much to stand. It was then that I realized my clothes were gone and all I was wearing was a hospital gown. There was thick, stiff taping around my ribs, and my hands and knuckles were swathed in white gauze. I poked at the crusted scab along my scalp line and the raised knot at the back of my skull. I could feel scratches all over my face and looked under my gown to see my legs and arms equally crisscrossed. The swelling on my throat suggested that it was bruised too. Silently I regarded the white ceiling. I must have looked very ugly.

Perhaps most people would have spent the next few hours calling for help, or attempting to break open the window bars. I just lay there, watching the ceiling. My mum was dead. A man had killed her. I had killed a man. Someone had paid a man to kill me. Someone wanted me dead. I had killed a man. My mum was dead. I hurt. Over and over. And the dawning memory that someone was responsible for this. Somebody had done this to me.

I was left alone in the room all day. It was many, many hours later that the door finally unlocked, and into the room stepped a tall, fair man with a clipboard. I watched him seat himself in the small chair beside my bed and scan my face for tears. He reminded me of a snow-cat with his soft groomed hair and restrained grace. Neither of us said a word. He took a pair of wire-rimmed glasses from his lab coat pocket and put them on his nose with long, delicate, thin-knuckled hands. My mum would've called them violinist hands, but she was dead.

"Marilyn Aske," he said, his gaze directly on me. "Do you know where you are?"

"I think I missed the sign post on the way in."

He looked at me gravely. "I understand that you are grieving and confused, Mara, but reacting with sarcasm is not healthy, and not tolerated here. You are at Arden House. Your father and the High Court judge decided that the best thing for you would be to stay with us for a length of time and see if we can help you."

"Arden House?" I didn't have the energy to care.

"It's an exclusive penal group home. It was set up twenty-four years ago for youths in your sort of...situation. I've been assigned as your specialist carer and primary doctor; my name is Dr. Obadiah Ayer, and we'll be working together daily to help you get better."

"Get better...? Youths like me?"

"Youths who should technically be going through trial and then incarceration. Those diagnosed with problems such as psychiatric disorders or mental illness, and who have a history of violence. The program at Arden House cares about and rehabilitates youths who have been branded as dangerous criminals by the outside world, and who would normally be thrown into prison if it wasn't for us."

"That's very admirable, but there's been a mistake—"

The doctor carried on as he couldn't hear me. "You should understand that the Arden House is *very* selective; it is incredibly difficult to secure a place here. Even such an influential man as your father considers himself lucky that we took you in. But we specialize in cases such as yours and so we were delighted to—"

"Cases where there's been a terrible mistake and the person is innocent?"

Dr. Obadiah Ayer shook his head slowly. "Mara, you were charged with the first degree murder of your mother and a man identified as Enrico Tagliavini. There was no mistake. However, as is the nature of our treatment, your sentencing has been postponed indefinitely...as long as you cooperate with us here in Arden House. It is perfectly within your rights to refuse our help, in which case we will arrange for transportation to the nearest prison facility. But it is our first priority here to give you the help *you* need."

"What about a court trial? What about a lawyer?"

"We have some of the best psychoanalysts, doctors, and therapists in the world, and we are sponsored and work in partnership with the largest businesses and scientific boards in the developed world to help give you the best chance of recovery. Our advanced program of care and rehabilitation is cutting edge, progressive, and the top of its field. We're breaking new ground every day with our individual methods, and our success rates are phenomenal. We don't believe in subjecting you to court, or prison, or hospital; they can't give you what you need. So there is no need to worry about any of that anymore; for now, rest, look after yourself, and grieve. You are safe here. And we'll introduce you to the rest of the house when you're ready."

"There was a man who wanted to kill us both," I whispered. "He was working for...for 'them,' he said. I can't stay here; I need to find out who they are, what they want."

His smile was carefully neutral, his hands on his knees. "Marilyn, this sort of attitude is what has been wrong with you all along."

"There was this dark blue Porsche."

"There was no car mentioned in any police reports. I should also mention that you've been diagnosed as a pathological liar."

Well, that was accurate at least. But I said, "You diagnosed me whilst I was sleeping? No wonder my truth-telling skills were limited —"

"Not to mention your issues with paranoia, repression, uncontrolled anger, and an inability to fully understand the consequences of your actions. Your flawless social interactive ability has allowed you to disguise and camouflage your problems well on a surface level, which meant you weren't diagnosed until too late. But none of this is your fault, Mara, and we can help you overcome all these problems which hold you back. We will help you to develop into your true, unstunted, good self."

Words had deserted me. Finally I managed to say, "You don't understand."

"That's the thing. We *do* understand."

"No, you don't! I...I know...." And suddenly I was stuttering, something I'd never done in my life. "I...but...look; the only thing wrong with me is an inability to...to...I'm not some sociopathic killer. I...and I demand a l-lawyer or

36

something because this is all a terrible, terrible mistake. No, I...I need to talk to my dad...*they* set this all up, someone wanted...I'm *innocent!*"

He interrupted in a soft tone of finality. "I'm afraid that's impossible. Who would want to harm you and your mother, except you? The police combed both your house and the surrounding area, and it could only have been you. I'm sorry, Mara. I know it's hard, but you must learn to accept responsibility for your actions. You broke. But you're only a child. Here, we understand, we don't blame."

I lifted my hands to my head, then quickly put them back in my lap. "Stop saying that. Just...just be quiet!" I swallowed. "I mean...I mean…wait...I'm eighteen, I'm legally an adult, so how can I get away with no sentencing?"

"The desires of powerful men such as your father and the board members of Arden House can never be ignored. But you must relax now. In half an hour, a nurse will come and —"

"I want to see my dad."

"He and I don't think that would be a good idea, and he's a busy man. Besides, it's time to discard the life you had before."

His face looked the image of helpful concern. I'd seen the image on my own face often enough.

"No...."

"Don't look like that, Mara. It's time to focus on building the new world rather than keeping yourself trapped in the old wrong one." He stood up, the conversation clearly over. "The first stage of the program starts now; we'll keep you in solitary for a while until you've dealt with the last of your grief, before transitioning you to the house. I'll be visiting you every day to check how you're doing. I know this is hard on you, but we at Arden are sure it will be worth it in the end."

I kept looking at him.

"Any last questions before I leave?"

He was at the door before I said abruptly, "You called me Mara. Why?"

His back stiffened, one hand on the door. "Your file listed that as your nickname of choice."

"It's not."

"My apologies; the filing system was erroneous." He left.

Until yesterday, I hadn't been called "Mara" in years...the name had died alongside a father-daughter bond. Yet he had known about the intensely personal nickname. Had my father told them? It seemed like the most likely answer...yet why would he have? My thoughts slowly began to click back into gear and start again. My instinct was that I needed to escape this place as soon as possible, yet I knew I had to find answers. Was it coincidence that the forged confessional note had also used that same abandoned nickname? Did it have anything to do with the dark blue Porsche?

Call it instinct, but as someone who'd spent most of my life watching and adapting to the people around me, I knew something was strange about Ayer and this place, that they knew something they were keeping from me. I knew they had answers, and I knew I wanted them.

The next few hours were spent lying motionless on my bed as the light streaming in from the window dimmed and bruised to the color of old apples. The soreness washed in and out of my body, in and out. No tears fell; I wouldn't let them. Ayer had said I was "socially flawless." I would be flawless at Arden House. I would be the best patient they'd ever had; they would trust me like everyone always did. And when I had all the information they had to offer, I would leave and discover who had sent that killer after us, and why.

I forced myself to smile. And I was ready.

***

Much later, a nurse entered with a plastic bowl of chicken soup, thick bread, and orange juice. She watched me swill the food around for a while before unlocking the door nearest to me, revealing a cubicle bathroom. She kept the door open as I cleaned my teeth and took a brief shower, and I didn't bother arguing. In fact, I kept my posture meek and submissive and my face tired. I even let her hold my head under the shower jets and systematically scour all the green dye out of my hair with foul smelling chemicals. It was just a hair color. The nurse then redid my bandaging and retreated into the doorway again, hands on her thin hips as I changed into a pair of plain grey sweatpants, a cotton sports bra, and a t-shirt from under the sink. I didn't look into the mirror.

After the nurse left, I saw she'd placed two new books and a red rubber ball on my bed. I eyed the novels unenthusiastically; Kafka's *Collected Stories* and *The Odyssey*. If they thought I was going to gain some sort of thematic message and understanding from their choice in novels, they were probably mistaken. Reading was a sore spot on my intellectual scoreboard, though a scrupulously hidden one. Still, I picked up the Kafka as it was shorter and started to flick through. Clearly Arden House's most pressing concern at the minute was to challenge my literary boundaries.

For the next two days I was brought equally boring meals, books, and hygienic necessities three times a day. The nurse was always the same, but she never opened her mouth other than to convey orders. She was careful, clearly mindful of her duties, and responded minimally to me, even when I acted as affable and softly fearful as possible. Her lack of response only increased my interest in her. She was of average height with soft grey hair that was noticeable because she walked with a lowered head, and she spoke with an educated BBC News type of accent.

I had too much time to dwell on this; by the time Dr. Ayer visited again, I was in danger of going stir crazy. Luckily, he had brought with him a file full of sheets with questioning and tests for me. We discussed them briefly, and as we started with the examinations it was clear I was being given some sort of emotional health test. I made sure I gave mundanely perfect answers. It was clear he had guessed my strategy; there was slight amusement in his eyes as I anxiously suggested that the ink blot looked like a candy floss machine, and I insisted I associated newborn kittens with my mother. Perhaps he appreciated my dazzling wit. (It had been known to happen.) Either way, he never betrayed any impatience or disapproval.

More examinations followed when we were joined by another doctor, a tall, shark-eyed American woman named Robertson, who took urine and blood samples, recorded my blood pressure, heart beat, reflexes, and checked out my ears, mouth, eyes, etc. As she did this, Dr. Ayer sat down and attempted to discuss the latest Scorsese film with me. Internally sighing at his obvious efforts to build up a rapport, I gave him some earnest smiles and a heartfelt analysis of the film symbolism, and he left looking satisfied.

The fourth day the nurse finally revealed her name to be Mrs. Shäfer, and on the fifth day she removed the taping from my ribs and scabbed knuckles. She also handed over a new iPod Touch along with breakfast. The iPod was empty.

"What music do you want on it?" asked Mrs. Shäfer.

I reeled off pieces by Verde, Puccini, Faure, Rachmaninoff, Elgar, Chopin, and Tchaikovsky.

"I thought you liked '80s rock and British or Scandinavian electronica," she said, frowning. Her reluctance to give me the songs I requested confirmed my paranoia. The music I had named had all been the music I had listened to as a young child, records I used to watch my mum singing along to in the kitchen or listen to the cellos practicing next door. Arden House clearly knew everything about my background; I had no secrets. I had nothing, just me.

"Whatever: to be honest. I don't like music that much," I replied casually. "Unless I'm feeling ironic; then I listen to *Rage Against the Machine.*"

"Um, well, if you're a good girl and try and get well soon, you can have any music you choose," the nurse replied, discomposedly pocketing the iPod.

On the sixth day, Dr. Ayer brought more testing; this time, IQ stuff. Being good with numbers always showed itself better on intelligence tests than any creative based intelligence, yet I still felt a new, proud pressure to do well as I scribbled my way through the papers.

"How are you feeling today, Marilyn?" Dr. Ayer asked as I finished the last of the questions. "You appear to have regained much of your energy, but I expect that's because it's very confining in this room."

"It's not too bad." I lied more instinctively than anything, adding in a softer, trustworthy voice, "I do feel I'm ready to be let out of here soon, though. I want to start the program properly, you know? Join the others, start getting better. I think I'm ready."

"I'm sure you do, Marilyn. But you must understand why we are proceeding with caution. We need to be positive it's the right time when you join the house program; we can't have more upset than necessary in there. Besides, before you are ready to recover you have to fully put aside your grief over your mother. Grief only damages people, holding them back in a state of constant stasis, and not all the doctors are sure you've understood this yet."

"Do I look like the distraught grieving daughter?" I queried, eyebrows raised.

"Do you often think of your mother?"

I smiled. "No."

He smiled back sympathetically. "Although you can use expressive grace and vulnerability to a wonderfully manipulative effect, remember that one can only tell outright lies when emotions aren't in the way. Remember that. And also remember that you shouldn't be feeling any shame. The new sense of freedom you feel is natural. Yes, death is sad, but *you* didn't die. You lived. That is good and to be celebrated."

I smiled and stretched out my legs, rolling my shoulder blades to release the tension. "You make stellar points, Dr. Ayer, and I'm sure you must speak the truth because you are a doctor and all. In fact, it's uncanny how right you are; I now feel like we are connected on a higher level or something. However, despite your pearls of wisdom, the only emotion I'm feeling right now is cabin fever from being stuck in this room."

As intended, he laughed, and I along with him.

He left shortly afterwards. It was the day after that he continued the conversation, saying "Marilyn, you must understand that these angry, sad, fearful emotions are not helpful; they are there to tie you down. They have been bred into you, to fester and explode and break down. Only once you can separate yourself from them can you understand. You have so much to potentially achieve in life; to do that, you must decide to truly live, and to live for yourself, as was naturally intended."

"I understand."

"Tomorrow you'll be re-situated in the main house with the other youths. It won't be easy there. You will be given a strict routine to follow, with classes, chores, physical training, and weekly appointments with a variety of doctors, psychoanalysts, and teachers. We will have a daily session in my office. I'll be in the house four hours a day, and you must always come to me if you have any worries or questions. Do you accept this?"

I nodded. He mirrored my nod with his own.

"All right, I think that's all for today then. And don't worry about tomorrow; you'll be with other youths just like you, all of whom just want to develop into better people." He collected his papers with those long delicate hands. "Any last questions?"

"How did I score on the tests you gave me?"

He didn't look surprised at the question, just pleased. "Flying colors, Marilyn...you passed with flying colors. Did you expect it any other way?"

When Dr. Ayer and Mrs. Shäfer came to transfer me the next day, the pallid early morning light was ripening to blue, reflected in the hard wooden floor. Mrs. Shäfer bagged the few personal items I had as I made charming comments that she in no way appreciated. Finally, Dr. Ayer opened the door and we walked out into the white, vast, empty corridor. The smell of disinfectant made my eyes water and I couldn't help but appreciate the psychology of the action as Dr. Ayer led me through the twisting corridors and flights of stairs, and past the various identical locked doors. I didn't see another person until finally we were on the ground floor, passing through another corridor that led off from the main, where there were adults murmuring inside rooms and walking around in lab coats with files and boxes. Computers hummed and generators buzzed...it reminded me of an expensive private laboratory. Dr. Ayer typed out a six number sequence into a wired pad on the largest door. Rather than watch the door open, I automatically memorized the number sequence. It had always been pedantry as much as paranoid instinct to memorize all of Club Luna's security numbers.

The door whirled open to reveal a plain square concrete courtyard surrounded by a high brick wall, wire, and a tall modern building standing on the other side of the courtyard. We stepped out into the cool fresh sunlight coming in over the walls, breathing in the early spring air, before I followed Ayer into the opposite building. Two security cameras swiveled to follow our movement across, and red flashes along the tops of the wall told me that there were alarms wired around the perimeter. Clearly, Arden House's methods weren't *too* different from the penal system. Then again, it was believed that I was a psychopathic murderer. The chances were strong that the people I'd be living with were also psychopathic murderers; perhaps security cameras were a wise idea.

***

Dr. Ayer typed the same number sequence into the door pad and we were standing in a homely hallway at the foot of carpeted stairs. The house décor here was so different from the previous building that it was grating to the nerves. It was designed to look like a very expensive mansion. The walls were manufactured panel wood, and I could smell detergent and polish in the air. Everything felt too clean and expensive to look comfortable or authentic.

"Well, this is Arden House," said Dr. Ayer. "Would you like a tour first, or would you rather join the other habitants in the breakfast room?"

Funnily enough, I was not eager to meet with the other "violent and mentally ill" teenagers I was about to share a home with, so I suggested the tour. Mrs. Shäfer left for her office and Dr. Ayer showed me around the place on his own. Arden was more like a mansion straight out of a holiday brochure, full of bathrooms, a kitchen, a dining room, a breakfast room (which I opted not to look in), a utility and laundry room, and a large living room complete with TV, sound system, DVD player, Xbox, Nintendo Wii, and several desks with Mac computers but no Internet. The second floor was full of the staff offices, the biggest belonging to Dr. Ayer and the other specialist carers. There was also a nurses' office, a solitary "resting" room, a spare room for when the night nurses finished their shifts, a testing room, and a top quality gym...which permission was required to use. The third floor was full of classrooms and a miniature library. At the two separate ends of the third floor there were steps leading up to the boys' and the girls' bedrooms. Dr. Ayer led me up to the girls' side.

"It goes without saying that it is forbidden to sneak across to the boys' rooms, and vice versa," he said.

"That's fine; I'm not here to expand my social circles," I replied.

"You'll share a bathroom—there it is—but the only other girls here at the moment are Clodagh and Jaid. They're sharing the room next to yours—here—and this one will be yours."

I was shown a rectangular little room, complete with two single beds and a chest of drawers. Dr. Ayer put his hand on my shoulder as I looked over the necessities already stocked in the drawers; deodorant, toothbrush, toothpaste, feminine hygiene products, a hairbrush. Everything had been prepared.

"As you see, at first we don't allow any personal items," said Dr. Ayer. "They come as rewards for good progress. But if you make a list full of the rewards you'd like — makeup, music, designer labels, and other such things — we'll take it into consideration for when you deserve it. But for now, you may just have this." He handed me back the silver iPod. Now there was a single track on it; Nina Simone's "*Feeling Good.*" I almost rolled my eyes. Surely this attempted process of stripping away and rebuilding my identity would only be effective if it possessed more subtlety than that of a sledgehammer? Had it even worked on the others here?

Dr. Ayer's tour finished, he sent me to Mrs. Shäfer's office, where I was given the "standard clothing," my schedule, and an educational program, which had been put together with the help of school reports. As it was my first day, I was out of lessons. Instead, I had an hour to get settled in, then had to report to the kitchens for extra chores until my settling-in meeting with Dr. Novikov.

Arms full of clothes and class plans, I sat on the end of the bed in my room. However, within minutes the sound of two other girls making their way up the stairs could be heard, so I grabbed one set of clothes and headed into the bathroom, locking it behind me as the girls, laughing about something, walked into their own room. I waited until they had gone back downstairs for class, and when I was sure I was completely alone, looked up directly into the bathroom mirror. A stranger looked back at me with a strange, closed-off expression. With dull ash-brown hair, pale angular features, and too-pale eyes, the only real color in her appearance came from the faded bruising and reddened scratches. I didn't even recognize my reflection at first, but when I did, I wanted to scream.

Of course, I didn't. Instead, I quietly observed my natural hair color. I hadn't seen it for years. I hadn't been missing out on much, though. With one final, scrutinizing look at the mirror, I had a shower and changed into the grey sweatpants and white t-shirt before heading down to the kitchen. A nurse there directed me towards the washing, pointed me to the list of laminated instructions, and left me to work by myself. It seemed strange to give me that sort of trust already, before I'd earned it. However, I was just grateful for something to do, my muscles and brain craving work.

"You must be the new girl."

Startled, I wheeled around from the sink, a dicing knife in my hand. A male around my own age leapt back from the knife. "Jesus Christ, I was just trying to be friendly!" he protested. "No need to try and stab me in the bloody face!"

"Oh…sorry!" I lowered the knife and gave him my most guileless smile. My twinkle power was still intact, at least. "Sorry, you just surprised me!"

"Do you respond to all surprises like that?" he demanded indignantly.

"Well, not usually, but you know the stereotypes one gets about a home for violent, crazy youths."

He scowled. "I'm not crazy."

"I'm sure that's what Norman Bates said, too."

"Who? And I'm *not* crazy; you're the one trying to poke a knife through people's skulls."

"We all go a little mad sometimes. Haven't you?"

We both looked at each other, and he started to laugh. Instantly I grinned back, strangely relieved. A sliver of confidence returned.

"You'll fit in around here all right," said the boy, much more warmly now, and turned back to the fridge to fix himself a glass of orange juice. I asked a bland question about the brand of the orange juice and continued to watch him closely. He was only a couple of inches taller than me, and he didn't look like the average angry teen criminal. Instead, he was glowing with life and hungry, kinetic energy, with deep glowing cinnamon-coffee skin, spiking rust-brown hair, and brightly black restless eyes. Then again, this was a house for seriously *rich* bad kids; had I expected them all to look like an average ASBO thug?

"So, what are you in here for?" asked the guy, turning back to me. "It's got to be pretty messed up if they put you in Arden; we're all born killers here."

"Not me," I said pleasantly. "My story is a bit more boring, mainly because I'm innocent."

He grinned disbelievingly. "Yeah, yeah sure! I mean, don't get me wrong. You do look a bit too...you know...wholesome compared to the rest of us, but that just means it's more interesting when you snap. By the looks of those bruises on your neck, it was pretty vicious last time. Even if you do look about as vicious as *Bambi*." He frowned, seeming to struggle with this apparent contradiction.

"Why is it that every single person I've met lately feels the compulsion to decide what I'm like deep down inside? It's exhausting."

The distraction worked and he immediately laughed. "Well, you should be more like me then. No one offers me advice; no one dares, you get me? Like, when me and my cousin first arrived here, I was pretty bruised up too—worse than you are now—but people still left us well alone. There was one ugly bruiser of a kid—don't worry, he's long gone now—who tried to return me to the hospital. But we properly showed him."

I suspected my expression was similar to that worn by a squirrel seconds before it became road kill.

"Don't worry though," the boy added. "All the people in here at the moment are pretty all right. Especially my cousin; you'll like her." He smiled at me, eyes catching my own, and I smiled back, wondering how crazy his family had to be that the pair of them ended up here.

"That's good to know. I don't think I'd survive in a fight here, especially not against you!"

He laughed louder, relaxing. "No! But I'd never fight against you, so don't worry. I only fight blokes and nasty bitches. Besides, even with your knife, you couldn't hurt *me*. I'm Levi, by the way."

"Charmed. I'm Marilyn. And I'm sure I couldn't hurt you. I'm not much of a fighter. I'm more the peace type." Or the arsenic-in-the-Ribena type.

"Well, that's cool," said Levi, now obviously in friendly mode, "because I'll look out for you in here, don't worry."

Immediately after his words, he tensed up again, looking above my head. "And if *he* gives you a hard time, just tell me and I'll bloody kill him. He's a mean, piss-ugly bastard."

I instantly swiveled around, alarmed, as a taller male with the broad shoulders and hard physique of someone who *did* fight entered the kitchen. Despite Levi's gritted words and wary posture, the newcomer barely glanced over at us, just rummaged around the pantry for food. Yet I was still wary; the guy looked hostile, tough, even though I'd noted how his eyes had slid past mine as if unable to make direct contact. I tried not to feel intimidated as he took his time choosing food, aware of both of us watching.

"Do you see what he's doing, Levi?" I said, in a falsely fascinated tone. "Have you ever seen when animals try to assert dominance in a new social setting?"

Levi looked a bit confused, and the new guy shot me a disinterested look, eyes still not quite meeting us as he turned back to his pile of cereal bars and fruits.

His expression irritated me. I did my best David Attenborough impression as I continued. "And here we have a special sub-species of the disaffected youth, known as the angry white male. Not a rare specimen by any means, but nevertheless they tend to have their own charm. Now, we wait for the AWM to respond to the interlopers...."

Levi was laughing as the guy finally looked at me, his brow furrowed and jaw tight. His long, deep blue eyes still didn't quite meet mine, though, as he said dismissively, "I see Arden has imported a new species of pet clown to entertain us all. Just what we needed."

He grabbed his food and walked back out.

Ouch.

I couldn't help but stare after him. "I'm going to need some aloe for that burn," I commented. "He's smarter than he looks, right?"

Levi glowered. "That's not saying much."

True. Now he had been much more the stereotype of a sociopathic killer. Perhaps around five-foot-ten, well-built and broad-shouldered, he'd looked a few years older than me and Levi, with short, black hair, hard, pale, plain features, and a brutally straight nose that looked as if it had been punched in a few times. He wasn't anything special to look at, and the flat, bored indifference in his eyes hadn't helped, but he looked like he could take some real punishment without flinching.

"That's Jason. He's a wanker," muttered Levi, also staring after him. "One of these days I'm going to beat the crap out of him, you'll see."

"And I'll be standing right behind you, pretending I'm not there."

He laughed and nudged my shoulder with his own. "You're funny, Marilyn. I gotta get back though, next class is starting soon and I'm supposed to be taking a leak. If I'm caught skiving they'll send me back to Dr. Gauk, and he always wants to talk about feelings and crap. He has yet to realize I'm a man, therefore a *machine*."

"Ah...identifying with machines; the first symptom of craziness," I responded, and he nudged me again, grinning happily.

"So perhaps I lied; maybe I am slightly crazy. But that's how they *want* us to be, you know. They don't want us to get better. Not the *right* kind of better, anyway."

"Then what do they want?"

He shrugged, his eyes suddenly becoming too intensely bright. "Something else. I don't know what. I just know that they keep me and the other special ones here as the others come and go. We stay because we're different; we're the ones they want, the ones who aren't ever getting out of here. And I can already tell you're one of us."

"Do you give this welcome to everyone, or am I just lucky?"

"Ah, you'll see soon that this is no normal rehabilitation program. I've been in juvvie and all the normal crap, and this isn't how it's supposed to be. They just keep us here and monitor us as they perform their own tests, make their own conclusions, teach us their own crap. And they *want* us to know it's different, that we won't escape from them unless we change."

I'd had enough. Nodding and smiling still, I detached myself from him and began to walk away. That would be the last time I joked about someone being crazy.

"I'll be careful, then," I promised.

"I've freaked you out, right?" he asked with a sharp laugh. "Who knows, maybe you'll be one of the ones they don't care about."

"You've not freaked me out...I'm just so glad to have made a new friend. But I'd better go find Dr. Novikov now," I said, and turned to knock straight into a tall, dark girl marching into the room. She shot me a look that sized me up and down, and then directed her forceful attention onto Levi.

"Levi," she announced, "we're going to be late for class again. And if you think you're skipping our bloody laundry duty afterwards, I'll kick your ass. I'm pissed off with doing everything for you." She then looked back down at me guardedly. She had the same arresting model-worthy features as Levi, but with darker skin and hair, and the same "screw you" attitude stamped across her forehead. She had to be the cousin. Past her, a heavier girl with an overgrown white-blonde Mohawk hung back on the edge of the kitchen. She looked slightly younger than me, although I had no illusions that this would give me any advantage over her.

"You must be Marilyn," said Levi's cousin. "Dr. Novikov is looking for you." She leant on the cabinet beside Levi with a fiercely territorial air.

"Hey, Jaid." Levi obliviously slung a casual arm around her. "You just missed Marilyn tearing down Jason; it was epic. Oh, did you notice Jason cut his own hair last night for no reason? How weird is he?"

"Completely psycho," replied Jaid, still occupied with her unsubtle look-over of me. "He's cut it in exactly the same style as that new male nurse's hair now. Probably trying to mess with the guy…Clodagh overheard the new nurse whining to Ayer that Jason was stalking him." She stopped, pointedly looking at me. "You still here?"

A power play already, then. I appeared not to notice and said "Awfully sorry to interrupt, but do you know where I could possibly find Dr. Novikov"s office?"

She folded her arms much as Levi had earlier. "My, my, aren't you well-spoken? He'll be in the third office second floor. We'll see you later, no doubt."

I left with a nod at the blonde girl who had to be Clodagh. She muttered "Goodbye," revealing a Northern Irish inflection and little teeth that slanted inwards.

Dr. Ayer was also in Dr. Novikov"s office. After I sat down and was handed my new schedules, Novikov began to take the usual blood tests and skin samples whilst Ayer took over the conversation.

"What do you think of the house?" was his first question.

"Very nice," I replied, somewhat predictably.

He smiled gently, and said "I'm glad you like it. I do hope you'll be happy here and not too...upset." He said the word delicately, making it clear what he meant.

"Grieving is pointless," I reminded him. It was what he wanted to hear. But there was an oddly painful feeling in my stomach even as my face remained open and agreeable.

Dr. Ayer patted me on the shoulder. "You mustn't forget that, Marilyn. You've only got yourself."

"Right, we're done now," said the other doctor, Novikov, packing away the equipment. "Class starts tomorrow, so finish all your settling in today."

"You may notice the difference in our teaching methods from your old school," interjected Ayer. "Arden House receives enough private funding that we don't have to follow the government's own restrictive education system, and instead can use our own highly personalized and more effective one."

"They should put that in the brochure," I said, getting out of my seat.

"Wait," said Novikov as an afterthought. "Do you need any sleeping medication? New habitants usually require a higher dosage."

"Thank you, but I don't have any trouble sleeping," I replied. Ayer gave me a private, soft-edged smile, impossible to read.

"You're not having trouble sleeping?" Novikov repeated, staring at me through his thick glasses.

"Do you think I should be tormented by nightmares?" I asked, to my own surprise. "Do you think it says something about me that I'm fine?"

"I'll let you decide what that says about you, Marilyn."

I left.

The rest of the day passed slowly. Another nurse sent me to clean the bathrooms along with Clodagh, the heavy blonde girl. Rather uncharacteristically, I did not feel like communicating, so I pretended I was shy and worked manically fast, making the silence between us both seem less awkward. She kept mumbling little remarks in a girlish tone every once in a while, as if trying to talk. "The hot tap comes out cold at first." "That's where Sylvia cracked her head on the wall. Can you see the blood stain?" ("Oh...why yes I think I can.") Between chores, I ate dinner as fast as I could in order to escape the table. Everybody else seemed to have the same idea, wandering in at separate times, nobody bothering to talk except for Jaid and Levi, who murmured together in the corner. Afterwards, as the six others went their separate ways for organized leisure time in the evening, I just went to bed. A nurse cornered me as I crept off and gave me vitamins, informing me that after tomorrow I'd be expected to take part in leisure time. It wasn't until I was alone in my small plain room that I started to shake; I didn't even know why. I got into bed and curled up as small as I could until it stopped. Novikov's earlier words echoed in my head and I didn't want to go to sleep. As a child I'd suffered constantly from bad dreams. Now, I didn't. This had to be a good thing, right?

Trying to ward off sleep, I began to plan how to find out what information Arden could possibly give me about the Porsche and the murderer. How would I find it out, and how would I get out of here if this place didn't have anything? What would I do once I was out? How would I find *them*. Strategizing made me feel better, calmed me down, and soon I fell asleep anyway.

As before, I did not dream.

CHAPTER THREE

Dr. Luo was the doctor assigned to teach my first lesson, economics. A bored lizard of a man, his eyes kept flicking to the clock as he handed the seven of us our individual work assessments. Levi and I were both in year thirteen and were each handed a red file, whereas Jaid, Clodagh, and the American boy Sebastian were in year twelve. The other American boy, Teddy, was in year ten, while Jason, who was apparently a couple of years older than high school, was given "special" work. Probably special ed work.

I sat at the back of the classroom behind Jaid and Levi. Sebastian and Teddy also sat together yet not speaking, both playing on Nintendo DSs under the desk, and Jason and Clodagh sat on their own, as I did. I peered down at my textbook, but Teddy quickly caught my interest instead. He was a small, frail boy, black with neglected overgrown hair and a lazy eye, and seemed to be unable to stop fidgeting or focus his attention on one thing at once. His eyes constantly flickered out to study everything around him, his brain almost ticking out loud in a self-unaware way. There were millions of scribbled jottings all over his hands and forearms—calculations, notes-to-self, ideas—all oddly organized and ordered down his skin, and when he thanked me for passing over his work, I noticed a slight speech impediment. The difference between him and Jason, who sat opposite him with his arms folded, legs outstretched, and staring out the window, was rather evident. Unlike Teddy, Jason barely seemed to move, and when he did, it was always with deliberate precision and innate control. I distrusted the unchanging expression of stony, bored hostility he always seemed to wear in group situations. He reminded me of a predatory creature lying in wait, and I knew if there was anybody who posed an immediate threat to me, it was him.

Perhaps I shouldn't have annoyed him quite so readily.

Dr. Luo seemed content to let us work on our projects with minimum interference while he sat at the desk with his laptop. As far as I knew, there was still no Internet in Arden House and I was unable to find any other distractions, so in the end I had no option but turn to the work I'd been given.

"Do you need any help? Economics is pretty boring," said Levi, turning to whisper to me. Jaid scowled at us both, but continued working steadily.

"I'm fine, thanks," I smiled. "Economics is actually one of my best subjects."

He sighed. "God, what kind of criminal home is full of supergeeks? You're as bad as Jaid. At least she's got the excuse of being an Asian stereotype."

"You think Jaid and I are bad because we work hard, but not because we're in a criminal home?" I asked teasingly, and he flashed me a wide sharp grin as Jaid swiveled round again, the scowl more pronounced.

"Levi, stop with your BBCD flirting and shut the hell up. Focus on your work; you're already the thickest person in the entire class, even with Mr. High-School-Drop-Out sitting in the corner."

"Relax, Jaid, they won't chuck me out of Arden if I fail; I'm much too good looking to waste on the general public," he said, making her glare more. She suddenly turned her attention to me.

"And I suppose you think you belong here now, too? You think that the Little Miss Perfect, Little Miss Superior routine is working? You don't belong here; there's nothing special about you."

I didn't know how to respond, partly because I was taken aback, partly because my strategy was normally to let people come to whatever conclusion they wanted about me, and then just carry on my merry way, doing whatever I wanted. Clearly that wasn't going to work in this situation.

Luckily, Levi interrupted. "Stop it Jaid, you're just being a bitch because—"

"Oh, of course you're fooled by her little sugary act she's got going on," Jaid hissed. "You're an idiot, Levi, and you always will be. She doesn't belong here, she won't get better; she's just a regular killer. The sooner she accepts it, the sooner she'll get out of our way."

Had everyone in this classroom killed someone?

"I'm not a killer, it was self-defense," I said very quietly, and Jaid snorted in disgust, turning her back on me. As I kept my head low, I felt that dormant knotted anger starting to uncoil along my veins. The memory of hitting and hitting and that red dirty fury reared its dizzy, vague head, and suddenly I was feeling unsure of myself again, and very alone.

It was then that I saw Jason's face was turned in our direction, watching the three of us with a glittering awareness in his startlingly deep blue eyes. Furious with myself, I made myself wink at him and blew him a kiss, making him instantly turn away, eyes lowered. Then I waited until I was back in control before tapping on Jaid's shoulder, my eyes wide and earnest and scared.

"You're right," I whispered desperately. "It's all an act. I don't belong here; I'm so scared all the time, and I know that they are going to find out I'm just a pathetic imposter and send me back home. I *can't* be trapped at home aga—"

"I don't what to hear this." Jaid brushed off my words, but I saw uncertainty in her stiff shoulders.

Levi nudged her, smiling into her face. "See, I told you you're still the Alpha fem around here." She shot him a look, but the way he smiled at her seemed to thaw out the hardness slightly. "Now look after your pack, all right? That includes all of us."

"Pack? I doubt I'll ever be part of that," I said with a hint more strength than I intended, but she didn't seem to notice. Instead, she coolly said "Maybe, but you're one of us now...at least temporarily. If you want, me and Clodagh requested the TV room after chores...no one will stop you from joining us. If you want."

I was officially baffled at the quick turnaround, but without hesitation I thanked her. "That's so kind of you!"

She was suspicious at my enthusiasm. "Well, the film will probably suck. Mrs. Mudiraj always chooses right crap for us to watch; nothing above a PG12."

"They probably figure we provide enough profanity and violence in real life," said Levi as he turned to me, that infectious sharp grin still in place. "But you know, so far we've been severely lacking in scenes of a sexual nature. How about we fix this problem?"

We both burst out laughing, making Jaid roll her eyes and turn back to her work. Dr. Luo immediately quietened us down and as the class continued, I smiled to myself. I was back in control, back inside a comfortable role, and had temporarily overcome the distracting obstacle of Jaid. I couldn't afford to think of anything other than getting out of there, and that meant being the perfect patient first.

Jason was watching me again. Slowly I raised my head and this time pulled an exaggeratedly helpless damsel expression, fluttered my eyelashes provokingly. He turned away yet again, his face dismissive, and I bared my teeth at the vulnerable uncovered back of his neck. It was only then that I saw he was still watching me, only now in the window reflection, and his expression promised trouble.

"Jason's been watching you a lot today," said Jaid as we flopped onto the sofas of the living room. "Why?"

I shrugged, picking out a film from the collection. "Clearly I'm irresistible."

"He's the newest one of us besides you," said Jaid. "He's even more of a head case than all of us put together. On his first day, Levi, Seb, and Ferdinand—Ferd's long gone—tried to, I don't know, initiate him or something. He didn't react well; half killed Ferd, knocked Levi out, and broke Seb's nose. It totally messed up the house dynamic for ages after."

"Shit. What did the doctors do to him?"

"Didn't even put him in solitary. They didn't care; they found it interesting, wrote a bunch of notes, and asked me why I tried to end the fight. Asked some questions about Jason challenging my place, generally trying to stir up more shit between us." Her lips thinned as she thought this over and I popped the DVD into the player, Clodagh switching channels.

"They want us to fight, you think?" I asked.

"No, they just...they just want us to keep to ourselves, believe that we should deal with our own, individual problems. Focus on ourselves, all that stuff."

"They don't want us to feel defined by the past or by our social position to others," mumbled Clodagh.

"Whatever," Jaid sniffed. "They barely tolerate mine and Levi's relationship; they say it's unhealthy and holding us back and stuff. But whatever. Levi and I have been together our whole lives, that's never going to change."

"You and Clodagh also seem to be friends."

Clodagh had a surprisingly girly smile as Jaid sighed. "Clodagh is friends with me because she doesn't want to be my enemy," she said bluntly. "Same as how Sylvia was, only Sylvia was just annoying with it. Clodagh's pretty low down in the house hierarchy; all the doctors except Dr. Ayer pretty much ignore her. The only person lower than her is Sebastian. He doesn't even have to see his specialists anymore. He'll be gone within a week."

"We have to be the most self-aware bunch of violent psychopaths ever," I said, glancing at Clodagh's reaction to Jaid's analysis of her. She saw my look and nodded, not remotely concerned.

"It's true," she mumbled. "I'm a talented parasite. I've learned to embrace it."

A brief look of contempt passed through Jaid's eyes before she grabbed the TV controller off her and switched on the film. As the credits started rolling, the small camera half hidden in the corner of the room glinted and caught my attention. Even now, they were watching us. Analyzing. This was certainly no rehabilitation center. I tried to watch the film but I had far too much energy, so I made my exit amid lots of apologies and headed towards Dr. Ayer's office, intending to ask if I could use the gym...which would probably be the first time in my life I'd ever used a gym.

As I climbed up to the second floor, a low conversation could be heard coming from the first office. It was Dr. Luo talking to one of the nurses...Mrs. Mudiraj, I thought her name was.

"So Obadiah is really convinced that these are his final six, then?"

"Apparently so, but he still needs to wait until the other board members confirm. Until then, we'll begin to move them into the third stage. On Monday we'll start the new physical exercise program and the class lessons can finally shift to the prepared phase three material."

"Aren't you worried it's a bit risky to start so soon? The cousins are proving to be very resistant, and the Aske girl has only just arrived. I doubt she'll be responsive enough yet."

"Obadiah thinks so; he believes she's already one of the most ready. He also believes the cousins are nearer than we think...that's why he's a genius, he spots this sort of potential. Like Jason Lucas; didn't you want to kick him out of Arden at one point?"

"Not just me, we all had doubts about him. I still do, no matter how much Obadiah says he's got him under firm control."

"Trust me, Lucas is the one who needs this program the most."

"And Sebastian Modine-Pound is being sent away tomorrow, right? Juvvie?"

"Back somewhere or other in the US government system, much to his parents' disdain."

At the sound of someone coming out the door, I noisily hopped up the rest of the stairs, and appeared to just notice Mrs. Mudiraj as she walked out the office.

"Oh, there you are!" I said happily. "I was just wondering where Dr. Ayer is?"

"He's assessing Sebastian's progress at the minute," she replied. "Go and wait in his office."

I didn't, of course. I went upstairs. As I climbed out onto the landing, a movement in the corner caught my eye; Jason straightening to his feet from the shadows. I jumped, but he was already moving away. Had he been listening to Mrs. Mudiraj's conversation too? A pressure was building up at the back of my skull and in the pit of my stomach, so I spent the rest of the evening cataloguing the entire house, taking an inventory of all windows, doors, locks, alarms, and searching for the weaker spots in the security...of which there were none. This managed to help keep away the sleep for many hours. And when I woke up the next morning, Sebastian Modine-Pound had already left Arden House. No one even seemed to notice.

***

In my daily session with Ayer the next day, he didn't mention anything. Instead, he took the usual tests, and then commented that I appeared to have managed to integrate into the house very well.

"You are starting to embrace your special strengths," he said, the satisfaction in his tone giving me a taste of what Stockholm syndrome must feel like. "You are realizing the person you could potentially be."

"As clarifying as always, Doctor."

"Actually, I tell you what, Marilyn. Let's kick start today's session with some more light-hearted fun questions for you. If you could have a magical power or any sort of supernatural improvement, what would it be?"

I cleared my throat. I didn't enjoy being asked unexpected "fun" questions. "How whimsical you are, Doctor. I guess...well, I used to watch the X-Men cartoons when I was a kid, and I always wanted to be either Mystique or Warren Worthington, aka Angel. I could never decide which. Like, in the third film when Angel flies out of the window; that was great." Belatedly, I realized I was telling the truth.

"You sound like you've given this thought."

I shrugged. "Doesn't everyone wish they were something better and more powerful?"

He looked steadily at me for a second before replying smoothly, "Of course they do. Few get their wish granted, though."

"It's called being human."

A few days later, our classes began to change. It started with a documentary the greyhound-like Dr. Gauk made us watch, analyzing and dissecting the problems of not only the current and past governments, but the theories of political forms of democracy and rulerships in general. It used as an example how the current British and American governments and law systems were irreparably flawed, and basically came to the conclusion that democracy was nothing but an idealistic theory that could never be put into practice. Strangely enough, the documentary made me think of Adam: his righteous indignation with the state of the world, the loss of power he felt, and his frustrated inability to do anything about it. But then thinking of him just reminded me of how his father had so easily handed me over to a stranger when promised a free pass from jail and a foothold in the corporate ladder.

Dr. Gauk then brought out graphs and correlatively showed us the rise of capitalist businesses, tycoons, and corporations, and explained how they controlled the majority of the power in the world: controlled and influenced the government more than the individuals who voted for the parliament ever would.

"And what does this teach you?" asked Dr. Gauk.

"That a single person is irrelevant in this world and can't do anything to change it," replied Jaid instantly.

"Wrong," said Teddy suddenly, jerking his hunched back straighter. "That's the easy way out answer. Think about it properly, Jaid."

"Think about my fist up your—"

Teddy hurriedly continued. "It tells us how all power is essentially up to the individual who agrees to follow and uphold these systems of power. When an individual lets himself be reduced to being part of the collective, he has nothing. But it's always one individual creating businesses, influencing legislation, creating any sort of change. When we act as a mass, the...the *system*, the collective power, can strip us of our power. It's how they create their own power. When we act as individuals, we strip them of *their* power."

I tried not to roll my eyes as Dr. Gauk prompted, "And how do you feel about this concept, Edward?"

Teddy looked slightly startled. "I feel like I'm being shown that I already have all the power I needed, without realizing it. And that I should be more aware of myself, and not let others take away my strength again. The world is created and controlled by individuals who understand how to use their power."

"I couldn't possibly comment on your personal opinion," said Dr. Gauk calmly, "but that is a logical concl—"

"No, it's not," interrupted Levi, looking around him. "It sounds nice, but it's bullshit really. I mean, if everybody was to suddenly start loving themselves and be all individual and refusing to follow the government and shit, then there would be absolute chaos! And if society can't function and breaks down, then we would have no progression as a culture and our civilization would be over."

Levi was becoming wound up; Jaid placed her hand protectively over his and said calmly, "Levi is right. We need collective standards in order to progress those very standards… and to protect those who are perhaps not as able as the rest of us."

"Good points, Levi and Jaid," said Dr. Gauk briskly. "But I would argue three basic points. Firstly, you didn't deny that the progression or regression of a society is still always created and dictated by a few key individuals; society will always be forced to tag along behind those few with power. Whether this is a good or bad thing is irrelevant; it simply is. Secondly, this means that there will never be 'chaos,' because ordinary humanity has a basic need to follow, to have a collective to keep them safe and in comfort. It is instinct to reject the dangerous aspects to individuality — the freedom, the power — and instead keep oneself bound in social structure. Therefore, thirdly, when there *is* an individual who rejects collectivism, he will be the rare exception and thus the one who triumphs. Society teaches us that chaos is a bad thing because chaos creates the individual and sets him free. In a chaos-restricted society (which all societies are), power will thus always come from the chaos. You all have the potential for chaos. This is a good thing."

"This is bollocks," said Levi.

At the same time Teddy said, "This argument seems self-serving."

I spoke without thinking. "What a wonderful thing to teach criminals in a rehabilitation center, Dr. Gauk; it's the system that's flawed, not us. We're all precious, special little angels."

Dr. Gauk didn't smile. "I expected some of you to have negative reactions to this concept. So let me put it to you this way. The six of you, as you've probably all noticed, are all above average intelligence, and all but one of you are from wealthy, self-made families who gained their money in the business and science sectors." (Clodagh looked sneakily at

Jason, who ignored her.) "Yet all six of you have had your lives unfairly determined and controlled by the state. You have all been failed, and all become failures in return. That is because you were all special, individual cases, with potential and ability that didn't fit the regular mold. Thus you were failed by collective standards. You have been rendered powerless because you allowed the power to lie in the hands of others. The government, the family, the expectations placed upon you, the *system*. Systems only work because people choose to believe in them and enforce them. Power lies where you *choose* it to lie; and it is the people who realize this and *wield* their power for themselves alone that will take back and own the earth. And that is what the graph shows you."

Silence.

"Must be in the footnotes," I muttered to Teddy, who was staring stricken at Dr. Gauk. I smiled tiredly at my own joke as Teddy then looked for footnotes. There was a new knot of anxiety at the back of my skull as Dr. Gauk's words echoed round and round, and I knew I was admiring them.

Dr. Gauk was just about to continue with the lesson when Jason spoke up from the back in his most expressionless voice. "I guess you think that morality is also a method of collective repression over the individual power?" We all looked at him in surprise. He never spoke when he could help it, and never willingly. I hadn't even been entirely sure he knew how to string a sentence together, let alone debate on ethical issues.

"Organized religious morality is a method of social control, obviously," interjected Teddy, his awkward enthusiasm grating. "But if morality was kept separate from church, state, and law, it would be the opposite of individual repression."

"It wouldn't exist then," said Gauk shortly.

"Morality is just a pretty little tool that people use to feel better about themselves," sneered Jaid. "They use it as a faux self-empowerment, to pretend they are better than other people, and hide how trapped their lives really are."

"My head hurts," whispered Clodagh.

"That's because you're in class with a bunch of bloody philosophers," Levi said, grinning. "I understand now why Van Gogh chopped his own ear off."

"Van Gogh was an artist, you dipshit," said Jaid.

"I can still sympathize."

"I see you're all getting tired," Dr. Gauk said. "So we'll finish today's lesson with one last point. We've all agreed that society benefits from having a collective moral system. But what happens when the collective moral system clashes with something that would be morally imperative for the individual? For example, justice when enforced by a lone individual is repackaged as vengeance and judged 'bad.' Why? And how many of you agree with the morality of vengeance?"

The response triggered by his words was immediate; an electric tension shocked the room. Even Jason was looking fully at Dr. Gauk, eyes narrowed and mouth tight. All six of us had had a personal, hostile reaction to his words, which was anything but a coincidence. I swallowed painfully. Lingering at the back of my brain was the suppressed, bloody vision that I punched down and down into, breaking the man who'd killed.... I swallowed again, and looked back up as Dr. Gauk smiled coldly.

"Is vengeance wrong, and why?" he asked, and with that, the lesson was succinctly ended.

Vengeance sets you free, I thought. But I was still stuck there, no closer to any answers, or finding out about the owner of the Porsche, or who the "they" who tried to kill me were. I was passive as ever. Weak. I had to escape this place.

CHAPTER FOUR

The classes continued. The next day, there was a completely new woman with an Italian accent talking about ethics. We were still unnaturally hushed as she started off with regular school topics of ethics, and then branched out into the rise of business ethics. Much of it touched upon what Dr. Gauk had said, hammering it all home. Then there was a history class, focusing on recent political and military strategic history, then natural science, economics....

As soon as the lessons for the day were over, Mrs. Mudiraj and Mrs. Shäfer directed the girls upstairs to the gym, and the males to the courtyard for fitness. In the next few hours, we had our health monitored and recorded. Our times on all the gym equipment were recorded, and we were timed against each other on the treadmill. I came last, of course. We were told our weakest areas, our fitness targets, and how to increase our fitness levels, and then were sent down to the courtyard as the guys passed us to go to the gym. Levi was leading, looked incredibly pissed off and shooting glances at a spectacularly unobservant Jason, while Teddy trailed miserably behind them both. We were all already sweaty, cheeks flushed and shirts sticky, yet in the cold damp courtyard, a square jawed white "Rhodesian" talked us through physical biology and athletic care while making us do sit ups, press ups, and agility tests around obstacle cones. He then taught us several drills for hand to hand combat, and pushed us through aggressive fighting sequences, partnering me up with the willing Clodagh when it was needed. By the end of the day I was more exhausted than I had ever felt in my life, and I could hardly breathe, every muscle in my body screaming from physical exertion.

Finally we were allowed to go back inside the house. The three of us stumbled straight up towards the showers, too dazed to speak. Jaid got to the bathroom first and went for the shower as Clodagh and I slumped down against the wall outside, preparing to wait. Clodagh keeled over and weakly spewed her dinner up on the floor. A few seconds later, I gingerly held back her soft fringe and rubbed her shoulder while she wheezed and retched. I was very good at comforting people; I had often done the same with my mother. I sighed. The bright orange overhead lights were making me feel decidedly sick as well. Finally Clodagh righted herself with a dim groan.

"You'll feel much better after a hot shower," I said distantly.

She gave a small pant of agreement and closed her eyes, leaning against me with her pale clammy face strangely content in its suffering. She even took my hand. To hide my discomposure, I looked over the titles of the new books on the hallway shelves. They were all self-defense manuals, biology texts, texts on genetics, the private sector, economics texts, psychology, strategy, and lectures on self-awareness, self-control, game theory, business, and so on.

Clodagh followed my gaze and said breathlessly, "We were chosen, Marilyn, we really were. And finally, it feels like everything is in motion, and we are going somewhere. We're all changing and it will be good."

"I don't want things to change anymore," said Jaid, stepping out of the bathroom with a rush of hot steam. Her long wet black hair dripped onto the landing as she stood over us in a towel. "I'm sorry, but wherever this is going, whatever is happening to us, it's not good, okay? I don't like any of this. When we came to Arden, I thought we wouldn't have to deal with any more constant bloody problems." She lowered herself down to sit on my other side and spoke again, her voice harsh. "I'm sick of this. Of plans and people and motives and schemes. I just want to be left alone. Maybe then, I'll get some bloody peace."

"Completely alone?" I asked, and she defensively corrected herself.

"I meant alone with just me and Levi. No one else."

I touched her bare knee, trying to convey sympathy as normal, but my brain didn't seem to be working properly and my motions were awkward. I felt too...confused...and I didn't trust myself to speak, so I kept quiet and kept on patting Jaid's knee, feeling raw and useless.

"It's ironic, isn't it?" I managed at last to find a topic I would be able to speak about with ease. "How an institutionalized program is teaching us how to be individual. Would the doctors really appreciate it if we attempted to be truly individual and...overtake them, or something? Really, they just want us to be selective in our self-empowerment."

"I don't care," said Jaid tartly. I rubbed her knee again.

"Don't be sad, Jaid," Clodagh spoke up from my other side. "You'll see soon that there is a point to all this, and you'll be happy again."

"You should go next for the shower," I said quickly, motioning to the bathroom. Clodagh smiled and got up, dragging her fingernails up my bare arm as she did so. It was rather strange, and when I looked back at my arm after she'd gone, I found reddened scratch marks. Jaid leaned back against the wall and watched me inspect my arm incredulously.

"Why did you let her have the first shower?"

I shrugged.

"It made you look weak. You think it makes you look like you care about her, but it doesn't. I know it's a pretense."

"If you say so."

This answer didn't please her either. "So why do you do it then? Why the constant acting, the false personas? Do you really think we're all going to be BFF"s forever and live happily ever after when all this is over?"

I couldn't think of any answer to give so I just smiled and nodded. She rolled her eyes and looked away.

"It's pointless trying to talk to you properly."

There was silence for a few minutes, before I had this strange urge to speak out loud, to vocalize myself.

"When I was a kid I used to…lie…because I had to. In order for me to…I don't know. Survive, to be left alone and to get my own way, without people tampering with me. And to make people acknowledge me. But now… it's not because I have to. It's because I can. Because it works. I like it."

"It's a power," she said.

I shrugged. "Yeah, I guess. I mean, I don't see it as a fault in me anymore; it's who I am."

I immediately stopped talking and looked at my knees.

"Everyone is changing," Jaid commented to the wall opposite us. "Except Levi. He said that we'll be safe as long as the two of us stay together, fight them, refuse to change or do anything they want. He'll always put me first, no matter what happens. It's just how he is. He doesn't ever want us to be alone in the world."

"He's pretty special," I said softly. "You're lucky you have each other."

"Are we?"

There was stubborn conflict in her face as I nodded. "When I was younger, if I'd had someone...if I'd had the opportunity to not be alone anymore. I mean, I think that...even when being alone becomes a key part of your identity, it's still not.... I mean, I know it sets you free and all that, but...." I broke off.

"I always figured that too. Now I'm not so sure." She tugged my knee against hers, gripping her hand around my ankle. Her comradely actions shocked me and I kept utterly still as the two of us continued to lie against the wall, unwilling to expend the energy to move. Unwilling to move away from a freely given physical touch. Inside the shower, Clodagh was singing Muse, and Jaid's breath was warm against my ear. For a few minutes I had a vision of friendship, the three of us, perhaps even the six, sitting together, working together. But then as Clodagh walked back out the shadow, accidentally kicking Jaid and causing her to flare up in retaliation, reality resurfaced. And although I laughed at my daydream, I also felt ashamed.

***

Life inside Arden continued as a revolving door of new lecturers, teachers, and lessons, everything we would need for "success and survival in the outside world." The competition between the six of us was increased and we were never given a chance to rest or relax with each other, only time to compare ourselves to each other. It sounded pathetic to say, but the most constant thing in my life, the thing I found myself taking root in, were the daily sessions with Dr. Ayer. Even if the meeting was only for five minutes, as it was sometimes, he was always there, sitting behind the desk and ready to talk in that practiced, serene way of his. Asking me questions, taking his tests, genuinely interested in the answers I had, even when they were lies. Especially when they were lies. I wouldn't allow myself to ever like him, of course. I told myself it was because I was waiting for him to slip up, to reveal to me why he was so interested in us. But in part it was also because he wouldn't let me get close to him even if I'd wanted it. He kept himself distant and instead spoke what I called "brochure words" over again. Familiar words by now, about never relying on anyone else, about me having power while I remained detached and in control of myself.

There was little time to remember the confused, bitter memories of the outside world.

The program continued to push and push at us and we barely had enough energy to eat, let alone resist. Class lessons continued to pull us in all directions; we learned in detail about security, modern military, psychology, and political history, exercises in critical thinking, the physics of light, medical basics, the cycle of plants. In some ways I loved it. No, I know I loved the information, the focus, the feeling of complete mental and physical exhaustion. All of us loved it to a degree, I think...even Jason, although he kept himself that silent, solitary figure at the back. I loved that in this world, I was good. No, I was one of the best. The outside world was irrelevant.

We were all taught how to increase our speed, our reflexes, and then they started on the fighting techniques — all to protect ourselves without the need for killing in the future, of course. It emerged that Jaid and Jason were already rather adept at forms of martial arts; the instructor mentioned something to Jason about his obvious Jiu Jitsu and wrestling background, and Jaid had been doing Muay Thai for years, while Levi was a fairly decent boxer. The three of us who were completely untrained were kept separate and taught alone. I had no particular skill at fighting and I had no intention of honing that part of myself, either. Teddy was also completely hopeless, but at least he tried hard. Rather than practice fighting, I took to running on the treadmill.

"I feel like this time around, when I face the world, I'll be able to do it properly," Jaid commented at the end of one particular workout. Levi's panic-stricken expression at her words was only noticed by me.

It was thus a huge shock when the routine I'd fallen into was disrupted again. For some reason, I woke up in the middle of the night with a tight knot of panic lodged in my stomach, and my limbs tangled up in the sweaty blankets. I had not dreamed of anything, but my skin was slick with sweat as if I had; my hair was tangled and I needed fresh air and water. As I sat up in bed, rolling my aching shoulder blades, a metallic glint fell across the window as if a dark blue car was driving past. Hurriedly, I jumped out of bed and headed downstairs to the kitchen, the only place where the windows opened up fully. The downstairs was hushed and dark, empty except for the gurgle of the heating system and humming electricity around me. The kitchen lights were still on, however. Assuming someone had just forgotten to turn off the lights, I started to drink from the tap.

"Having trouble sleeping, Marilyn?"

I spun around quickly. Jason sat beside an open window in the furthest corner of the kitchen, watching me. The security camera above him had been violently knocked upwards so it now faced the ceiling. As usual, Jason had the animation of a rock, yet there were dark circles scoring his flat eyes, and something seemed different about him tonight. Weaker. Aware that I wasn't wearing a bra, I crossed my arms across my chest, but he didn't appear to notice, turning back to the window when I didn't reply.

"Yeah, light sleeper," I agreed, glad that conversations with Jason only ever lasted a second or two, and turned to head back upstairs.

"I'm surprised. I thought you were having the time of your life here in Arden." Confused, I glanced back at him as he added, "Don't you just feel so damned lucky to be here and all special and shit?" His eyes met mine then shunted past, arms folded and his face tightly challenging. "Well? Don't you?"

"But of course, sweetheart," I said in my most artificially innocent voice, just because I knew he'd dislike it. "Why wouldn't I love it here? Don't you know that Arden wants to give us a second chance and give us future prospects in a failing world? I'm so darned lucky I can hardly believe it."

"Do you think that's funny?" he asked slowly, a slight crease between his brows, trying to figure me out. "Because it's not."

"Well, you're the resident expert on humor, so I'll just have to accept your word on it."

He leaned forward, his nostrils flaring. "That's it, accept my word as well. You seem to be talented at accepting things. Like accepting the fact you're in Arden, without even knowing *why*."

"It's so cute when you try and intimidate me. But accept the fact that your words mean less than nothing to me, and go pick a fight with someone else."

"Oh, I see how it works. You don't do fighting, or confrontation, in case you don't get your own way. You employ other methods. Like accepting things. Do you accept the fact everyone thinks you killed your mum? Looks like it. You certainly employed other methods on her. Like poison.

Poison got you your own way, didn't it? Got rid of your mother and got you accepted into here."

It felt like he'd sucker punched me in the stomach. My mouth dropped as I searched for words, the kitchen suddenly feeling incredibly overheated. He suddenly shifted, as if aware he'd gone too far, but his gaze was unwaveringly frowning, fixed to my left as I tried to find a response. "It...I...that would.... I didn't accept.... I never...not as it seems." I halted, my brain dizzied. And then I simply said "You're wrong."

"No, I'm not. You're not even bothering to look for the connection between Arden and your mother's death, even though you instinctively *know* there has to be one. And the only logical reason you're not looking is because you don't care about truth or justice. Or are you just glad she's dead and out of the way now, so you get to be some pretty little butterfly set free from the cocoon?"

My mouth was open, heart yammering, as he said one more final brutal sentence. "Ayer has a very informative file on you. The only thing I'm still trying to figure out is if it means you're strong or weak that you had to resort to poisoning your mother with a cup of herbal tea."

With a strangled noise, I picked up a glass and flung it at his face as hard as I could; he stood up and swiftly caught the glass mid-air, placing it aside as I leaped forward to hit him in the face. Eyes narrowed, he knocked my hands away easily and pushed me back, trying to say something. Furious, I lashed out again, and this time my hand made contact with his jaw, hard. He swore and instinctively brought his fist up just as I moved in to hit him again. His fist connected with my mouth and pain exploded through my face as I went flying backwards into the kitchen counter and then toppled over it, smacking the floor. I heard his indrawn breath as utensils clattered down around me, but then I heard no more as suppressed memories roared up to engulf my senses. The last time I'd been punched, been knocked to the ground...sudden pain.

I'm a real showman, me.

And I could see him standing over me, his fingers around my neck, squeezing. I could see my mother, but she was dead and her bottle green eyes couldn't see me. She was dead.

"Marilyn?" Someone was urgently calling in the distance, but I couldn't breathe because his latex clad fingers were still closed around my throat, pushing in tighter and tighter, and I was terrified. I didn't want to die, I just wanted to live. Heat gagged me as I frantically scrabbled along the floor, trying to get away from him. It felt like I was being suffocated in plastic and blood. I struggled harder.

Hands pinned me to the floor. "Marilyn, you need to breathe!"

Sweet dreams till sunbeams find you.

I screamed.

Sweet dreams that leave all worries behind you.

I bucked up, screaming,

"MARILYN!"

Wait...the voice wasn't the Showman's. I blinked, gasping for air. Tears and sweat blinded my vision,

"Marilyn, breathe! You need to breathe, okay? Just breathe. Slow breaths, that's good. You're fine, Marilyn, just breathe. You're safe here, it's just me."

I lay with my eyes tightly closed and forced deep slow breaths in and out. In. Out. As I calmed down, I became aware of strong, calm hands on my solar plexus and stomach, slowly massaging up the center of my rib cage and back down to my stomach. Jason's low voice was soothing above me. I opened my eyes, but he wasn't looking down at me, rather at his hands rubbing my abdomen. He looked badly shocked, his eyes narrowed to frozen slits of blue and his lips a tightly compressed line. Guilt radiated from him.

"I'm sorry," I rasped, mortified. He looked sideways and our eyes met for a second before he shunted his gaze back to his hands.

"You need water," he said finally, removing his hand from my sweaty t-shirt and standing up. I sat up on the hard kitchen floor and touched my stomach sickly.

"I don't, I'm fine. Just...the flu...that's all it was," I said, more to convince myself. "It couldn't be anything else." Humiliated, I climbed to my feet and wondered why my face was aching so much. I touched the side of my mouth and blood came away on my fingers. I couldn't help but look at Jason, who was backed up against the side counter away from me, all his usual indifference gone as he looked bleakly at the blood.

"I'm—" he started, his jaw rigidly tight.

"I'm sorry!" I blurted, more automatically than anything. And then I was furious at myself for saying that word, so easily falling back into the same old weak, terrified apologetic state. I was better than that now, wasn't I? Or so I had thought. I turned to leave, blood dripping down my chin.

"Wait, Marilyn—"

He tried to step in my way, but I dodged and broke into a run for the stairs. I wanted to cry, or scream, or punch something. It felt like everything had crashed back down around me. And all because Jason had hit me and I had reacted in my usual pathetic, weak way. Scrubbing my face with shaking hands, I climbed back into my bed and pulled the sheets over my head, pressing them down into my face as tightly as I could. Jason could use this incident against me. He had seen me weak. I had forgotten that I *was* weak. Which meant that I had to change, properly. And I had to regain power, both over myself and now, over him as well.

And I knew how I'd do it.

Sleep was a long time coming.

***

The next morning I had an ugly bruise and a lip that was bright red and swollen to twice its normal size. I was inspecting it in the bathroom mirror when Jaid walked in.

"Oh my god!" she uttered. "Who did that to your mouth?"

"Just a little accident, won't happen again," I said breezily, although it hurt to talk. Make up would have hidden the bruising, but I didn't have any anymore. And I was transfixed, unable to look away from the color of the ugly bruising.

"Who did it?" Jaid repeated, yanking me to face her. "Was — was it Levi? I swear, he only hits out when — dammit, I'm not putting up with his shit ANY longer — "

"It wasn't Levi!" I protested. "I knocked into my wardrobe door in the middle of the night, that's all!" She glared fiercely at me, and I looked back earnestly until she finally let go of my arm.

"You better not be lying to me. He needs to start taking responsibility for his own messed up actions; I can't keep on covering his back forever, you know? We all need to grow up."

To my relief Jason wasn't in the breakfast room, we shared no chores, and he barely looked up during class, so the rest of the day passed without any action. No one else commented on my bruised mouth once they heard the story. Levi was too distracted by his own thoughts to even notice it. And my plan to equalize the score was already formalized by the time evening came. I was going to break into Ayer's office.

As I lurked outside Ayer's office studying the key lock, Mrs. Shäfer cornered me and dragged me to her office, where she demanded to know what was wrong with me, her lips pursed as she applied Savlon to my mouth.

"A very talented wardrobe," she said after I finished my tale, lashes lowered. "Look, Marilyn, the staff are discouraged to become involved in your personal interactions, but I feel it is my duty to advise you against fighting Jason Lucas in the future."

"No, I hit the—"

"I'm serious, please listen to me. Jason is a very angry young man, and has created unhealthy defense mechanisms to deal with this, as well as how to cope with his... ineptitude at connecting with people. Of course, a girl like you would find a way to...get underneath this. But you need to stay far away from him, and keep out of trouble. Just wait. Things will get better. Trust me, just wait."

"Wait for what?" I asked. She hesitated, and pursed her lips even more tightly, apparently having an internal debate.

"Just keep on your guard. Besides, Dr. Ayer has been considering allowing you to have some personal items, and we don't want Jason Lucas to ruin that for you."

I laughed slightly. "Why Mrs. Shäfer, I didn't know you cared!"

"Of course you didn't," she retorted. "And you still don't; that's the problem with people like you."

I grinned, still not quite understanding what she was getting at, and pocketed two paperclips and a plastic name placeholder from the desk as I left. I used to feel guilty when I did these things. Now I felt guilty when I felt guilty. And yes, I also overthought things.

I waited until about three in the morning, when the night nurse was taking a break from patrolling and sneaking a smoke outside the kitchen. I slipped to Dr. Ayer's office, where he kept the file cabinets. Jason had read a file on me that was in Ayer's office, had he? Well, there had to be files on all of us. Jason would not hold that sort of weapon over me again. And if there were any extra files on Ayer and what Arden House was doing to us, even better.

The door to the office was locked, of course. But the lock wasn't anything special; when I was a little kid my mum had installed a similar one on her door. I was just thankful there were no security cameras on this floor, or in the office. However, I was still jiggling the clip and plastic card in the lock when Clodagh spoke from behind me.

"You need to get the wire at more of an angle."

My response was to almost trip over my feet in my haste to stand up in front of the key hole.

Clodagh raised her eyebrows and soundlessly giggled at me, saying "Here, let me." Taking the wire, she carefully toggled the clip inward. Glancing back at my surprised, anxious expression, she rubbed away a coy smile and said, "I figured that after Jason floored you, you were gonna go after him this way. I mean, no offense, but you don't seem the type to fight back to his face...more the scheming type."

"Yeah, but I can do this on my own."

"I'm not doing this for you. You think you're the only one he's floored? Besides, you suck at jimmying locks." As she spoke, the door clicked open, and she shot me a triumphant look, the eagerness slightly malicious. "Here we go."

Inside the office, I got to the file cabinet first; thankfully, it wasn't locked. Inside were folders full of alphabetically listed names. I easily found all of our files, mixed up with others belonging to names I recognized—Sebastian Modine-Pound,

Sylvia Schenk, Ferdinand De Villiers—and others I didn't, like Meekyeong Song, Caroline McReary, and Adrianna Zhou. I eyed my own file first, then figured I had to prioritize and pulled out the file for Jason Lucas. Clodagh pushed close against me and peered over my shoulder as I read.

The first thing I saw were the clipped in photos and mug shots that appeared to begin about twelve years ago and had all been taken officially by the social care regulations. In all of them, Jason was looking fully into the camera. As a child he'd glared like a caged animal; by the last photograph, it was the familiar expressionless, bored stare. I rifled past the photos. Jason Lucas, twenty one years old, diagnosed by several therapists as having severe behavior problems including a lack of ability to empathize, communicate, or emote, not to mention an anti-social disorder that had led to various violent outbursts over the years. However, several times as a child he had shown remarkable progress with several therapists, although circumstances and a rotating care system prevented his recovery with those therapists from being taken further.

I put down the file, jaw tight. Clodagh picked it up instantly and flipped it back open.

"He read every single thing in your file," she reminded me. "That's just how it goes; you're either a victim or a victor. This way, we'll both be victors, so read up."

I touched my still-aching lip and looked back at the file. His criminal record listed GBH, battery assault, obstruction of justice, joyriding "without a license," as well as three counts of first degree murder.

"Check this out," breathed Clodagh. "Has been placed in an estimated eighteen social homes from the age of six, listed below...I'll skip that...received a stable foster home at the age of seventeen. Limited documentation about his birth mother and life before he was placed in care, except possible neglect cited as a source behind behavior difficulties, and his birth father was actually the key suspect in a high profile serial killer investigation. Oh, but the case had insufficient evidence."

I turned the page, edging the file back into my hands. Jason was brought into Arden on Christmas Eve, for the first degree murder of his foster parents and an unidentified other man. He had been on the run for four days before he was caught.

"Well, what do you know?" whispered Clodagh, reading just ahead of me, and I soon saw what had made her react. It was documented how Jason not only insisted he wasn't guilty for the murders, but had tried to tell the courts he'd been set up, and that the third victim had been a hired hit man who'd also attempted to kill him as well as his foster parents. When Jason had first been caught by the policemen he wouldn't stop speaking about a blue Porsche with a number plate that didn't exist on record.

My throat had gone dry. "Clodagh...Clodagh, I need to read all the other files at once; this isn't just about Jason anymore. Can I look at yours now? I need to...I think something is up."

Clodagh looked at me mulishly. "Why? What would you do for me in return?"

A noise on the stairway made us both jerk round. The night nurse was back on patrol and approaching up the stairs; I didn't have much time.

"Look, Clodagh," I whispered urgently, touching her elbow. "Please go and distract the nurse...just give me five minutes here. I swear I will tell you everything I find out if you keep her away, and I'll owe you a favor."

Clodagh looked uncertain. "How do I know—?"

"Clodagh, I need you, I'm trusting you," I interrupted. "I know that goes against everything we're being taught at the minute, but—"

"I'll do it," said Clodagh quickly, rubbing her mouth. "I'll puke on the nurse for you."

She left and I heard her stagger from the bathroom opposite and then out to the nurse, getting her to lead her up the stairs to the bedrooms. I grabbed the other files and spread them along the desk, not daring to steal them out the office. I rifled through the first file: Clodagh Van Der Broek, sole child of a top Sinn Fein politician and the Belgian socialite son of the founder of Genetech Inc. Then I found one of the patterns I was looking for; Clodagh had murdered her family. One day she had crept into the bedroom of her father and mother and slit their throats with a kitchen knife. She then proceeded to carve the letter "P" into her father's face. However, unlike Jason and myself, Clodagh confessed straight away, and it was she who referred herself to Arden. There was also no mention of a mysterious third party, or a Porsche. Disappointed and frustrated, I put the file back and turned to Levi Ghelani's. Skimming his various young offender cases and the various domestic problems between his British-Malaysian mother and Indian father brought to the British court system, I found the part where he and his cousin tied up her parents and their visiting friend and tortured them to death. (Levi had been legally living with his aunt and uncle since the age of fourteen.) Both Levi and his cousin Jaisudha "Jaid" Khanna had declared they were innocent, blaming the visiting friend, identified as Enrico Tagliavini, for their guardians' murders. They had insisted police track down a non-existent blue Porsche for answers.

Bingo.

Glossing over the part of the file that detailed evidence suggesting that Tagliavini had been tied up and subjected to extreme violence hours before his eventual death, I turned to the file of Edward Stanley Goldberg — aka Teddy. A faint disturbance on the bedroom stairs made me freeze, but it was followed by the sounds of Clodagh stopping the nurse and leading her back up the stairs. I picked up the pace, flipping through Teddy's file. He had killed the grandparents who raised him...there was no mention of a Porsche, but he did claim he was innocent. According to Sebastian's file, he had shot his parents and three half-siblings in the head on holiday on the French Riviera. Just as I was opening up Sylvia's file, there was another, more insistent motion upstairs, followed by the sounds of Clodagh protesting and someone descending the stairs in a hurry. I shoved the files back into the cabinet, but in my haste knocked over the sole ornament Ayer kept on his desk; a tiny snow globe I'd never bothered noticing before. I grabbed at the globe and shoved it back onto the desk, but not before I saw the writing printed on the bottom: *For my darling Diah, in case you ever entirely forget what home is. Love always, Mom.*

All that was inside the globe was a white and blue lioness stencil and a picture of a white building. With no time to contemplate this, I rushed out of the door, lunged across into the toilet, and hid behind the door just as the nurse stormed back onto the landing, followed by Clodagh.

"I'll call Nurse Udrea," the nurse whispered threateningly.

"No you won't," replied Clodagh in her calm, high voice. "You'll do your job. Don't you want to make me feel better? You didn't complain when it was Levi asking." I heard the sounds of someone slamming against the wall. I stepped out from behind the door.

"There you are, Clodagh!" I exclaimed. "I was so worried you'd been sick again and couldn't find the nurse!"

Clodagh looked back from where she had cornered the frightened nurse, her hand splayed across the nurse's chest. "Yeah," she said, smiling at me. "I found her."

The nurse quickly shook herself free. "I'll get you some paracetamol," she said shakily.

"Don't bother; Marilyn will look after me."

The nurse shot me a nervous, humiliated look and hurried back down the stairs. We heard the sour male nurse Udrea asking what the noise was and her noncommittal reply before Clodagh followed me back up to my room. Her head was held higher than usual. My room suddenly felt too small as she sat on my bed and waited expectantly for me to tell her what I had discovered in the files.

"Why are you staring at me?" she asked at last, the petulant tone creeping back into her voice, and I smiled and looked away.

"Oh, no reason. And I didn't find out much, I was just being paranoid."

She looked unsurprised at my words, her lips downturned. "Okay." However, she looked suddenly so vulnerable and disappointed, I found myself speaking again.

"But...I'm not sure. I may have found a pattern. All six of us currently in Arden are here for the murder of our guardians, yet we also definitely murdered another unknown male as well. Four of us, excluding you and Teddy, blamed the other unknown male for our family's murder. In two of the cases the other male was identified as an Enrico Tagliavini. Four of us reported being stalked by a Porsche. The files also contained information and photographs about all of us, dating back from before we had criminal records. It's obviously not a coincidence."

"Teddy and I do fit the pattern!" was all Clodagh had to say. "All six of us are definitely murderers, and all six of us were provoked into the murder. We fit."

"Right...but it's not just that it can't be coincidental how we all survived similar situations and arrived in Arden. It's that the doctors had all our files and yet apparently failed to notice that we were all stalked by a dark blue Porsche, or that this Enrico Tagliavini has supposedly been killed twice. The doctors had to be aware of it!"

"The Arden program was probably just specially designed for a specific type of patient profile, that's all," said Clodagh with a remarkable lack of concern. "And Arden isn't interested in our lives before we came here; there is nothing to be gained from—"

"There is *nothing* in this program to suggest it has been specifically designed for a spontaneously family-murdering teenager," I interrupted stiffly. "In fact, the doctors do their best to keep us from discovering how similar our cases are to each other. They must know we are innocent...and that we could provide testimony to each other's innocence. Instead, we are being kept here."

"You forget though," Clodagh said casually. "None of us are innocent."

"It was self-protection! Or justice...but, that's different, right? Anyway, what if it was Arden House who hired the men who killed our families? If it was Arden that set up the whole situation so that it would bring us here? I know it sounds ridiculous, but—"

"But who cares?"

I halted. "What?"

Clodagh tilted her head to regard me in that sly way of hers, and got to her feet with a lopsided smile. "I'm just saying, Marilyn. What's the problem? We were all brought here for a reason, and you don't know that reason. But you know it's for our benefit that we're here. They care about us here, they see who we are. This is just you being unable to let go, being too weak to fully make the transition. Finding problems, finding moral quandaries, anything to stop you from looking properly at yourself and embracing what you see. From moving on with your life. So just let go; stop being afraid of this new opportunity."

There was a fraction of silence before I said pleasantly, "I'm sure you're right. Anyway, I'm exhausted now, so goodnight, yeah?"

Clodagh nodded. "Anyway, you've now got the information you need on Jason Lucas to bring him down."

Jason. He had seen the files as well; he'd seen the pattern first and realized something was wrong with Arden. And then he had deliberately goaded me into looking up the files, so I'd see something was wrong too. He wanted me to know too, and had known exactly how to make it so I found out the truth. Why?

I lay back in bed. The fact that he wanted me to know as well as him meant that the next move was mine; he would be waiting for my reaction before he could continue with whatever his plan was. Well, he'd have to wait; I would play this game on my own.

The next day I made efforts to be especially charming and warm to everyone, with mixed success. Levi came down to breakfast clearly wound up and on edge; he and Jaid were sitting separately and Levi looked feverish, as if he hadn't slept. Jaid kept her dark eyes on her toast as I sat next to Levi and coaxed him into a better mood. Jason sat slightly separate from the rest of us, and although normally it was impossible to tell if he was feeling any particular emotion, the glacial posture of his body and his determined way of looking everywhere except at me suggested some sort of emotional state; I just wasn't sure which. When the entire breakfast had passed without a hint from me that anything was different, he calmly turned to Jaid and Clodagh and icily stated something which, judging by Jaid's aggressive if fruitless reaction, was extremely offensive. I knew then it was fury he was feeling. I quickly went to class with Levi so Jason couldn't find me, and then hurried out after, escaping into the empty courtyard for fresh air and relief. I still wasn't sure what I wanted, I just knew that a confrontation with Jason — or anyone, Arden included — would not benefit me until I was in a calmer state of control. My last confrontation with Jason was still raw in my mind, sapping at my strength.

The security cameras whirled overhead as I tried in vain to think of ideas of escape and action, but all I could feel was claustrophobia and entrapment, and my mind was all over the place. The camera whirled to face me directly and I automatically started to jog around the damp concrete perimeter, looking as if that had been my purpose all along. It was then, as I jogged and eyed the cameras along the top of the wired brick wall, that I had an idea. The frigid wind was colder than usual and blowing northeast, so I positioned myself accordingly, and then began to sprint on the spot, pulling off my jumper as I worked up a sweat. Just as the wind tugged, I let go. The jumper flew straight up onto the security camera, snagging and snapping across the lens, stuck in position by the various wires. I did a dance of victory and then ran to the wall corner underneath my jumper, where there was now a blind spot from any of the cameras.

"Oh no," I said aloud, for the benefit of any sound receptors. "My jumper is trapped! I had better climb up this wall and retrieve it!" And grinned.

The brick was smooth and hard to climb, and the jumper was right at the top of the wall, a fair way up. I had just rammed my toes into the small crevice and heaved myself up when behind me, Jason said, "There's a pressure alarm triggered if the wall is touched above two meters."

I jumped back down next to him,

"I'm just getting my jumper," I explained sweetly.

"Let me help you get it without sounding the alarm."

I gave an exaggerated expression of shock at his kind offer, which didn't seem to please him at all. Instead, he carried on pointedly, "Come on, I'll teach you a balancing trick I learned from one of my foster brothers who was in a circus. You do need that jumper, after all." He added the last bit with a certain amount of woodenness that could either have been a sense of humor emerging, or simply terrible acting. Still, I couldn't help tensing up as he stepped closer to me and lowered onto his haunches.

"Get on my shoulders," he said to the ground.

I didn't trust him at all, I didn't want to go near him, but I said nothing. In the end, he glanced up, irritated, and his eyes narrowed. "I'm just trying to help you look over the wall so we know where the hell we are and what security surrounds us. I didn't mean what I said to you last night, but if you need to equal up and hit me before you can do anything useful, get it over with."

"Your persuasion technique needs work, sweetheart," I said, but moved to climb onto his shoulders. His face looked cautiously relieved as he helped me kneel on his shoulders. His back and shoulder muscles were hard and tense underneath me, and he didn't appear to have much difficulty standing up under the camera a foot away from the wall. Still, even kneeling on Jason's shoulders, I was nowhere near tall enough to see over the wall, scope out the cameras, or even reach my jumper.

Precariously, I started to shift up onto my feet. Instantly, his hands came up and gripped my thighs painfully tightly, keeping me secure as I stood up, hands sliding to my knees as I straightened. However, no matter how I craned my head, the wall was still too high to see over. I could only just see the tops of the taller buildings. I lifted up onto my toes, and briefly saw other concrete buildings and wire, but then staggered and almost fell off Jason's shoulders.

"Stop that, you'll fall!" ordered Jason below me, breathing harder now. "I have a better idea; how good is your balance?"

"It's only nearly failed me once so far."

"Fine; spread your arms out." He started to lift me slowly up off his shoulders. I could feel his muscles straining as I was first two inches off his shoulders, then another one, another...and suddenly I was above his head and could see over the wall. My hands flew to my mouth as it dropped open.

"What is going on here?" demanded a voice from the door, that of Dr. Novikov. With a startled yell, I promptly lost my balance and fell backwards. Jason rapidly let go of my knees and stepped away, reaching up and seizing me hard around my waist so I whacked into him, and both of us fell into the ground, me on top of him.

"Oh Jesus Christ...Jason, are you okay? I've killed you!" Half winded, I scrambled off him, causing him to groan as he caught his breath.

"That hurt," he wheezed, yet he didn't seem too bothered as he rolled up to his feet, me hovering next to him. In fact, he seemed remarkably even-tempered as we turned to Dr. Novikov, who was bearing down on us suspiciously.

"Marilyn? Jason?"

I instantly pointed grievously to my jumper, still dancing up over the camera. "The stupid wind put it up there, and I knew Mrs. Shäfer would be pissed off if I lost it; and then Jason came along so I made him help."

"And I agreed," added Jason, slightly unnecessarily, frowning again.

Dr. Novikov looked between us, unable to decide on whether to focus on me or Jason, who was looking straight at him and barely bothering to conceal his impatient disdain behind the normal impassive mask.

"Well, just get back inside," Dr Novikov said at last. "Marilyn, you're supposed to be in the kitchen with Teddy. Jason, you're on laundry duty."

"We need to talk about Ayer's files and what you saw over the wall," murmured Jason into my ear as we headed to the kitchen. "Somewhere private. Now."

"I'll come find you later," I said. He looked as if he wasn't going to accept this answer, but then I smiled sunnily at him. "We can make it a date, sweetheart," and he backed up and walked off, predictably stiff.

I waited until about two in the morning before creeping into Jason's room. He wanted to make sure it was private when we talked, didn't he? I was unsurprised to see that Jason slept by the furthest wall, lying on his stomach with his hands up around his head. Levi was snoring lightly on the bed opposite him, sprawled out on his back with the sheets kicked off.

I crouched down beside Jason and whispered into his ear. "I said I'd find you later."

Jason opened one eye, apparently having only been dozing, and, unbelievably, almost looked somewhat irritably amused, though against his will. But then his eye moved down to my busted lip, and he sat up as humorless as ever.

"The middle of the night? This is a bit of a petty power struggle, Marilyn," he said in a low rumble.

"It's a bit of a petty power *win*," I retorted.

"Nice try."

"Nice *win*."

He said nothing more, although he still looked equable compared to normal as he got out of bed and searched for a t-shirt. And yes, I looked at his body...unfortunately, I was not inhuman. Once his t-shirt was on and his charms remarkably diminished again, he led us both to the boy's bathroom. As I sat down on the end of the bathtub, blinking at the sudden light, he leaned against the back of the door. I waited for him to speak. He waited for me to speak. I raised an eyebrow and smiled questioningly. He made an irritated noise and, as if he'd intended to start the conversation all along, asked "So what did you see over the wall? Location? Are we in a city or the countryside? Roads? Security? How hard will it be to escape over the wall?"

"It's going to be practically impossible to escape that way...or any way," I said, although I already had ideas forming about how I could do it. "This building is in the middle of a massive complex, and there are two other lower new-looking buildings to the side of us, built out of plain concrete, and wire fencing everywhere. Beyond the buildings I saw a massive pair of electric gates, with electric fencing surrounding the property. And...I think I saw guards, plain clothed though. Men were sitting outside. Cameras. I saw some trucks by the gate, and unloaded crates and boxes next to them. Wherever we are, we're surrounded."

"But beyond the complex's electric gates?"

"I...I didn't have enough time. I think I saw roads, but not major roads, small roads. Woods, trees...it looked like we are in the countryside, maybe? But it's all beyond the high fencing and guards and the blocks." I stopped talking, as the reality of our situation sank in. Jason frowned, deep in thought.

"And you read Ayer's files on everybody?" he pressed on.

"Yeah. And I think I figured why you want me in the loop, too."

He looked at me cautiously, but didn't reply. I was starting to think that he had no problems communicating whatsoever, he just chose not to. I continued.

"My guess is that you wanted me to look at the files because you've already started planning your great escape, only to your chagrin, it turns out you need someone else to try and escape too, to create a diversion perhaps, or even to help watch your back. Am I right?"

"Let me get this straight; you have just discovered that the same people who have trapped us all here for a reason we don't know, also were the ones who hired hit men and murdered our families. And you only see this information in terms of...of *currency*? Why I gave it to you, how I will use it against you."

"I'm being practical," I said. "And realistic; if you led me to the truth out of the goodness of your heart, you would have also led Jaid, Levi, and the others to the same place. You didn't, which means that you have a specific reason for wanting me to know. Because you see me as the most able to help you escape, and I'm the one most likely to escape besides you." I paused, and then added, "You believe Arden definitely ordered the hit men?"

97

"It's a logical assumption," he said. "But regardless, Arden wants us all here for a reason, and they have cut us all off from everything else, completely dependent on them."

"Jaid and Levi might know more about what's going on," I said doubtfully. "They tortured that hit man for information."

"They didn't torture him for information," said Jason shortly. "It was Levi, and he didn't bother asking questions; he just wanted to cause pain."

"But if we all pool information—"

"No, Marilyn," he said, frustrated. "You *know* this can't turn into some group-hug kumbaya affair, so why are you still pretending? Didn't you read? Levi and Jaid tortured the hit man to death. Clodagh's mother was a chief patron and investor in Arden, and Clodagh requested to come here of her own free will. Teddy's father created the biggest science technology corporation in the western world, which has major ties with a man called Wrexham, one of the founding Arden Board members—I used Ayer's office computer to research them. Whatever is going on here, chances are they already know, or simply don't care. Or, like Levi, they are liabilities. They won't escape; they'll just stop us from escaping. Six people trying to escape would be a joke...we'd be found out instantly. Us two, we're the best. We're the ones who can do it."

I was silent. "The others deserve to know what Arden did to them."

He looked at me oddly, as if trying to work out if I'd meant what I just said. I myself was trying to work that out too.

"Fine, escape," I said. "But I need to find out why Arden wanted to trap us all here first, what they wanted with me."

"What good will answers do?" he demanded. "The only thing I care about is getting as far away as possible. Figured you'd be the same." But there was a look of deep simmering frustration in his eyes that said his ignorance bothered him badly. Despite this, he leaned against the door with his customary lack of movement and continued to look stubborn. That was when I figured out what made him seem so daunting. He never fidgeted, or had any of the usual reactions that characterized other people; he always seemed still and controlled. It seemed preternatural. And I could never tell what he was thinking.

I looked down at my knees.

"You were right though," he said suddenly. "I did want you alone to see the files so we could work together. You alone."

I wasn't listening. For the first time in a long while, I was thinking of the outside world. I would have nowhere to go if I escaped. I knew I'd never be allowed to see my brothers again. Fiona and my dad wouldn't be happy if I went all Shawshank on this place; they certainly wouldn't be happy if I turned up at theirs. In fact, Dad probably thought he'd finally gotten rid of me when I was sent here. Not that I blamed him. He had his nice world...I just didn't belong there, just as I didn't belong in Arden, or with Adam, or any of the many worlds I'd stolen my way into. It was just me. So why did I care about answers, or justice, or vengeance? It would still just be me alone. I had to care about getting stronger, about getting out of here.

Jason made a sudden movement above me, then folded his arms across his chest. I looked up, but his eyes were still fastened on the wall above my head.

"I never apologized for hitting you," he said stolidly.

"I hit you first," I replied, not particularly caring and unable to bother pretending otherwise.

"Not an excuse, Marilyn. You're a girl."

I laughed slightly at him and his eyes fastened on mine. "You mean, I'm weaker?" I said. He opened his mouth, frowning, but I cut in. "Whatever. Besides, it's not the fact you hit me that you're so sorry about, but my pathetically dramatic reaction afterwards. I guess I have made less progress than we both thought."

He looked completely taken aback for a second, but then shook his head slightly, brow still furrowed,

"No, that's not it—"

He was about to carry on when the door behind him swung open and a half asleep Levi gaped at us both.

"What the hell are you guys doing in here?"

"Shush!" I whispered, standing up. "I'm just leaving."

"Hold on," he exclaimed, and blocked the doorway entrance. I was suddenly aware I was standing in between two taller guys, and felt a pang of apprehension. "Hold on, Marilyn...what were you doing all tucked up in here with *him*? Are you and him...?"

"Oh...no, Levi, you've got it wrong...," I started.

"Don't bloody lie to me!" he said, his voice getting louder as he continued to stare at me in that horribly injured way. "God's sake, Marilyn! Are you two...? What the hell is wrong with everyone? Marilyn, how can you be so stupid? He's a psychopath who doesn't give a damn about anyone except himself...like everyone else here!"

"No, Levi, you've misunderstood the—"

"Let me bloody speak!" he snapped, turning on me. "First Jaid, now you. What the hell?"

I reeled in confusion at his upset anger, seemingly out of nowhere and fueled only by itself. "Jaid and Jason?"

"Hardly," Jason muttered.

"Why do people always feel they can treat me this way?"

"Listen, Levi—"

"Don't tell me to listen, bitch! I've seen what *listening* has done to you all! I've been the only one *hearing* since I got here, and there's no point anymore. Even you, Little Miss bloody Perfect, you're the same. You talk and talk but you're not hearing! And why the hell do you act so nice to me if you're just banging the psychopath over there? Felt sorry for poor pathetic Levi, with his silly wants and needs?"

"Shut up, Levi," said Jason in a low voice, as I could only gape wordlessly at him.

"Or what?" Levi turned on Jason, energy spilling out with his every movement. "Or what? You'll make me shut up permanently? You dumb brute, that's the only way you know to respond, right? I know you did something to Jaid, made her turn her back on me!"

Jason looked bored. "Just get out."

"I will," muttered Levi. "I will." He moved back to the door, and turned one more time to me, his black eyes chaotic and burning. "You've shown your true colors, Marilyn. But you don't even have to worry; I won't tell anyone about you two hooking up in here, because I just don't even care anymore. You're all changing. I'm through with it; I'm through with all of you."

As Levi stormed out, I met Jason's eyes, mine wide in amazement.

"Don't worry, Levi will have forgiven you by morning," said Jason dismissively, reaching past me to re-shut the bathroom door. "He just can't control himself, especially now that Jaid is through with him. He's irrelevant now."

I shook my head at him. "You're a cold bastard."

He stared me down. "I never deny what I am," he said, nostrils flaring. "You, on the other hand, lie and pretend...and manipulate and manipulate...and you seem...*proud* of it! Like it's the best—the only—part of you! Though of course, now you'll get all innocent-eyed and insist that I'm wrong. You'll try and make me feel like a dumb cruel animal and I'll back down and *you'll* win. That's your normal trick, right?"

"I'm going to bed," I said, turning back to the door away from the onslaught. But it was as if he couldn't hold his words in anymore.

"Of course you're not going to bother fighting back. You won't argue because you think your power comes from the perception you're some submissive, delicate innocent flower they can easily control. You *want* to seem weak; it unbalances people, makes strong people weak, lets you get away with anything. It makes people want to protect you. But it's a lie! It took me a while to figure that out, but I've got it sorted now. Like most people, your only priority is yourself, and you don't give a damn about everybody here. Yeah, this place is perfect for you."

"I miss the days when you never spoke," I said.

He let me push past him but followed me out into the dark hallway.

"Come on Marilyn, tell me I'm wrong—that you don't like it here, that you don't secretly want to stay...and you can quit the wide eyed act now. I'm immune."

I said nothing, just worked on fighting the instinctive reaction of backing down and agreeing with him. I refused to be like that in front of him. He raised an eyebrow, the corridor shadow falling over us both.

"Arden is teaching us to embrace who we are in order to improve our lives," I said sweetly, carefully. "And if anything, I've embraced my ability to ignore the words of those who simply don't mean anything to me. Now, I'm going to bed for a nice, deep, dreamless sleep."

"No," he said through gritted teeth. "I pointed you towards Ayer's files; I helped you look over the wall. Now you have to listen to what I — "

"And that shows how little you *do* understand me," I interrupted, unable to stop my voice from getting higher. "Because if you did, you'd know that *nothing* could ever make me listen to a person like you. You led me to the files; now I have no further use for you. I will escape on my own, without you, and you can go back to brooding by yourself and trying to whittle other people down until they are as weak and confused as you, and you get to be the strong one, just how you like it."

His jaw snapped shut wordlessly and I walked away. I waited until I was in my room before punching the bed repeatedly. I'd do it myself. I'd do everything myself for myself; that was what I'd always done. And it was what I was best at; it was when I was strongest. When my talents were able to work best. I'd just been too deluded to realize that before I'd come to Arden.

***

It was the grimy, early hours of morning and I was still pacing my room when suddenly all the alarms began to screech and wail around the building. I joined an equally awake looking Jaid and Clodagh outside and the three of us hurried down the stairs, where the bleak-eyed nurses crowded into the hallway. Through the open front door we saw Levi being dragged off the concrete ground by three security men and a doctor I'd never seen before. His hands and knees were ripped bloody and his eyes were wild; he was

103

yelling as they dragged him backwards into the opposite building.

"I'm not changing! I'm not playing by their rules anymore! Jaid, help me!"

"He tried to climb over the wall!" Udrea yelled over the alarms to the nurses, as more men in lab coats ran into the courtyard in case assistance was needed.

"Get back to your rooms!" yelled Mrs. Mudiraj, pushing the three of us back up through the front door as Levi was pinned against the wall and Dr. Luo bent down and gave him an injection of some sort. Instantly he seemed to fold.

Mrs. Mudiraj kept herding us back up the stairs, stressing, "Bed! Now!"

I turned to Jaid. She was deathly pale, her eyes glittering in the dark. She looked betrayed, clenched with disappointment. Jason was nowhere to be seen, but Teddy stood alone at the top of the stairs, a look of not-quite comprehending fear in his eyes.

I quietly led the way back up to our rooms.

I didn't sleep that night, just sat in my bed with my knees up under my chin. Was Levi trying to escape my fault? What would they do to Levi now? They wouldn't punish him badly, would they? Not if Dr. Ayer had really taken so much care to bring us all to Arden in the first place.

I was angry, too. I just wasn't sure why. Perhaps I was angry at how hurt Levi had been, how he'd allowed himself to be hurt by me, and whatever Jaid did to him. That he had been fooled by my stupid sparkly act. That he looked down on how we were all changing.

***

Levi wasn't at breakfast the next day, and the atmosphere was strained between everyone. Jaid in particular was completely silent, and there were puffy scratch marks down the side of her face. Even Teddy, who usually had problems picking up on moods, left his DS upstairs to stare at us all in a dejected manner. It was later, when Dr. Ayer had finished giving me my daily injections, that I got the chance to ask him what had happened to Levi.

"He's been placed in isolation for a while," said Dr. Ayer. "He was very distressed; we thought it best to give him time to recover alone."

"Can I visit him? He's been brought to the medical room on the second floor, right?"

Dr. Ayer gave a mild shake of the head. "I don't think a visitor is a good idea, Marilyn. People only heal true when alone. Besides, Levi is being kept heavily sedated by the nurses."

"Please?" I said quietly. "Please let me."

His pale green eyes were curiously soft as he asked, "What's wrong, Marilyn? You seem to be struggling with the program lately. Are you having trouble completing it?"

For a second, I was desperate to confide in him, ask him to relieve all my fears...beg him to just tell me that he was a good man, that this was a good place and that I could stay here safe and cared for, and how I was changing was good. That *I* was good. But I knew I was just feeling vulnerable after Jason's attack and Levi's attempted escape. So instead, I whispered, "You don't understand, Dr. A. I blame myself for Levi; I knew he was upset before we went to bed, and I need to apologize. Maybe he'll be calmer if I apologize. And I know he'll want his friends with him; Levi needs company. He's not like the rest of us, he destructs when he's on his own."

Dr. Ayer's eyelids flickered. "Yes; a significant character flaw that should've been spotted and corrected before now. Still, last night would suggest he is curing himself of any dependent tendencies. We are choosing to see his little episode as belated progress, and are confident he will recover fully."

"So can I see him?"

"Fine, I'll inform Mrs. Shäfer."

He smiled, waiting for me to depart. But I had another question and for once, I was going to ask it.

"Dr. Ayer... you keep telling us that we were specially selected for Arden because you feel we are worthy of your dreams and so on, but when will we actually know what it is that we were selected for? What is the end result you want?"

He delicately began to sort out the papers on his desk. "I'm afraid you aren't ready to hear those answers yet. When you find out that answer, then you will be ready for the final stage and to start again with your life."

"I don't want to fit back into my life."

"Your new super-life will be different. Stop worrying, Marilyn, you will achieve your purpose if that's what you really want. Now, go do your chores if you want to see Levi."

"Yes, Doctor." My jaw ached from keeping it so stiff.

***

Jaid and I were chopping vegetables for dinner, with Teddy setting up the dining table in the adjacent room, when Mrs. Shäfer told me I was allowed to see Levi for ten minutes. Jaid promptly accidentally sliced open her finger before folding her arms and hissing at Mrs. Shäfer that "it's nothing." She watched me leave with an accusing look, ignoring Teddy's whine to know where the butter was. I didn't care about that though...I was too focused. When Mrs. Shäfer let me into the medicine room, Levi looked very young and pale in the white iron bed, his thick brown hair rumpled and sweaty. He was hooked up to a drip and I thought he was sleeping at first, but his eyes opened as I approached the bedside.

"He'll be a bit dozy," said Mrs. Shäfer. "He needs to get used to his medication." She seated herself next to the open door with a paperback. I placed myself on the end of the bed and steadily returned Levi's gaze, his eyes sleepy and alarmingly soft. It was as if I was Jaid or someone else, and the unguarded smile he gave me was downright terrifying.

"Did you come just to see me?" he asked drowsily.

I swallowed. "Yes." *Lie.* I had already caught sight of where Levi's medication must be, in the cabinet over the sink. Just where I remembered it being. "I wanted to apologize to you about the other night."

"No," he said, trying to sit up. "I'm sorry...I screwed up massively. I just felt all this...anger, and I couldn't control it, you know? I'm always like that. I get so angry it feels like I'm going to burst into flames and I can never help it. Talk to Jaid, and she'll...." He stopped, with noticeable effort. "I'm an idiot."

Ashamed of myself, I leaned forward and touched Levi's shoulder and smiled. "I'm an idiot too. Here, let me get you some water."

I stood in front of the sink with my back to Mrs. Shäfer and turned on the taps loudly. She looked up and then back down to her book. Under the noise of the water, I quickly opened the cabinet and found what I was looking for. Quickly slipping the Ambien and Valium under the jumper, I got the glass of water and took it to Levi, who was struggling to keep his eyes open.

"I want to make sure you know something, Levi," I said, and paused to give Mrs. Shäfer an embarrassed look before shuffling close to Levi. "Just that...I want to make sure you know there is nothing going on between me and Jason.

Nothing at all. We were just talking...at least until you got so angry." I leaned over Levi, elbows on my knees, and smiled shyly.

He breathed in sharply and laughed shakily. "I really do screw everything up, don't I? Maybe I do need help. Maybe that's why I'm here, you know? God knows my life has been nothing but one screw-up after another, nothing changing. I need to control myself. Jaid will be relieved to hear me say that...I've done my best to screw up her life too. Yeah. Maybe I should just stop fighting them."

"You should sleep, Levi," I whispered, and leaning over against his shoulder, nuzzled his cheek. He breathed deeply against my hair and didn't notice me slipping the now emptied pill bottle under his pillow, along with a few pills scattered down the side of the bed and under the bed sheet. Once I was back in my own bedroom, I removed the rest of the tablets from my socks and hid them in my bar of soap. I refused to feel guilty. I needed this.

CHAPTER FIVE

While the five of us ate breakfast the next day nurses rushed up and down the stairs, and finally it was announced that Levi would not be returning to us for a while. He had been caught stealing extra sleeping medication, and a specialist nurse was arriving to treat him for his serious addiction.

Jaid's expression made me either want to cry or punch something, but I continued eating my cereal. Very soon, I knew I'd done the right thing, because by the end of the day it was apparent that I was going to have to create an escape plan from Arden even sooner than I'd thought.

As soon as we had all finished our breakfast. Dr. Luo and Dr. Ayer guided us into the main classroom, where they both stood at the front with formal postures. Sitting at the desk between them was a man I'd never seen before. He looked like an aging military man, with a black crew cut shot through with grey, and a build that must have once been muscular, but now was turning to fat. He wore an expensive business suit and wore tinted glasses. Clodagh, who was sitting next to me, sat forward in her seat eagerly, and the hair on the back of my neck stood on end. She repulsed me.

"Congratulations," said Dr. Ayer. "We've decided it's time to move you into the fourth step of your rehabilitation, hence the abrupt change in schedule. One of the key concepts of Arden is setting you up for life, which of course, includes a career and a place within the world. So let me introduce you to Mr. Harald Wrexham OBE, CEO of LPD Inc., and co-Chief Director of the Arden Board. You see, Arden works in collaboration with many successful multinational corporations and industries, all of who have invested in you. Wrexham acts as mediator between the Arden Board and the business world, and will be helping the representatives of companies select who they wish to sponsor. He felt that in order to make the best matches, it was time he came down personally to meet all you and to help tailor the last few steps of rehabilitation even more to you and your possible future business partners. So, Wrexham, anything you want to say about the upcoming few weeks?"

Mr. Wrexham's thick lips were slightly twisted as he surveyed us. His spectacled gaze remained on Jaid a fraction of a second too long before it turned to me. Instantly a spark of recognition caused his lips to flatten before they quickly snaked back into the same self-satisfied smile. How did he recognize me? I realized Ayer was looking at the two of us cautiously as Wrexham stood up, lips now relaxed and smug as he addressed the room.

"Well, it's good to finally meet you all," said Mr. Wrexham in a deep, decidedly Etonian-educated accent that contrasted with Dr. Ayer's higher undistinguished voice. "The Board went through a lot of youths before finding the six of you, and so I have a deep investment in how you are faring. Now I've met nearly all of you, I know that it was a very wise investment."

Almost discontentedly, Dr. Ayer took over again. He told us that over the next week the most important benefactors and representatives from top controlling institutes and organizations would be visiting Arden House to meet with us and decide what they wanted and who they were most interested in sponsoring. Once this stage was complete, we could finally move on to the second to last stage. We'd be moved to new, separate locations for our final individual training, and then, finally, we'd be complete.

"So, please continue your routine as normal today," finished Wrexham. "It will be interesting to see you in your natural modes of being, and the first clients will be arriving in a week."

As I left the classroom I could see Jason trying to catch my eye, approaching me. I avoided him and headed to the laundry room, where I was on duty, and started to empty the machine and sort out the clothes. I had no intention of aiding Jason with his escape plan, or telling him what mine was, and there was no way he'd manipulate me into doing either. Manipulation was MY game. So I dumped the clothes out over the floor and got to work sorting them.

"You must be the young Mara Aske."

I looked up over the washing machines. Instead of Jason in the doorway it was Mr. Wrexham, with Ayer standing behind him. He held his hand out to me and I stood up to shake it, correcting my name without further comment.

"How are you liking being in Arden with my good friend Obadiah?" It took me a second to remember that Obadiah was Dr. Ayer's first name.

"I like it a lot," I said sweetly, and saw the smug amusement in his face, like he was laughing at me.

"That doesn't surprise me," he replied. "Tell me, have you no hope of rejoining your father after you've been released from Arden?" Behind Wrexham, Ayer's hands twitched spasmodically at his sides.

"I don't think so," I said, still smiling.

"A pity. I met your father back in the day — only once or twice though. I would've thought Brendan would be very proud to have a daughter like you. No doubt he is *very* anxious for your return."

Was he insulting me? What was he implying? Feeling a little sick, I just continued to smile — with a hint of shyness, of course — and knelt back down to the laundry.

"Ah, and this fellow must be Jason Lucas."

Jason walked past the two men with a basket of clothes in his arms. He dumped it at my feet and looked back to the men and nodded briefly, eyes automatically sliding past them as was his habit. Mr. Wrexham didn't seem inclined to talk to Jason however. "Well. It was interesting meeting you, Miss Aske, and do give my regards to your father when you next see him. I can tell you've got more in common with him than just a pair of captivating eyes. No doubt you use them to good advantage, just as he did. Now if you'll excuse me?" He allowed Dr. Ayer to lead him out to the rest of the facilities. My skin was still crawling after his voice faded away into the hum of the laundry.

"Why do I get the impression he knows something I don't?"

"Because he's a dickhead," said Jason, now crouched down to sort out the new basket. I stared after Wrexham, with his smiling secrets.

"Marilyn? It doesn't mean anything that Wrexham knows your dad. Your dad is a brilliant businessman; it makes sense that he's met him once or — "

"Yeah, I know."

He continued to separate the clothes piles on the floor as I sat opposite and rested my chin on my knee, still feeling rather sensitive about it all.

"Come on, Jason," I said at last, forcing my tone to be conversational. "We both know the only reason you're here helping out with my chores is because you want to bully me into either telling you my escape plan or helping you with yours. So get on with it."

"Is this you trying to be straightforward with me for once?" he asked, finally closing the door behind us and standing to face me. I shifted to the side a little, as it was less intense.

"Clearly I'm growing as a person. You were my inspiration."

His nostrils flared. "Stop sulking. We need to get out of here before Arden starts selling us next week, and I have an idea that will get us both out. I'm stupidly trying to help you, so will you be sensible and listen to what I have to say?"

"Has anyone ever mentioned how marvelous your skills of persuasion are? Or what a shit liar you are? You have no interest in helping me, and you wouldn't be trying to include me in your plans unless you had no other choice."

He frowned. "I know that it's impossible to escape this place alone due to the security set up, so yeah, it may not be all altruism, but I'm still—"

"Just go away, Jason. There's no way I'm trusting you enough. I can imagine your idea of 'working together,' and I'm not causing some diversion or standing guard as you escape, and then I'm still stuck here in an even worse situation. No matter how you spin this, I know that I'm just a pawn in your plan and I'm not having it. I'll escape on my own."

He looked thoroughly pissed off now, his shoulders tensed and back straight, but a part of me realized that I had no fear he'd snap and hit me again. He was just pissed off. "I'm not trying to spin you; that's your talent, not mine. I'm just telling you that I've worked out the only plan that will get me out of this place, and it needs two people to work. Equal partners, both acting at the same time, both escaping at the same time. It can't be done alone. Trust me, I would if I could." Some stunted emotion flickered through his eyes before he continued. "Besides, the doctors will never expect us to work together, so there's an extra element of surprise."

"They would never expect it if you were working with Teddy, either. Why me?"

He gave me a look, apparently not particularly wanting to answer.

"Jason?"

"I have greater chances of escaping if I base the plan around you and me. That's all. Look, I'm just asking you to work with me to benefit yourself."

"I'm not creating a diversion," I said quietly. "We're completely surrounded in here; the only possible way to escape is via diversion. Right?"

"No, I don't need a diversion. Trust me."

"I don't trust you; that's the problem."

"I figured," he snapped coldly back. "But I can guarantee we'll both have the opportunity to get out; I'm not quite that much of a bastard. And then once we're out, you can come back here for the others, or get the legal systems involved, do whatever you want. I won't care by then."

I hadn't even thought about the others. I couldn't stand the sight of any of them, yet they'd remain here with my consequences affecting them. But I couldn't think about that. Perhaps I'd come back for them, like Jason said. Who knew?

I swallowed and looked at Jason, who was looking his most intent.

"What's your plan?"

"It's not all completely sorted; I need you to—"

"Tell me what you want us both to do," I said at length. "If I like it, I'm in. If you're a means to the end, I'm not going to ignore it."

"Good," he said heavily. I smiled back with my blandest smile and sat down on the floor, waiting for him to explain. He rubbed his mouth in a movement out of character for him. "The drugs you stole and framed Levi for; do you have enough Ambien to knock out two adults?"

"Yes."

"Okay, good. The nurses trust you enough to let you near their tea." He seemed almost distracted as he switched focus suddenly. "And you have a personal appointment with Dr. Ayer tonight, right?"

"Is it the first rule of Serial Killer 101 to memorize everyone's schedule?"

He gave me a look. "I'll take that as a yes. You need to ask Dr. Ayer if you can have a personal item for your good behavior, and ask him for white hair dye. I mean, because you like to dye your hair and stuff."

"How do you know I like to…?"

He waved the question away impatiently. "Your file pictures…horrible green hair. And you need to ask for the dye *today*; Mrs. Mudiraj does the house shopping tomorrow morning and we need to act tomorrow evening, or we'll have to wait another month."

"You still haven't explained anything yet."

A tightly compressed smile half revealed itself before he lowered his head. He levered himself to the ground opposite me, stretching out his long legs alongside mine, and then began to explain, his voice quickly switching back into the methodical yet oddly intense manner of his.

The plan was good. He had planned every possibility, honed the plan, and had obviously spent long hours obsessing over every possible detail. I questioned him extensively, which he didn't seem to mind, and then put in my own suggestions, suggesting changing things around, showing my own skill for details. He accepted these adjustments without difficulty or annoyance, which surprised me. And then we were both sorted. My throat was dry, and I was aware that my eyes were giving away my excitement. What we were going to do was suicidally risky, but I wanted to do it. And Jason had known I would feel that way. Besides, if the plan didn't work, I knew I'd find another one, with or without help.

"I'm in." I smiled.

He looked relieved and rubbed his mouth again. "Okay."

We both sat in companionable silence, lost in thought.

"Once we're both free you'll never have to see me again," he said, almost distractedly. "You can go back to having everyone worship at your feet. Won't that be good?"

"Stop ruining the fact we just got on for like, a whole hour," I said, and surprisingly enough, he gave a cautiously suppressed smile.

"Okay. But it was only fifty-two minutes; we could never get on for a whole hour."

I was pulling a face at him when the door swung open and Mrs. Shäfer hurried in, out of breath and clearly looking for us. When she saw Jason and I sitting close together amid the laundry, her expression was comically alarmed. Jason never sat down when speaking one-on-one to someone. He needed to hold some sort of advantage, often physical, so he always stood. I smiled at Mrs. Shäfer and casually stood up.

"Hey, Mrs. S. Can you believe Jason didn't even know how to sort out colors from non? I just saved the entire household from a pink disaster."

Mrs. Shafter was eyeing Jason with dislike. "How curious for someone who's been doing his own washing since he was seven." Jason's jaw tightened as Mrs. Shäfer continued. "I know there are no rules prohibiting certain relationships, but—"

"Mrs. Shäfer!" I laughed slightly. "Have you not *met* Jason? Granted, he has a nice ass, but it doesn't completely make up for the personality defects. You have nothing to worry about, so please don't punish me just because I refuse to be an uncommunicative, broodingly tormented misanthrope and wander the corridors alone!" And then I exclaimed, as if the thought had suddenly occurred to me. "Oh no, please don't tell Dr. Ayer I was hanging out with Jason! Oh, please Mrs. Shäfer! He said I could have a personal item if I was good, and I *have* been good! Please don't tell him, he won't let me get my item then!"

She instantly consoled me. "Don't be silly, sweetheart. Obadiah wouldn't punish you—"

"Yes he would!" I said fretfully. "Oh, this is all my fault!"

"Don't worry," she insisted kindly. "I won't mention anything about finding you with Jason as long as you promise not to do anything like it again."

I instantly agreed and left with her, but not before surreptitiously grinning at Jason, who regarded me with an air of deep irony.

"Nice ass?" he mouthed, and I winked, making him look highly discomfited. *Excellent.*

First things first, however: Preparations for tomorrow.

***

It was so easy getting the white hair dye it was almost a disappointment. After the usual injections, blood tests, and vitamins, Dr. Ayer placed his hands on his knees, as was customary, and asked whether I had any further questions.

"Well, I don't like the color of my hair. I never have; I prefer unusual colors. I always dyed my hair before I came here, so I was wondering if I could have some hair dye as my personal item?"

He smiled, showing small, even teeth. "Your hair is a nice enough color, Marilyn; you shouldn't feel the need to dye it."

"Thank you. I am aware of the pros and cons of my natural hair, but I want to dye it. I was thinking of going white this time; a shock of bright, white hair. Cool, right? And very symbolic and all that."

He barely thought it over, just nodded in a way that said "girls." However, just before I walked out the door, he called me back as another thought struck him. I turned, heart beating.

"Marilyn, a word of caution. Jason is not someone you want to get close to." He smiled ruefully. "I know we aren't supposed to admit to these sorts of things, but I do worry for you sometimes. We are all very fond of you, you know, and we don't want to see you get hurt because of others. Be careful."

My heart constricted and I left. I already knew I had to be careful. And not just because Stockholm syndrome had been invented for people like me. No one must suspect Jason and I were planning something.

The next day dragged on for an eternity. Levi was still being kept in the isolation room, and none of us were allowed to see him until he admitted to ODing on pills. The whole house was subdued as I spent the day doing chores, helping Mrs. Mudiraj put away the groceries in the kitchen, and finally taking my hair dye upstairs along with a palmed knife. And when the afternoon finally started draining into night and the artificial lights of the house buzzed on, I went to the living room for my last evening in the house. Clodagh and

Teddy were also there, Clodagh reading and Teddy on his DS. I sat down on the armchair opposite and switched on the TV. After a while, Jaid marched in, scanned the room, and lay down on the carpet to listen to her iPod. When she realized I was watching her, she just raised a threatening eyebrow.

"What are you listening to?" I asked.

She didn't reply, but budged slightly to the side of the carpet and offered me an earphone. Feeling guilty as hell, I lowered myself down next to her and took the offered earphone.

"High on the wind the angels they fly, Hovering over her grave."

"Darkening Sky," said Jaid, her tired face resting down.

"I'll dig this hole as deep as my love,
And bury her memory away,
And bury her memory away."

The elegiac song didn't seem like something I'd ever have associated with Jaid. Was it Levi's?

"Can I listen?" Clodagh asked, and Jaid turned, placed both earphones onto the carpet, and dialed up the iPod to full volume before placing her head beside it on the carpet again. Clodagh copied us, curling up along the floor with her arms around her chest.

"Teddy?" I asked, and he looked across at me awkwardly before shaking his head.

"I don't understand music much," he said, flushing slightly. "I can identify chord schemes though, so it's not like I...but I don't think it matters, right?"

"Right." I turned and regarded Jaid and Clodagh lying on the floor, and suddenly felt annoyed that I'd been lying with them a second ago. They looked stupid. I stood up abruptly and walked out, past where all the nurses were hovering anxiously in the hallway. And when I returned with a glass of water, my "friends" were all back in their previous places, with their DS, novel, and iPod.

***

As soon as the digital clock beeped eleven, I stood up with a yawn. "I'm going to bed."

Through the door I could see Mrs. Shäfer and the male nurse Udrea coming into the corridor, preparing to start their night shift. As I made my way up the stairs, I found Levi sitting on a chair beside the medicine room, eyes turbulent as ever.

"Night, Levi," I said.

"I don't suppose you want to sleep with me?" he asked.

"Sorry, no."

"Is it because you're a dyke like Clodagh?"

"No."

"You want that psychopath Jason instead?"

"I just don't want to be with you like that, Levi. I don't want anything like that."

He shrugged. "Whatever, it wouldn't mean anything. I just figured that we were both stuck here, nobody cares about us, our families have all buggered off. Don't you want somebody to touch you? Just make you feel good again, natural like?"

I turned away from him to head up the next flight of stairs. "I don't want, or need, anybody else to make me feel good, Levi, and neither should you."

"Yeah, but wanking gets boring after a while."

As I placed my foot on the first step, Levi suddenly spoke again, his voice clearer. "I know you're up to something, Marilyn. I know what happened to my sleeping pills, and I know...." He broke off as Clodagh walked up the stairs behind us, tilting her head to the side.

"Feeling better, Levi? Less like a suicidal druggy nutter?"

"Piss off."

"Make me."

"I'll see you tomorrow," I interrupted, and set up the stairs hurriedly with Clodagh trailing after me. Once Levi was out of sight, Clodagh yawned delicately, and as we reached our rooms she took hold of my arm, sitting us down on my bed.

"He's so exhausting to deal with, isn't he?" she said meekly. "And he's being surprisingly resistant to Arden's teachings. I don't know how Jaid ever coped with him leeching onto her for so long."

"All people are exhausting," I replied, not in a good mood and too tired to hide it.

"Yes they are," she agreed. "Back at home I spent hours locked in the bathroom just so I could be on my own. That was before my dad removed the locks."

I removed my arm from her hand and stood up.

"I want to go to sleep, Clodagh," I said apologetically.

She looked around my bare room. "Okay, sure. But I'm glad Levi's finally given up, you know? He can tell finally that he's lost you and Jaid and Teddy, and everyone has changed now. He's no longer trying to stop everyone else from changing just because he can't. It makes things easier, I think."

I started pointedly exchanging my top for the pajamas. She watched me.

"That's why it's of no use, you know; if you try and escape now." Her tone was quiet and conversational. I turned to her, her hazel eyes oddly distant.

"Excuse me?"

"It's too late for us. But just because you're too stupid to realize what's been happening, I'm not going to let you try and get out of here."

"You want to stop talking now, Clodagh."

"I know you've been scheming ever since you saw Ayer's files. Thinking you could escape or some bullshit. Be the greatest, the favorite, and ruin things for the rest of us. Why are you pretending to fight this place? It makes no damned sense at all. What were you worth before you came here? What would you have ever achieved in this world? The doctors *value* us; they want to create something in us that is special. *I* understood that from the beginning...why can't you? Why are you worthy of any of this?"

"We're not discussing this," I said, keeping my ground with difficulty.

"Yes we are," she said quietly, stepping up to me. "And I'm telling you that your little plan tonight won't work; I'm not letting you."

"You have no say in what I do," I said, frozen into honesty, but it seemed to be the wrong thing to say; she flushed an ugly, mottled color.

"I've been told that before," she said in a muffled voice. "At least, that's what my da used to tell me. 'You can't stop me; you have no say in what I do. Now come here and give your lonely ole da a kiss.' And it was suffocating. It really was; I spent half my life on my back, being suffocated. Are you trying to suffocate me, Marilyn? Do you want me on my back?"

I felt sick.

"It won't work," she said, stepping closer to me. "The first decision I ever made— no, the second, sorry—was to come here. Because I knew for the first time what I wanted...power. To stop being so...human. But now, I'm here and I find it's full of people like *you*: stupid, trapped victims, who have no clue what is about to happen to all of us, or the gift they are being given and do not deserve. How can they be favored ones? How is that fair?"

Internal alarms were screaming inside my head as I asked slowly, "What do they want with us here, Clodagh?"

She placed her open palm on my chest. I flinched backwards, losing my ground.

"Stay and find out. Either way, you're not leaving this room tonight. I'm in control here."

I took a deep breath. "I don't want to fight you, Clodagh. Please just go to bed."

She sneered at me, stepping up close, and deliberately ran her hand down my chest again. "Make me. Be somebody."

"No!"

I snatched up her wrist and attempted to fling her into the wall. She was too heavy, however, and only staggered slightly before grabbing my wrist back and heaving me back against the wall. I grabbed the deodorant bottle from the bedside table and whacked her on the head.

She staggered back again, letting go. "You can't fight me," she said, and I tackled her.

She effortlessly tripped me over her hip, and as I smacked into the floor, she knelt on top of me, gripped my hair, and punched me in the mouth. Apparently I'd never learn that physical violence wasn't my forte. I could taste my own metallic blood along with panicked dizzy memories of The Showman as she pressed her hand down over my mouth.

I began to wildly struggle, buying myself time, trying to calm myself down from the memories. I had to refuse them. I would be strong. I brought up my legs and scissored her midriff, wrenching myself over whilst flinging her off me and into the wall with a crack. As she spun back round, clutching her head, I stood up, my back pressed against the wardrobe.

"If you want me, come and get me," I said.

She bared her slanted little teeth at me. "I want everything," she retorted, and lunged.

I dodged and swung the wardrobe door out right into her face. She fell back with the impact, hands flinging to her face, and I yanked both her feet out from under her. She smacked the bed edge on the way down and toppled onto the floor, her head banging the ground. Hoping no one heard the noise, I quickly straddled her and forced her arms up behind her back, but she had been knocked unconscious.

I stared down at her face, the blood leaking out from her pale blonde hair onto the dark carpet. My hands were swollen and cut, with her blood on them. Circular. It was all circular.

I had to get out.

Biting my lips against the overwhelming panic, I rolled her onto her stomach and used my thin pajama bottoms to knot her hands and feet together behind her back. I stuffed a sock into her mouth and used a t-shirt to bind it into place, with another t-shirt over her face. I then struggled to fit her into my wardrobe before shutting the door on her and keeling over with panic.

Furious with myself, I gave myself a quick slap and dragged the bedside table over and jammed it under the wardrobe handle, while making sure there were still gaps so Clodagh could breathe. I didn't want her to die. I wanted her to live, me to live, me to get out of there, me to change. Me.

But I didn't like this at all. What if Clodagh woke up before Jason and I were gone? She could ruin it all. As I stood worrying, Jaid clomped up onto the outside landing. Flinging a t-shirt back on, I cracked opened the door a few inches and called to Jaid,

"Hey, Clodagh's in here with me tonight. She isn't feeling well and wants me to play nurse for her. That okay?"

Jaid seemed distracted. "Better you than me. How did you mess up the lip this time?"

"Levi," I whispered, and shut the door in her clenched face. She would be occupied with her own thoughts now.

Now it was time to prepare and wait. The worst bit by far. I changed into fresh clothes and trainers, crushed the Ambien, and wrapped it in toilet paper, then sat back down on the bed, hands in my lap. My stomach hurt. And then finally, it was time.

CHAPTER SIX

Jason and I had timed everything out to the nth degree. There couldn't be any mistakes, or we'd miss our opportunity. I placed the Ambien pills and knife in my knickers, the white dye under my baggy sweatshirt, and headed downstairs to the kitchen. The camera in the hallway was motionless as I shuffled along, clutching my stomach as if I had stomach pains. Mrs. Shäfer and Udrea were inside the kitchen, Udrea fixing their customary cups of tea, having just finished their first patrol of the house. Tonight was the only night of the monthly rota where there were only two members of staff on night duty inside Arden House, which meant they had the shortest shift and would head back to the main building at 3:00 A.M. The shift would then be taken over by Mrs. Mudiraj, Dr. Luo, Dr. Kranselbinder, and Nurse Patel. We had to be ready before then.

"What's wrong, Marilyn?" Mrs. Shäfer said, glancing around as she smoked a Marlboro out the kitchen window. I bent over the table beside Udrea as he popped teabags into the empty cups.

"I've got lady pains," I moaned. "They always make me sick. Where is the paracetamol kept?"

"Top cabinet, but it's locked," said Udrea as the kettle pinged. He sighed irritably. "I'll get the key. Make the tea, Marilyn."

I obediently began to pour the water. As soon as Mrs. Shäfer flicked the ash out the window, the crushed pills were in the boiling water. Liberal amounts of milk hid the last of the powder.

"You're a doll," said Mrs. Shäfer as I handed over her cup, and Udrea grumpily sorted through the pill bag for me. I stayed with them, glugging down the paracetamol with water as they drank their tea. When I judged it was time, I started to groan again.

"Oh crap," I muttered. "I think I'm going to vomit again," and fled out the kitchen into the bathroom opposite. As soon as the bathroom door swung shut behind me, Jason stepped out of the cubicle with a cut off pipe in his hand. My adrenaline spiked like crazy. He gave me a quick look-over and, looking slightly reassured, stepped behind the door.

I was bent over the sink loudly retching when Mrs. Shäfer stepped in after me, the picture of concern. She didn't have time to realize there was no vomit in the sink before Jason smoothly stepped out behind her and had the hard pipe edge pressed against her soft throat. I drew out the knife from my knickers. She froze.

"Call for Udrea's help," said Jason in an undertone.

"Udrea...a little help," she instantly called out, voice only slightly quavering. I made the obligatory vomit noises. Udrea stepped through the door and straight into Jason's grip, the pipe against his throat as he was dragged firmly inside. Udrea's mouth opened in shock.

"Yell and I'll knock your throat in," Jason said coldly. I stood a few paces back, my knife out against Shäfer's throat. I was shivering with fear and adrenaline as we shoved both Shäfer and Udrea into the corner of the bathroom.

"I don't know what you idiots think you're doing." Udrea's eyes were fixed on mine as he spoke. "But you won't get away with this. It's impossible...you will be discovered in less than a few minutes...." He shut up. He appeared to be struggling to concentrate, his body clearly slowing down and eyelids drooping. It was the same with Mrs. Shäfer, starting to sag back against the bathroom wall. It was Mrs. Shäfer who realized we'd drugged her; she made a sluggish rabbit movement to get past me. I easily pushed her back down as Jason smashed Udrea's head brutally hard against the wall, knocking him out. Shortly after, Shäfer was out too, both of them collapsed at our feet.

"Makes you feel pretty powerful, right?" I commented, unable to keep the bitterness out my voice.

"Like nothing else. Come on, we don't have much time." Jason was watching my face, uncharacteristic uncertainty in his eyes.

"Sorry." I moved over to the sink and began to frantically apply the white dye to my hair as Jason methodically stripped Udrea and Shäfer of their clothes. The heat generator gurgled and bright lights buzzed overhead as I spread the dye as thinly as possible, so my hair wouldn't turn pure white but a grey color. As I began to scrub with water, I told Jason about trapping Clodagh in my wardrobe. He was less than happy, but just shrugged on Udrea's clothes without comment and turned to watch me struggle with washing out my hair.

"Here," he said at last. "Let me." He came over behind me. Nervy, I backed up too quickly and hit my hip on the sink, sloshing water onto the floor. He stepped away instantly, his expression rigid again, and let me dry my now dingy grey-white hair with paper towels. He then silently handed over Mrs. Shäfer's clothes, scrutinizing my hair from a distance.

"It will pass without close inspection," he said. I began to change and Jason faced the door.

This was the incredible, daring part of the plan, the part I still couldn't believe we were doing. Jason had explained how he'd noticed that he and Udrea were of similar height with dark hair. So he'd naturally made sure his hair was cut in a similar style and lost muscle weight to match his. Of course, Jason had said there were two problems; one, that Udrea had been barely used in the house staff before Jason came; he'd been distrusted and seen as a lightweight. Two, that a guard was never alone. But then he'd noticed I was similar enough to Shäfer in height to pass in the dark, or from a security camera's view. And somehow, a few weeks later, Udrea had been promoted to a regular staff member and Shäfer was his night duty partner for the most isolated shift a month. Go figure; I hadn't realized Jason was such a master manipulator.

"There's no way you could've fixed all that. They must suspect something; it seems too lucky." I had argued straight away.

"Does it?" he'd argued back. "None of them think we'd ever do something so risky...they think they've got us how they want us. And none of them would ever guess we'd partner up."

I'd been sold. From the camera angle, and in the dark, we'd look close enough to pass, and then we'd be out.

"Quick," reminded Jason. "We have seven minutes."

I changed into Shäfer's plain nurse uniform and solid black heels, and placed her glasses on my eyes and her radio on my hip. I dragged my kinking hair back into a bun, trying to straighten it with water. Jason heaved Shäfer and Udrea into the furthest cubicle, and replaced the piping behind the toilet cistern.

"You've clearly visited girls' bathrooms before," I whispered as he locked the cubicle from the inside then climbed out over the top.

"There's a reason they think I have anti-social tendencies," he replied seriously, jumping back down.

"If only they knew how misunderstood you are."

And both of us were out the door and walking confidentially down the hallway, security camera motionless and unsuspecting. It was surreal to say the least. This sort of thing only happened in films. I thought of Clodagh tied up in my room, of Shäfer and Udrea unconscious in the bathroom, and had the urge to laugh.

"Wait," whispered Jason, taking my elbow and pushing me into the shadows beside the staircase. "We are slightly early." We waited, Jason's eyes on his watch and his breath tickling my ear, before he pushed me back out towards the front door.

"Now."

I opened the front door; dark cold night air rushed in and we both walked out into the dark courtyard. The radio on my hip bipped 3:00 as we slowly made our way across to the other side, where the main building was. I raised my hand to cover a yawn and Jason looked down to fiddle with his own radio just as the opposite door electronically opened and Mrs. Mudiraj and Kranselbinder walked out, Mudiraj rubbing her eyes and carrying a cup of steaming coffee.

"Have Val and Luo gotten up yet?" she asked in passing, and Jason nodded, me still yawning. They walked on towards the Arden House, and we walked towards the other building. I couldn't believe that the last few minutes were the product of Jason spending hours studying the night shifts and staff transactions. It was all enough to make me realize how I'd wasted my time here focusing on the people. The door closed electronically behind us. However, there was another door in front of us, with a number pad. I pushed in the number sequence I'd memorized, the door opened, and I grinned. I'd remembered the correct numbers.

Once we were inside the main building everything was even more hushed, faint light spilling out from under the odd door and security systems, and the sounds of machines sliced up the silence. We hurried down the corridor.

"When you looked out the wall, you were facing southwest, so we go that way," he whispered in my ear, keeping so close to me that he kept knocking my side. We hurried until we reached the end door. Iron stairs took us down past another floor, and another, and into a cloakroom and large empty reception area filled with crates and storage. To leave there would be too much in the open, so we made our way out through another corridor and left through the fire escape. And then suddenly, we were outside in a concrete world of ugly squat buildings, delivery trucks, and wire fencing.

The polluted tang of midnight air cleaned my cramped lungs as we went at a walking pace through the complex of clearly new buildings. The place was mainly deserted except for the odd man or woman in crumpled lab coats smoking or yawning. Two security men with radios barely looked past their iPad's at us. They stood next to one of the low concrete buildings, which had a large placard nailed over the door saying "Testing 047-2." The adjacent building had "Samples" on it. I shivered. Jason's jaw was clenched as we kept on walking. What was happening here?

"Relax," I muttered under my breath to him. "You're too tense." His nostrils flared but he did as I said. Finally we were past the cluster of buildings, past all the stationed trucks and storage that lay between the building and machinery, and were in the loading area. I could see the high electronic gates just past all the trucks and cargo, and the guards walking alongside it. And through the gates, there was a road, and trees. Woods. Perfect.

Suddenly a high pitched deafeningly loud alarm rang over the place, and red lights began to flash around us. Jason uncoiled like a panther about to attack. I hurriedly clamped down around his waist, and stuck my heels in as he tried to move.

"*Stop it,*" I hissed. "Act natural; look around for the intruders like everyone else!"

"They found out too quickly," he hissed back through gritted teeth, looking around us. "We need to get out *now*— that way!"

We made our way out, pretending to look around and search as our radios went crazy on our hips, and people around us confusedly roused themselves. People were crossing buildings and peering out of the windows as security men all began to run around, clearing spaces for us to walk through. There were only two security men at the nearest point of the electronic fence, but the fence was firmly shut, and there would be no way we could take out the guards and steal their uniforms now.

"We're going to have to climb the fence," Jason said, staring into the distance, focused.

"Hey, you two over there, get back to the main!" The voice came behind us. We both ignored it and continued walking, tears of fear stinging my eyes. We were nearly at the fence, ten meters across from the guards who were all conferring with each other.

"Hey, you two! Stop now and turn round!"

One of the guards had heard the voice and turned towards us. I started to turn to face them, and then suddenly yelled "There they are!" and pointed to two figures walking around the back of the nearest lorry. Not the most sophisticated plan, but they all turned. As soon as they did so, Jason launched into movement, throwing me up against the wire fencing before running and launching himself up onto it. I scrabbled up after him, the wire biting into my fingers and knees as I climbed, but already Jason was high above me, getting further and further away as he scaled up with the single-minded grace of the panther I'd compared him to earlier. And he was near the top, but he was slowing down, looking behind…looking at me, yelling, and stopping. I could hear yells below us, and felt the fence being pulled and shaken beneath us as I kept going further and further, higher and higher.

And then there was a *whsst* as something split through the air beside me. Above me, Jason's body jerked horribly, and his fingers were ripped from the fence. I looked up in horror as he began to fall. I tried to pull myself to the side out the way of his body; there was another *whssst* as something narrowly missed me and instead hit Jason again, his body jerking like a puppet. His body crashed downwards into me, tearing me off the fence and into the air along with him. We both hit the ground, only this time I was on the bottom, and it hurt. Trapped under Jason's weight and barely able to breathe, I could only gasp at air as dark figures surrounded us. Jason was unmoving, pinning me into the muddy ground. Black splodges danced around my eyes as I tried to heave him off. Someone poked my head with the barrel end of a gun.

"That was pretty close, eh?"

"Too close."

"Dr. Ayer won't care; he'll be happy at how successful they were. Took them long enough to try and escape, but they outdid his expectations of how far they'd get."

"Nah, Ayer will be pissed we had to shoot the male GE."

"Oh well."

I looked up into the cold mesh of night as the man above me raised another gun and pointed it down into my face. I almost wet myself.

"That's right, honey," the man said down to me. "We've been waiting for you to try and escape for a while now; most of us doubted it was ever going to happen. It's the final confirmation that the program was working, you see, to make sure you'd be ready for the next phase. The final aptitude test, find out who would be marketed for the highest price. He'll be surprised that it's *two* of you though, eh?"

"Oh shit," said the other man suddenly. "I now owe Gauk three hundred quid."

They shot me with a tranquilizer gun...at least, it didn't feel like a bullet. Maybe I was dying though...strangely, I wasn't focusing on it either way. All I could hear was the static-filled melody of a song as waves of dark sleep curled around me.

"Stars fading but I linger on, dear, still craving your kiss."

"Get them both back to the labs, boys, and someone tell Ayer we have the winners of his little competition."

"I'm longing to linger 'til dawn, dear...,"

***

When I woke up, I was strapped down to a bed in the exact same empty white room I'd first woken up in, and I was back in the hospital gown. I lay there, breathing hard, unable to move my head to the side, but hearing the murmurs of nurses and doctors in the room around me, the snap of clipboards, the clicks of machines. Dr. Ayer appeared in my vision and seated himself at my bedside. He leaned over to pat my arm as I groaned.

"They shot Jason," I wheezed, and he looked grave.

"Only in the shoulders; try not to be overly dramatic, Marilyn. We're not trying to kill anyone here; in fact, quite the contrary. The Arden Board and I spent far too long selecting who would become our *Ubermensch* product to waste that now."

"You *what?*" As I stared at him in dawning horror, masked doctors appeared at the periphery of my vision, all comparing me to the clipboards. Dr. Ayer smiled comfortingly.

"I am very glad it was you and Jason who almost escaped first. I always saw the two of you as the greatest investment. Of course, I was slightly disappointed that the two of you chose to work together. Victims will always need each other; it's what makes them controllable. Why you still insist on perceiving yourself as a worthless victim is interesting, and will need further attention before you are finished and ready."

"Wh...what's happening?" I whispered. Dr. Ayer smiled as a tall man with a surgical mask lifted my face up to the light, tilting it this way and that. I was frozen, straining my eyes sideways.

"Don't worry," Ayer said, "you don't have much longer to wait before the second to final stage of your program starts. As expected, the attempted escape had the useful side-effect of finally forcing the bustling bureaucrats and posturing ethicists into action, and we can finally truly begin."

As I started to shake violently the chief surgeon flipped up his clipboard and skimmed the print on it. "M. Aske. Okay, this one is down as our Angel of Vengeance, prototype was Avenging Angel 305B. We all ready?"

Positive murmurs all around.

"The clientele will love the theatricality of this product," said another doctor, voice wry behind his mask as he stepped up to my bed and checked my bonds. "I hope she gets merchandised as deserved."

Dr. Ayer leaned forward in his chair. "There's nothing to fear Marilyn; you're just going to be unconscious for a short while. You're in the best hands in the world; our operating theatres are the finest, most expensive, and top quality you can get, and waiting there are some of the world's leading specialists and expert surgeons all ready for your individually designed genetic enhancement."

"Genetic...." I stopped breathing, turned my face up to the lights, and started screaming. This wasn't real. It couldn't be happening.

They gagged me. Ayer was trying to talk, but I wasn't listening.

"The Board and I...be more susceptible...further training once you...clearly the vision we have in you."

I wanted to keep screaming, but no more sound was coming out.

The doctors removed my gown and began to draw with black marker pen across my face, throat, chest, ribs, arms, and legs. One twisted my shoulders up and another scribbled along my spine and blades.

"Has Robertson arrived yet? She wants to oversee the shoulder and back muscle reconstruction."

The chief surgeon handed a nurse his clipboard and said to Ayer, "Okay, I think we're ready to start."

"Wait a second," said Ayer. "Let me explain everything to her, or she'll be scared."

The chief surgeon looked at his watch and nodded. Ayer smiled into my eyes, liquid excitement in his own soft green eyes.

"We haven't much time, Marilyn, so I'll be quick. What is about to take place is the most genius, innovative scheme, and it will change the entire face of the corporate and scientific new world. It will not only make all of us rich beyond imagination, but place in our hands almost unlimited global power. The Arden Board Organization is my dream; I made it come true, and the six of you are part of that: my superhuman progeny, the first faces of my brand. I have taken the two most popular, overpopulated, competitive industries in the world and am combining them to take them to new heights. It will knock all competition out the water; I will be providing the most in demand service of the world. The industry of genetic modification meets the world of hired force and violence; by combining the two, we are creating a service that no one and nothing else in the world can compete with. Military, mercenary, hit men, sabotage, bounty hunters, personal detectives, all will be second choice to hiring *you*. Our methods are top secret and have taken decades to perfect, but luckily, many top businessmen have invested in Arden Board. Many people have stakes in this venture. They know that to have a part in this venture will give them more power than top tycoons, criminal dons, *prime ministers*. In fact, the government is already aware of our scheme, and is powerless to stop it, Equally, those corporate powers and enterprises not involved with the Board are trying to do everything they can to put a stop to this. They know which way the power is turning. But most want a piece of this business, of what I'm creating, and the government knows it can't cross that. And you, Marilyn, you and the five others, you are what we'll be selling, owning, contracting. You'll belong to the Arden Board — the perfectly created killers for hire. The world will fear you and desire you."

He was breathing hard, his eyes gleaming. I could feel hysterics coming on. I started to laugh painfully.

"No," I said, "no, no, no!"

He looked at me like I was an obstinate child. "Marilyn, my love, you'll be one of the most powerful and rich individuals in the world. You've been so lovingly selected and cared for, and that will just continue, your worth will just increase. The world will want you, the most precious commodity to own. And we'll make sure no one will be able to emulate what we've done — the six of you are already fully patented, all our evidence and knowledge closely guarded, patented and protected. We will always win the competition!"

I couldn't keep control any longer. "You're crazy!" I screamed, the gag muffling my words. "You're crazy! You're going to kill us...what you're doing is impossible...you're going to kill me!"

"Come on, Marilyn. We'd never go through the modification operations unless we were 100% sure they would be successful. We've been creating and getting rid of the prototypes and testing stages since the '70s. We spent so much time on selecting you, making sure you fit all the criteria, maneuvering circumstances, getting you here — to waste it all on the most important part?"

"My mum...." My throat was as choked as an autumn gutter.

"It was necessary. After all, you could have the perfect genes, perfect health, the specific family history we were looking for, and been brought up in a certain way...but all of that is only good up to a point. We needed killers. Equally, we needed our killers alone in the world, abandoned by the government and the legal system." He paused to stroke my arm. "It was the first test, being able to kill some middle-tier hit man. And we gave you the gift of vengeance along with it."

"My mum...." Briny tears spilled over my cheeks. "My mum. How could you...?"

"Of course," he went on, "many of the youths we tracked down failed the criteria at some point. Most were killed by the contract killers. Some we brought here and realized they were unsuitable. Clodagh was different, of course. She used her mother to track the Board down, and put herself up for it."

"My dad...he didn't know...?"

Dr. Ayer looked up from straightening my sheets. "No," he said in a voice thrumming with satisfaction. "Brendan the 'Gatsby' does not have the slightest clue what we're doing with his daughter. Oh, he'll put two and two together soon enough; he keeps an ear close to the ground, for all his reformed ways. But it will be too late for him to make a difference."

I closed my eyes and started to cry.

"Obadiah, finish up," said the chief surgeon. "You're making the subject agitated."

Dr. Ayer rose to his feet, hands neatly at his side, as the chief surgeon placed his mask into position.

"I know you don't believe me right now, Marilyn, but I really do think you'll like the changes. We've chosen the most suitable abilities for each of you; you will be perfect."

When I'd seen films with this sort of scenario in it, the heroine was always able to escape in the nick of time. Perhaps it was because this wasn't a film—or perhaps because I was nobody's idea of a heroine — that this didn't happen. I started to scream; I struggled and strained my body against the straps. But even as I fought them, powerlessness drowned my brain, my inability to change or control anything. Still, I couldn't stop screaming, even as the nurse slotted together the anesthetic and applied the drip to my hand.

"Please no, make this stop," I screamed hysterically. "I will kill you, I swear I will kill you all! No, no, you can't make me…I refuse!"

Dr. Ayer said nothing, his eyes gleaming.

"You won't feel a thing until you wake up," said the chief surgeon, looking at me for the first time. "You may experience some discomfort then."

"NO! No…you can't…."

As I wept, my eyes were already closing.

CHAPTER SEVEN

The chief surgeon had a knack for understatement. I woke up swallowed in a crescendo of filthy red pain. I threw up over myself...repeatedly. The stench of sour vomit and chemicals gripped my hazed, drugged brain and clogged up my throat as I lay God knew where, disorientated and in pain. Strange nurses appeared and disappeared, bustling and fussing and changing sheets. A hit of morphine made me throw up again, and the pain still boiled and burnt through my flayed body. Cool hands were on my forehead, and I heard Mrs. Shäfer's distant voice. "It's okay, dear; the surgery was a complete success. You just need to rest now."

For the next few days, I drifted in and out of consciousness, between light and dark, flickering and hallucinating, and always tied down and hooked up to humming machines and drips. Nurses murmured, doctors spun, bandages were changed, casts replaced, stitches checked, drips fixed. Just to keep the nurses on their toes, I continued to vomit on a regular basis and had no control over my bladder. Indescribably humiliating: what a shame I wasn't fully there to enjoy it.

I didn't know how many days later it was — only that it still felt much too soon — that the sickening fog began to recede, the chemical pain killers began to be reduced, and the chaotic pain spiraling through my body began to settle into a constant red ache.

"Are you ready to get up?" Mrs. Shäfer asked me, and I realized I was fully conscious.

"Leave me alone," I tried to say, but my throat was so swollen that the words couldn't come out. I tried again.

Mrs. Shäfer busied herself checking the drip. "Come on, Marilyn. Let's try and get you standing up; it's dangerous to spend too long lying down. Your blood circulation will—"

"Did you ever read *Frankenstein* in school?"

She helped me sit upright and moved my legs to the side of the bed. I felt exhausted already.

"Yes."

"On a scale of one to Boris Karloff, how do I look?"

"You look like a very sickly, ill young woman who needs to get her blood circulation going again."

"*Dawn of the Dead*, then?"

"Just focus on feeling better, dear." She unhooked me from the drips, pads, and monitors and got me to my feet. "I'm glad you're okay," she added huskily, looking away. I ignored her and began to shuffle across the room. Dull pain radiated through my skeleton, flaring along my shoulders, back, and chest. "I made sure you were getting the best care out of the six of you. All the nurses wanted to look after you." She paused. She sounded stressed, her eyes shining as if she were blinking back tears. "You're being transferred to your new location tomorrow morning," she said. "I'm glad you woke up before that happened."

I was walking back to the bed when Ayer and the chief surgeon entered the room, the chief surgeon still clutching his beloved clipboard. I kept my exhausted gaze to the floor. Not yet, not yet.

"Walking already!" said the surgeon. "Excellent news." Dr. Ayer smiled at me, and I focused harder on the floor. I would kill him. I had never decided to kill someone before. But I would.

The two men watched me as I made my way back to the bed, not bothering to hide how out of breath I was. Mrs. Shäfer hovered anxiously in the background.

"All right then," said the chief surgeon, consulting his papers as Ayer sat on the chair beside the bed. "We've come to discuss the effects of the surgery you will be experiencing as soon as your body has accepted them slightly more."

"Explain as simply as possible," Ayer reminded. The chief surgeon cleared his throat.

"Fine, let's get straight to what you will find different with your body. First, the wings we designed are removable, and not quite finished, so at the moment you just have the two twin metal holes in each shoulder blade, with retractable wires, and the slot in which the wings go. We linked the ports up to your spinal cord and the rest of your CNS, of course. We also transfused some bird genetics with your shoulder blades, and used bird tissue as a genetic link, so when the wings are connected to you, they should function as a regular part of your body. You should receive the wings as soon as the final adjustments have been made and your shoulders are sufficiently healed, and then you can continue in your training. Questions?"

I attempted to twist my hand up behind my back to touch my shoulders. I could only feel the bulky plaster bandaging that covered my upper back under the hospital gown. Sharp pain made me abandon that idea.

"Marilyn?" Ayer prodded.

"I'll be able to fly," I said to him, and he nodded. Yeah right, that was possible. I didn't understand, I didn't believe, and I didn't like.

"The second change is more complicated to explain, so I'll simplify it as much as I can," the surgeon went on. "You are familiar with chameleons? Well, a chameleon has a special layer of cells called iridophores. They contain a crystalline substance called guanine, which reflects light, allowing chameleons to blend against the environment. Specialized cytoplasm controls this reflection of light. Basically put, you now have electronically controlled and activated skin cytoplasm hooked up to your heart and the CNS. We've adjusted your heart to make sure it can cope with the extra pressure, and to allow it to function as a control on the guanine. As soon as your body is healed, we'll show you how your body can now reflect light when it wants. However, don't test it out before we say so, as you need to be shown the correct, safe way to change your heart and control the electric switch, and the doctors need to be on hand to monitor the process."

"Did you make my boobs bigger?" I asked. "They definitely feel bigger."

The chief surgeon ignored the comment. "In short, the surgery was a complete success. No brain damage, no nerve damage, no additional trauma, and your heart should recover fully from the stress of the operation. Better than new!"

"Amazing, isn't it?" said Dr. Ayer gently. "I wanted to give you new reflexes as well as the abilities for flight and invisibility, but your body couldn't cope with anything more. Nevertheless, I'm proud of you, Marilyn. If you keep on progressing like this, you'll be in the final phase of rehabilitation in no time."

"What about the others? Will they be in rehabilitation?"

"Don't worry about the others."

Once Ayer and the chief surgeon had gone, I asked Mrs. Shäfer to use the en-suite bathroom. Time to assess the damage.

"Are you sure? You...you should to go back to bed."

I insisted, and we made our way to the connecting door. I wanted a mirror. No, I wanted to be alone. I stepped into the bathroom, shutting the door behind me, and switched the light on. Focused on breathing.

I could've looked worse. I still looked like me, just not a great version of me. Like I'd endured a lifetime of domestic abuse or escaped a crystal meth cult or something. My face was thin, sharp, and grey-tinged, hollowed out from pain and exhaustion. My hair, still dyed a greyish color, was sweat-sodden and shaved in patches along my temple and at the back of my skull. My pale eyes looked even uglier when blood-shot, and my throat was bruised and swollen, as were my lips and hands. My back, upper chest, and shoulders were all hidden under the bulky bandaging. There was also gauze and lighter bandages around my wrists, neck, knees, and down my spine to my ass. In the shaved parts of my head, I could see neatly stitched up cuts along the skin. I tried to give my normal sparkling smile without much success, so I gave up and just stared.

Mrs. Shäfer opened the door to check on me. As I looked back to the mirror, I noticed the roots of my hair were stark white. I was shaking badly, and behind me Mrs. Shäfer quickly forced her face into neutral, although not before I had seen the clash of emotions in her eyes. They were emotions I had no desire to acknowledge.

"We'll get you some more hair dye later," she said shakily. "And a haircut to hide the patches."

"Can I have a shower?" I asked. She hesitated, but just said, "Try not to wet your bandaging," and withdrew, shutting the door after her. I turned on the shower, then turned back to face the mirror.

Could I turn invisible?

No, it was a ridiculous idea. Impossible.

I held out my hands in front of me, started to breathe in and out, and as my heartbeat began to slow down, I focused inward, listening to the beat reverberating around my chest. It was comforting at first, strengthening...but suddenly I began to panic. What if my heart was damaged in the operation? Could anyone truly know the effects this would have on my body? What if...?

As I panicked, I suddenly felt a shifting motion in my chest, and a jolt passed through my heart like an internal spark igniting, or an electric reaction. A strange sensation crawled over my skin, like it was being wrapped in freezing cold cling film. My heart suddenly had to work harder, vibrations spiraled through my veins, and my blood began to *really* pump, the new mechanics of my body trigged out of their dormant state by my heartbeat and the electric current. And it started to sting. My veins felt like shards of glass were being passed through them. Shock at the pain fueled the reaction further, and my heartbeat sped up, faster and faster. My chest felt like it was on fire, my blood surging and spiking through my veins, and now it *really* stung. I looked across to the wide-eyed girl in the mirror as she became fainter and fainter, like my image was being washed away from the mirror.

And then...I was gone. Only my hospital gown hung in midair, wrapped around the contours of an invisible body. I waved my hand at the reflection, but the movement chafed my hypersensitive skin against the fabric. It felt like my skin was being scrubbed against hard, rough Brillo pads, and the bathroom tiles were jarringly cold and hard against the throbbing soles of my feet. Yet I was invisible.

Invisible.

I let out a grimace that was meant to be laughter. I was invisible! And suddenly I knew I'd have my chance to escape again soon. Because I was different now, they had changed me. I no longer belonged here, trapped in these endless cycles of pain and panic. I could escape.

There was a knock at the door.

"Marilyn, are you okay?" Mrs. Shäfer called.

"Yeah," I called back.

How to change back, though? Keeping my eyes on the mirror, I assessed my body and the way that my heart was thrumming, too fast and mechanical to be normal. I focused on forcing down the rate of my heartbeat, but it didn't want to break the pattern. I could feel the internal reaction to change back fighting against my heartbeat, but nothing happened. Frustrated, I hit myself in the chest. Instantly, an electric shock shuddered through my body as my heart reacted. The electrical stinging sensation across my skin was reducing, and my image was beginning to emerge again in the mirror. I peered at the reflection, my skin still tingling with tenderness; however, it only looked momentarily wind burned, and other than that I was the same.

"Holy shit." This was incredible. Yes, it had hurt like hell but I didn't care. I had a weapon now. I knew I could escape. I kept staring at my reflection. How fitting it would be, to free myself using the thing my captors had given me! I walked into the shower, water and stringent hair dye running over my sensitive skin. It was only as I walked back out that I remembered to hide the small, secretive new smile.

"Feeling better?" Mrs. Shäfer asked as I opened the door.

"Much."

"Good, but back into bed with you now, Marilyn."

"One last question, Mrs. Shäfer. Do you know how they are going to transfer me to the next location tomorrow? I hope it won't be too painful."

She looked at me cautiously before answering. "They decided not to put me on duty during the transfer, but I understand they will be taking you by vehicle, on the roads." She continued to look at me. "You aren't so stupid as to think of escaping again, are you? You won't have a chance. Besides, they will be taking you to their most secure location, where you'll continue your training with some of the best corporate mercenaries, ex-spies, businessmen, and hit men able to be brought into the Arden program; once you're there everything will be different. You'll also gain your wings."

"I know," I said, and allowed her to help put me to bed. Tomorrow I'd have my second chance for freedom, and this time I wouldn't mess it up.

When Mrs. Shäfer opened the door to leave, the faint sounds of high-pitched screaming could be heard in the distance. We both pretended not to hear. I'd learned my lesson.

***

Judging from the light outside the tiny barred window, it was still very early morning when they came to move me. I was awake, sitting in the middle of the artificial bedroom as the door opened and two big security men entered, along with a new nurse and Mrs. Mudiraj. Behind them, four more security guards stood in the doorway. They all wore armored vests, radios, and holstered guns—hopefully tranquilizers.

"Do as we say Marilyn; get up and put your arms out, there's a good girl," said Mrs. Mudiraj, holding up a strait jacket.

"Please don't make me wear that," I whispered starkly.

"She's a tricky one," said Mrs. Mudiraj to the other nurse, who was staring at me doubtfully. "Pay her no attention; she could convince you she was your own newborn babe if you're not careful."

The younger nurse nodded gravely and Mrs. Mudiraj continued speaking to me. "If you don't allow us to put the jacket on you, Marilyn, it shall be done by force."

I swallowed and held out my arms. She strapped me up in the jacket and twisted my arms up across my chest, making my bandaged shoulders ache anew. The guards brought out a dark hood, and I didn't have time to react before it was over my head and I was in darkness. I felt the two guards take a grip on my painful shoulders, and I was led forward out of the room. As I walked down a corridor, I could hear the distant pain-wracked screams again, only this time, I knew who they belonged to.

Clodagh.

"Some of the surgeries have had minor setbacks, a few unseen side effects," said Mrs. Mudiraj in my ear. "But all that matters is that yours was a success."

I swallowed again.

We went down through various corridors, flights of steps, and doors until the smell of fresh air and petrol hit me. My senses confused, I was urged up and boosted into the back of what seemed to be a large lorry or a van. I was then pushed through some wiring into what had to be a tiny cage of some sort. I focused on keeping my heart steady and not triggering the heart switch as the hood was pulled off my head and the wire cage door closed, with me inside it. The guard then walked back down past the other cages that filled the lorry and exited out the back, disappearing into the blur of grimy morning light. He slammed the door shut behind him and darkness filled the lorry.

I didn't know if I should be crying or swearing. I stood in silence, trying to decide which, as the lorry engine began to vibrate under my bare feet and the lorry began to move. I started to swear. However, we could have only been in motion for five or ten seconds, me pacing around the cage, when the lorry halted again. There was a flurry of annoyed voices outside the vehicle, and the sounds of someone being dragged.

"You can't put them in there as well! The angel GE is already in there, and you know Dr. Ayer's orders were to keep all of them separate! We were already breaking his order by putting those two—"

"It's not by bloody choice! The fire boy just burned his lorry to the ground and we're on a deadline here, so shut your bitching and help me get them onboard."

After more argument the exit door opened again. I watched men drag two hooded, bound figures inside and dump them in separate cages on either side of me before leaving again, still arguing with each other and the men waiting outside.

"What does it matter if they see each other one more time?"

"Ayer *expressly* said not to—"

"Ayer should've warned us about the reaction the boy would have when the goddamn meds wore off."

"Jaid? Levi?" I whispered out into the darkness.

"Marilyn, is that you?" Jaid's voice sounded hoarse, taut with pain from where she was curled on the ground, her hood still in position.

"Yeah, it's me. Are you okay? Levi? You okay too?"

"He's unconscious," she said, her voice low. "But I don't know why—just suddenly there were flames everywhere, but I still had my hood on. And he won't respond to anything I say. He hasn't ever since the...you know."

The engine of the lorry started back up and moved, rocking me back into the cage wall.

"Levi is fine, Jaid. He's probably just unconscious after the energy it took to create the fire. Maybe he passed out because of the oxygen it took to fuel the fire." I kept my voice matter-of-fact and sure, even though I was making up shit for all I was worth. "They wouldn't transfer him if there was anything wrong with him after the surgery. And can't you also hear him breathing? In fact, I bet he's just been tranqed up after the fire and is now dreaming of 'Lucy in the Sky with Diamonds.'"

Jaid breathed out sharply, and I could hear her wince as she raised herself to sit against the side of the lorry, as near to Levi as possible. She didn't argue. Hidden by the darkness, I shakily copied her and sat down on the floor, wishing my arms weren't strapped up against my chest. It was going to make escaping somewhat harder.

"I can't see Levi," Jaid said suddenly. "Can you see him? Is he moving yet?"

"It's really dark; I can't really see him either."

"I couldn't see him when he started the fire either, just heard.... Do you think he's in pain? What if—?"

"Jaid—"

"He should be awake by now. Levi? See, he won't wake up...I can't get him to wake up."

"Jaid, calm—"

"Don't you tell me to calm down! Levi needed me to protect him; he needed me and he was all alone. Ever since

153

we were kids he depended on me, and I've always let him down. They took him away and I've done crap all—"

"There was nothing you *could've* done, Jaid," I said, leaning my aching head back against the wire mesh. "No one could've done anything. It happened, and now we just need to prepare for what we want to come next."

Silence fell again. I listened to the sounds of traffic gradually immersing us.

"What did they do to you?" Jaid asked at last.

"Gave me invisibility. What about you?"

"They had a right party with my body." Her voice was flat and bitter. "I can still feel; they told me I've got a new skeleton. A new and improved one."

"Improved how?"

"Metal. My bones and significant muscles are some metal alloy—a real life Adamantium for me."

I closed my eyes. "A metal skeleton…?"

"I'm harder, faster, better, stronger. I can jump unnatural heights, bench-press a car, my bones are unbreakable, and my reflexes are robot quick. I just have to avoid metal melting furnaces, getting electrical shocks, and I have to pray that this type of metal doesn't go rusty."

"I'm sorry."

"Shut the hell up, Marilyn. There's no point in the eternal sainthood of sunshine routine anymore; the game is over."

I shut up. But she was wrong. The game hadn't even started yet.

Unfortunately, it wasn't too long before she started worrying about Levi again, calling out his name. "Can you see him, Marilyn?"

"I promise to tell you if he makes any startling disco-esque movements."

I could feel the force of her glare under the hood. "This is the real Marilyn showing, isn't it? You don't even understand what it is to care about someone else more than you care about yourself."

"I just think both you *and* Levi would benefit if you took control of yourself first. Look after your damned self, figure out what the hell is going on, and then you can look after Levi."

She sniffed. "I don't want to look after myself. Besides, I saw the scars they gave me. Like...lines, all along my legs, my arms, down my ribs, spine, hips...my face...everywhere."

I buried my face in my knees.

"I've heard Bio-Oil is good," I said. I sounded distant, even to myself.

To Jaid's credit, she managed a grimace of laughter. "God, this is crazy."

Levi spoke up from the other side of the lorry. "Yeah, we're like a nightmarish version of the *X-men*. The X-men meet Dr. Mengele."

"Levi!" cried Jaid, and I could hear rummaging and rattling as Jaid pressed herself against the wiring, trying to get closer to his voice.

"Are you okay?" Jaid demanded.

"Not really," said Levi, muffled under the hood. "I'm going to kill them. All of them." But the usual fiery emotion seemed missing from his tired, uncharacteristically fragile voice. "I swear, I hate them all. I will murder...." He broke off to cough for a painfully prolonged period of time.

"Did the fire damage you?" Jaid's frantic voice was exhausting in its intensity.

"No."

I asked, "Is that what they did to you? Fire?"

He heaved himself back against the lorry wall, his movements like that of an old frail man. "I...don't know. Maybe," he said at last, dazed.

"Maybe? How can you not know?"

"I think something is wrong. It's not supposed to...I...I just felt pain everywhere, and blood, and there was fire everywhere. I think I killed Dr. Luo. Not that I care. But it feels like...something is wrong with me."

Jaid began to babble frantic words of comfort, hope, guilt, and apology; Levi sat there lost in confusion. I pressed myself away from them against the back of the cage and wished myself thousands of miles away. I knew I should whisper reassuring words as I usually did. But I didn't. Jason and Jaid were right all along; I knew I was selfish. I always had been. Manipulating my mother, manipulating school and friends and everything. I didn't care about anybody else.

But now that was a good thing. It was good; I *couldn't* care about anybody else because I had to get away. It was necessary. In fact, it was no longer being selfish, it was being individual. Surviving. Living the ideal life, or something.

***

I'd estimated the lorry had been travelling for over six hours, and judging from the outside noise, had passed several motorways. Soon the surrounding traffic noises had died away, though, and the smell of fresh country air permeated the cracks in the lorry tarpaulin. The lorry stopped and we waited for another four hours before setting off again. Levi, Jaid, and I all sat in silence. I could hear Levi's harsh, loud breathing, and it sounded very unhealthy. Jaid was just stirring to ask if Levi was all right again when there was a huge CRASH, and with a violent jerking motion we were all lifted up and flung sideways. The cages swung to the left with the impact, us in them, as the lorry skidded wildly around us. CRASH. We hit something, the collision jolting through my bones as we were flung midair again until the lorry slid to a standstill.

"What the hell was that?" yelled the driver from the front, before more yells burst out around us and there was an almighty BOOM. Outside, a flare of exploding orange brightness swept through the new darkness and through the inside of the lorry, the heat assaulting our eyes. I got to my feet; the violent light that had filtered through the cracks revealed that the lorry had fallen on its side. I could hear the roar of fire surrounding us, and smoke stung my face. More yells sounded, along with the screeches of new cars halting and people running around...new cars and people running up to surround the lorry.

"They're running into the forest," an unfamiliar voice yelled. "Split up and track. You four...secure the GE's."

"They're trapped inside! Secure the perimeter first!"

"We need to get out!" I cried to the others, the smoke and heat beginning to overpower the darkness.

"No...they've come to rescue us!" Levi said.

I spat the taste of grit out of my mouth and struggled to my feet, arms still bound across my chest. "The police?"

"It's not a rescue team," Jaid yelled back from where she was trying to stare out between the cracks in the wall. "They're not wearing any uniforms...just black stuff."

"They must be Arden's competition," I replied, my chest heavy.

"They're coming this way!"

"This goddamned straitjacket!" Jaid screamed out of frustration, getting to her feet.

Frantically, I searched the fallen cage around me; there was jagged wire all along the side. I ran over and began to grate it against the thick fabric of the strait jacket. I glanced back to Jaid and yelled over the noise.

"Use your strength to stretch and rip it off!"

"I.... It hurts." She swore, nodded, and started to slowly push her arms out against the jacket, the fabric making a loud rending noise as it ripped down the seams.

As she did this, I rubbed my head against where the cage was jagged, trying to catch the hood on the wire and wriggle free. Finally, it caught and I managed to get out of it. As I did so, Levi, half hidden in the orange fumes and shadows, suddenly stood up, arms bound against his chest, and closed his eyes.

"No!" Jaid yelled, removing the fabric as the stench of chemicals and metal hit the air and reddish, clotted blood-sprayed flames shot out of Levi's blackened fingers and mouth. They raced across the white jacket and up his sleeves; the sizzling cloth flamed up and fell apart as Levi gagged and screamed in pain until he was able to wrench his hands out of the blackened jacket and drop and roll the flames out. When he stood back up, his bare torso and arms were badly burned, the skin scorched and bleeding, with deep blistered sores on his hands. As he used his new freedom to pull himself out of the blackened cage, I could see the grotesquely sewn up skin livid red over his heart and along his wrists, illuminated by the fire. Levi burst flames out of his hands against my cage and pulled the burning wire apart with a yell of pain before moving to open Jaid's cage. She strode out and slammed her weight straight against the back exit door of the lorry. A crack splintered down the middle. Tears falling down over the cuts that lined her face, she adjusted her position and slammed into the door again; this time it burst open and the outside chaos was revealed, as were the four people standing outside on the road and pointing their guns up at us.

"Step out of the lorry with your hands on your heads!" one of the men yelled. Jaid instantly swore and slammed the door shut again.

"My turn," I whispered, and Jaid pulled my jacket off, Levi clumsily ripping at the rest of it with his bloody hands. As I shucked off the rest of my clothes, I focused on speeding up my heartbeat until I could feel the switch in my chest heat up and switch into position, and suddenly the spark was ignited, the reaction within me taking place, and I was turning invisible. Jaid and Levi stared at me until the sensation of scalding cling film was fully stretched out across all my flesh.

Levi hissed, "Your bandages!" Jaid hurriedly reached across to also pull off the bandaging and plaster from my torso. It hurt like crazy, but I focused on her hands, which were swollen and bruised, her forearms bloody. Clearly her skin and normal muscle weren't genetically enhanced, just the bone. There was a line of stitching down the middle of each finger as she used her metal nails to cut off the last of the bandaging.

"You guys start making demands," I said. As Jaid hesitated, Levi promptly re-opened the door.

"We'll only come out if you promise not to harm us," he called to the men, and I crept out past the men in strange body armor into the middle of the wide deserted road. The men were all surrounding the lorry or watching the wooded area around us.

"Weren't there more GE's in there?" demanded one of the men by the lorry, his accent rather heavy.

"Check with Dozjek that we have all the other GE's."

"Come out and we promise we won't harm you!" yelled the main man to Levi and Jaid.

I ran down the road to where there were six powerful looking cars parked in a circle, blocking the road. We were surrounded by woods with pillars of smoky fire weaving through the trees and cutting us off from the rest of the world; the only way out was down the road, which was boxed in by the cars and full of men patrolling with guns. There was the sound of distant gunfire and as I ran to the nearest car, I saw the dead bodies lying sprawled on the edges of the road in the blood-spattered foliage. A man stood beside the nearest car, his back to me, his focus on a dead body curled up at his feet. As I grasped the car handle and hauled myself in, his head snapped around, but it was too late as I turned on the ignition and slammed down the accelerator. He yelled and lifted his gun to the car as I drove the car back towards the lorry.

The men guarding Jaid and Levi started to look around and suddenly, Jaid was twisting and roundhouse-kicking into the nearest one. He went crashing into his partner as Jaid spun and push-kicked the other; he went flying too far backwards to be natural. The rest of them dived out the way as I slammed on the brakes and spun the car around to the lorry. Levi and Jaid leapt into the back seat as guns sounded and men ran towards us. I yanked the car into reverse and began to drive back up the road, spinning the car around in a screeching J-turn and continuing up the road, past the yelling men and the other cars.

"Faster!" yelled Levi, waving around his burned hands. I glanced in my rearview mirror; already three cars were setting off in pursuit, leaving the burning lorry wreck far behind us. I used the handbrake to steer the car sharply into a minor road, and then went down through a heavily wooded area and back onto another twisting minor country road.

"You should've slashed the other cars' wheels!" Jaid yelled.

"That is not constructive!" I yelled back, driving so fast I didn't dare take my eyes off the road to check mirrors. "Are they still following us?"

"Yes!" Jaid swore repeatedly. "They are getting closer! Quick, turn left here!"

I did so, when a noise in the front passenger seat made us all start; a radio crackled into life.

"Team Delta, this is Team Charlie…the security has been broken. Arden has been secured but is already on fire; I repeat, Arden is already on fire, unidentified reasons, but their security has been blacked. Arden is abandoned. Ayer, his doctors, and the other board members have already fled the premises. They took one of the GE's with them. Fox and John have the other GE safely captured, taking it to — "

"This is Team Delta…three GE's have escaped with a radio and a car. Don't use the radios! I repeat, the GE's have escaped, do not use the radios."

The radio abruptly stopped. Jaid threw it out the window.

I finally looked into the rearview mirror as we swung back onto a larger road. Two black cars were racing down the black asphalt at a distance. We were entering a more built up area; it looked like the outskirts of a larger country town. More cars were started to pass us, all honking their horns at our speed. I glanced ahead as we entered the narrower streets of what was obviously an expensive suburb, with cars parked everywhere and stucco apartments soaring up high along the roadside. I steered down a narrow one-way street between the apartments, when suddenly Jaid gasped. Straight ahead through the block of apartments the street came out into a junction. On the other side of the junction was a brick bridge, and beyond that the glittering black of a river.

"Turn back, turn back!" screamed Jaid. "The junction is too tight...you'll go over into the water!"

"Get your seatbelts off!" I yelled. "And prepare to jump out!"

I lowered my speed as two cars came twisting down the narrow road after us.

"JUMP!" I yelled as we reached the junction entrance, and I jerked the car ninety degrees and slammed on the brakes, spinning the car around to block the junction exit for the cars behind. We had three seconds to dive out of the car and run to the sides before the two black cars slammed into our car at full impact. There was a screeching of brakes as they shunted the car across the road to smash into the bridge, and then all three cars toppled over and collided into the river.

The three of us scrambled back to our feet, preparing to run. However, two more black cars were already racing down the roads on either side, boxing us against the bridge. Without a word, the three of us sprinted to the broken edge and flung ourselves out into the air and down to the churning river, where the last wreckage of the sinking cars glinted in the night air. I had barely enough time to get into a diving position before I plunged into the freezing cold water, engulfed in darkness. The air was punched out of my lungs as I began to claw at the ice cold water and scramble my way back up to the surface. Slimy weeds slithered around my legs.

Finally I managed to heave my face above water to gasp at the oxygen, treading water. Fire burnt above me all along the edge of the bridge, and I could see the two black cars were gone. I swam through the slimy water to the river bank, trying to keep as close to the bridge wall as possible. I hauled myself out into the mud and rotten leaves of the overgrown bank. Someone approached from under the mossy underside of the bridge next to me.

"Marilyn?"

"Here," I gasped, and Jaid ran out from under the bridge. When she paused amid the tangled weeds and debris, looking around her, I realized I was still invisible. Indeed, my swollen heartbeat was still beating at the unnaturally fast, strong yet fixed rate, independent of my body.

"I'm here," I repeated, reaching for her forearm. She jumped before helping me up the bank. She too was filthy and soaked, and there was a hard glaze to her skin that looked almost metallic grey. Her forearm was abnormally cylindrical and hard. "This way," she said, and I followed her under the bridge, both of us shivering violently. Levi was waiting next to ladder rungs leading up to a sewer hole under the bridge.

"They'll be cordoning off the river, surrounding the exits by now," Jaid said through chattering teeth. "We can get into the sewers and hide; the tunnels will lead to other rivers, or the center of the town. If we follow the tunnels into the center of town, we should find a train station or something. If not, we'll follow the sewers out."

"They'll be watching the trains and the river exits," I replied,

"Then we'll hide until they aren't watching," Levi snapped, and attempting to locate my hand with his own raw one, tugged me up towards the ladder rungs.

"Wait," I said, arms wrapped around myself. "Wait. The three of us have been trained to work on our own. And if the three of us stick together, we make an easier target to find."

"You're right," replied Jaid, looking at where she thought I was standing, although her eyes were not quite in the right place. "It's safer for all of us if we split up."

"What? No! Have neither of you learned anything?" cried Levi, his face stressed and furious as he shoved Jaid towards the steps along with me. She looked at him mulishly.

"I've learned that they expect victims to work together," I replied. "And we'll never escape if we are too busy worrying about other people, protecting each other, acting as part of a mass rather than filling our own needs. So you guys go in the sewers, get separate trains, meet up at a later point. I'll head off down here, split their focus."

"What the hell are you playing at, Marilyn?"

"I'm invisible!" I stressed. "I'll be fine, I can bait them!"

"You're crazy," said Levi incredulously. "Jaid...Jaisudha, don't tell me you'll let her do this?"

"Think properly, Levi; your burns need medical attention," said Jaid, thinking fast. "I won't.... Let's go. She can do what she wants." She pulled herself up onto the bottom rungs, her hand gripping Levi's wrist, and turned in my direction. "We won't wait for you at the station, Marilyn, and we won't come and get you if you get captured. You're either with us or you're not."

"I know. I'll try and meet up with you later," I said. We all knew that that wouldn't happen...this would probably be the last time I ever saw them. But I was impatient to leave. I knew what I was now. If I was to ever be free and in control, I had to access it myself, and I knew how to start doing this: first, information.

Levi clearly wanted to hug me before he followed his cousin up the ladder, he just didn't know where I was. The blackened burns along his chest and arms were filthy red and leaking, the skin slaked away; he looked awful, and I didn't want to be touched.

"Dr. Ayer would be proud," he said instead. "I'll see you again, maybe."

"Yeah, try not to die," Jaid added, eyes flashing, and then they were gone.

I headed back down the riverside, sure that there would be black cars waiting somewhere along it. The cold of the night had now disappeared under my swollen, juddering heartbeat's unnatural chemical heat and my thrumming veins. And then I saw a sleek black car parked on the opposite side of the river, along the concrete pavement. A man in the black body armor got out, a gun in one hand, and spoke rapidly into his mobile as he walked down to the riverfront. In the distance police sirens were drawing nearer. I slipped into the river and swam across to the other side. The man was still patrolling along the water as I crept out into the grass. I could hear him speaking, with a faint Italian accent, into his mobile phone.

"No sign of them here, of course. Are the others searching in the town? Okay, right, yeah, he's making sure the town is surrounded from all entrances. The police should be here soon, anyway. You and Daniel keep heading up the north road with the other GE; at least that's one sixth of the money."

The man hung up and I followed him back to his car. As soon as I stepped out onto the gravel pavement, he stilled and turned around, his gun poised. The barrel of the gun was only a few inches from my shoulder, but his eyes looked straight through me. I stepped past the gun and kneed him hard in the groin, twisting the gun from his hands as he crumpled to the ground, hands cupping himself. Before he could yell out, I dropped down on top of him, balancing my knee against his throat, and calmly pushed the barrel of the gun against his forehead.

"I won't shoot unless you yell," I whispered as his eyes wildly searched the darkness for my face above his. He didn't yell, though he was sweating badly, pupils dilated. Clearly the gun was loaded. "In fact," I continued, "I'll let you go once you've answered some questions. So, who are you working for and what do they want with us? Why did they attack the lorry?"

He swallowed. "The Redstone Firm. Look, I don't know much, I'm just a foot. Let me go, I don't have what you're...." I pressed the gun to his forehead and he closed his eyes in fear and spoke in a rush. "All I know is that my team got sent back from Iraq to undertake this assignment. We were told to secure the Arden Building, execute all adults, confiscate all information there, and capture and contain six youths, codename GE's, who were all supposed to be recovering from serious surgery. When...when the GE's weren't all there, we tracked them down to elsewhere. That's it, I swear."

"Redstone...the private military company?" I remembered hearing my dad mention them when I was a kid; it was one of his biggest gripes that privately hired mercenary armies were often more effective, better trained, and better equipped than the British State Army these days.

"Yes...Redstone PMC," the man stuttered, eyes open and trying to locate my face again. "This is beyond my pay grade. Why the hell can't I see you? They didn't mention this part in briefing."

"Who is Redstone working for at the minute? Who hired them to get the GE's?"

"I don't know!"

"Are you being contracted by an outside client, or is it Redstone itself who wants the GE's?"

"I don't know anything! I just follow orders from my superior. Only the command at Redstone would know the client identity!"

I dug my knee further into his throat and he began to gag. I felt sick myself.

"It's the truth; this is just my goddamned job!" He hesitated. "But I know there were overseas clients trying to muscle in on our op...and when Team Delta stopped the lorry they were ambushed by another team of armed people. I...I also know Arden Board had lots of enemies. They'd broken lots of promises and deals with other companies. Unpaid debts, financial difficulty; there were lots of people gunning for it. People are angry."

"What's happened to the three other GE's who weren't in the lorry?"

"When we got into Arden, there were only two; one escaped with Wrexham, the other was in severe condition, too ill to move. They've got him under close guard at the minute."

"Where are they taking him?"

"Away. Please...please, don't ask me anything more."

Keeping the gun trained steadily against his forehead, I dug the mobile out of his pocket with my other hand. He didn't move. Hopefully he wouldn't realize I had no clue how to work the gun; blame UK arms restrictions.

"Call the people who have the GE...Fox and John," I said, thinking fast. "Tell them you need to meet them at a secure location outside this place, and tell them to bring the GE. The new plan is to use him as bait to capture the others." I flipped open the mobile, pressed "call" on the last received number he'd spoken with, and pressed it to his ear. "Don't tip them off," I added. My threatening voice wasn't remotely threatening, so I added, "Or you'll be sorry. Invisibility isn't my only new talent."

"Change of plans," the mercenary said into the mobile, face glazed with sweat. "Hamanci needs you to get back over here pronto, and bring the GE with you. The little bastards are playing games with us, so we're switching to bait. Take the northwest Crescent road, and I'll meet you at the first bridge on the E8 exit. Be careful, and don't use Souza's radio; they've taken control of that line."

He hung up and gave me the details of where the location was.

"I'm not your enemy, kid," he said at last. "This is just a job to support my wife and her two kids. It's nothing personal, just how the world works."

"Likewise, etcetera," I replied and paused, trying to remember the most painless way to knock someone out. Clean solid punch to the jaw, the Rhodesian had said; hit around the wisdom teeth, aim for the bone.

I nodded, drew back my fist, and punched him squarely in the jaw.

"Ouch!" I winced and shook my hand, but it seemed to work; his face fell slack and his eyelids closed. Thinking I should've asked him to climb into his boot first, I dragged his heavy form there myself and shut him inside after checking his breathing and fishing out his car keys.

Finally I was in the driver's seat of the black car and driving off towards the E8 exit. The car windows were tinted, but I remained on tenterhooks as we passed the river bridge, now taped off and swarming with police and armored Redstone men patrolling the outskirts of the buildings.

The exit was just beyond the end of town. I pulled up into a lay by and cut the engine. It was time to wait. Yet as I sat there, eyes on the road ahead, I slowly became aware of the pain my body was in. My skin had gone numb, my veins felt sluggish and forced, yet I could feel the painful pumping of my heart like a machine inside my chest, forcing the blood and chemicals through my body and swollen internal organs like a machine. My rib cage was powerless around my heart; my muscles felt as if they were being eroded raw. Suddenly there was hot liquid dripping down my face, down my chest, and trickling down my thighs. I began to gasp for air.

Deep breaths, I told myself, and began to clamp down my heartbeat until it was slow enough to disengage from that switch that seemed to be in my chest. My heart struggled to slow down, so I used the palm of my hand to hit myself in the chest again. The reaction was immediate again, the chemicals instantly halting, blood churning back to normal, skin painfully shifting back to its natural state. Dizzily, I checked my reflection in the car mirror, just to be sure I was back. The image staring back at me would've given anyone a nasty fright. I looked like one of the undead, or a ghoul or something, with bloodshot red and ice eyes, and shining trails of blood running profusely down from my nose, mouth, hair, and ears. My chest was too covered in thick crimson clotted blood to see the damage done to the skin underneath, and when I looked down, my thighs were also streaked with blood...too much blood for it to be menstrual. I held my hands out away from me and pressed on the air conditioning, but it did no good. *I refuse. I refuse.*

I allowed myself ten minutes of waiting before I steeled myself and turned invisible again. The same numb sluggish feeling covered me almost immediately, and a fresh hot nosebleed trickled over my lips as I tried to stay focused above my grinding heart. The other car would be coming soon, so I took the keys out of the ignition and the batteries from the mobile phone and radio, tossed them all out into the hedges, and sat on the car bonnet to wait.

Just as I was starting to wonder if the mercenary had stitched me up, I saw an identical black car driving into the road ahead. It pulled up into the lay a few meters ahead of my car and stopped. I walked over to the car and peered in through the window as a man in a black coat got out of the passenger seat. The man in the driver's seat gripped the wheel, attention alert as the other man headed to the car I'd just deserted.

I moved my attention to the person lying cramped up and motionless in the backseat, and then swore to myself. It was Jason. His arms were swathed under a straitjacket and he was ice pale, his skin and now-shaved black hair plastered with unclean sweat. Even the bones in his face seemed different; sharper, more jutting, hungrier. There was dirty bandaging around the back of his head and ears, and his eyes were badly swollen, their expression drowsy. Under each eye there was a chillingly precise cut, and there were other straight knife cuts along the bridge of his nose, all along his hairline, around his temples, above his lips, and across his jaw. They looked like scabbed red wires stuck into his skin.

"It's empty!" called the man behind me as he peered into the deserted car. The driver in the front cranked down the window, frowning.

"It's filthy in here," called the first man again, now switching to the back seats. "There's mud and blood everywhere."

"You think the GE he had got away?" the driver asked as the first man pulled out the dead mobile from the car, frowning. I was just about to open the door to the driver's seat when I glanced back into the rear window one last time, and jumped violently. Jason was staring straight at me with disorientated eyes, his scabbed nostrils flaring. How could he see me? But even though his entire posture was moved to my direction, his eyes were a few centimeters off from mine. He was staring at my cheekbone.

Just as I was starting to take it as coincidence and move away, he made a sudden gesture and mouthed "Marilyn?" I stopped, dumbfounded, as he jerked his head towards the other car, where the man was now walking down to the boot. "Stop him," he mouthed, and his eyes rose to fully meet mine. "I'll take care of the driver."

I didn't have time to doubt Jason's ability to do as he said because the other man was about to discover his colleague in the boot. I stole up behind him as he reached for the latch. However, as I approached him, he suddenly spun around and shot out his fist. It just missed my neck, scraping along my shoulder, and was enough to push me off balance. But when a muffled crash from the other car distracted the man, I lunged forward and knocked into him, kicking his legs out from under him and swinging him over my hip, much as Clodagh had done to me a lifetime ago. He tumbled back into the car, but flipped back up as I started to drag his gun out of his holster. He grabbed me around my neck and flung me down onto the ground, him on top of me. But as he reached for his gun I head butted him square in the face; he drew back, I elbowed him in the throat, and was finally able to grab the gun, whacking him in the head with it. He fell down as I ran back to the other car.

The driver was now slumped motionless over the steering wheel. When I opened his door, he tumbled out onto the ground, revealing a bloody mess of a neck and a dead radio. Unnerved, I looked back at Jason, still in the backseat. Blood strung down from his crimson, oddly bulky mouth, and was smeared across his bare chest, his straitjacket discarded. He wasn't even panting; it was like he'd never moved. There was a horribly vulnerable look in his hooded eyes as he watched me get into the driver's seat. I hit the accelerator just as the man behind us discovered the lack of keys in the other car and started to run after us.

"Go that way and head off the third junction," said Jason, his voice barely audible and still oddly muffled. "There are no men there."

I drove at a dangerously high speed for a while, heading off the third junction and taking as many turns and twists as possible until I felt a safe enough distance had been put between us and the town. I was sure no one had followed us, but I kept up the pace as we went through endless villages and long country roads. The hedges and dark trees blurred into one under the night atmosphere and formed a secluded, isolated world around the travelling car.

"Slow down."

"I'm all right, thanks."

"No, I said...." He stopped and expelled his breath sharply.

I glanced into the mirror. "Did you see Clodagh or Teddy before they got you?"

"I saw Clodagh. She's dead. The operation...whatever it was they did...it was killing her." As I processed this, he continued to speak, asking as if against his will, "Marilyn, why did you rescue me?"

"My fault you got caught, teaming up with me. Figured I could at least get you out so I could...I don't know. Make things right. Start anew."

"We need to switch vehicles," was all he said in reply, but he sounded flat and unhappy.

"More car-jacking. Excellent."

"Slow down now, Marilyn...we're safe from Redstone. I didn't survive in order to die in a car crash."

He was starting to sound more like his normal self, so I ignored him.

"Marilyn, slow down!"

"Chill out; you don't understand what a pro driver I am now. I did a J-turn and everything!"

"Just slow down."

I laughed suddenly and he frowned, but then I stopped because shooting pains in my chest were making it hard to breathe, and heat and sweat were attacking my body. I tried to ignore it and carried on down the road, slowing down.

"Stop," Jason spoke up from the back. "Stop. Something is wrong with you, Marilyn. What is it?"

"I...I...." It was hard to hear him over my thudding heartbeat, over the stench of electricity.

"Pull in here and get out!" he snapped, lunging over the seat to grab the wheel from me. I pushed him back, and he growled as I pulled the car off the road and into a stretch of woods and hedges, hiding the car from the road view.

"Marilyn," he started, breathing heavily, chest spasming.

"Don't follow," I gasped as I lurched out of the car and stumbled into the woods. I tried to clamp down on my heartbeat, but it wasn't working; my heartbeat was too fast, too strong, too disconnected, and my vision was blurring, blinding.

"Slow down!" I screamed, and hit myself violently in the chest. I felt a distant spark, and hit myself again, harder. And again. An electric current seized my body, and suddenly the invisibility was leaving, receding away as my heart finally slowed down, clenched up. Slower...slower.... Jason ran through the foliage behind me. I looked up at him, fully visible, bloody rivulets seeping down my skin and my heartbeat deafening my ears. I cried huskily, "It worked!" Then my heart stopped and I keeled over.

***

When I awoke I was lying underneath a canopy of dark green fir trees with the soft lilac dawn light washing over my skin. I slowly lifted up my head and rubbed my eyes. Dirt cascaded off my limbs and back down to the dank bracken floor. Every inch of my body ached, and when I touched my lips, my fingers came away bloodier. Tears pressed against the backs of my eyes. A hazy memory of somebody pushing hard, sharp lips against mine, forcing oxygen into my body, drifted into my head and then back out. I was alone in the woods. Someone had placed a stiff car blanket over my naked body and winched a dirty bandage across my blood-mottled chest. I lifted up the rest of the fabric. My legs, my arms...all covered in dried blood. It looked like a dark red mesh of shattered cobwebs laid across my entire body. Whatever modesty I'd once had was now truly gone. I stared unseeingly at the pale color of my legs underneath the red, as the cold fresh morning air crept along my skin and made me shiver.

"I didn't move you in case it triggered your heart or something," said Jason from behind me. "Don't sit up yet."

"I'm fine," I murmured, using the last of my energy to shift over onto my stomach under the blanket. I sighed and protectively snaked my arms through the dirt up around my painful chest, clean air washing my bare, raw shoulders.

"You're not fine," retorted Jason as he dropped to his haunches beside me, bare-chested and clean. "Do you even realize how close you came to...?" He bit off his words and just looked at me, uncharacteristically agitated. I smiled tiredly as his fingertips reached out and traced the lines of pain along my shoulder blades and spine, the feather-light touch at odds with his grim voice. "We need to find you shelter...and warmth," he said.

"But we're on the run from the mercenaries, remember?" I said, turning my head to the side.

He rubbed his cut mouth, staring with his frown still in place. "They're not a problem anymore. Careful...I said *careful!*"

I sat upright to face him; he shifted to support me with his shoulder and held the blanket up on my shoulders.

"What do you mean, 'not a problem anymore'?" I asked as he secured the blanket firmly.

"I'll explain later. Marilyn, I think you gave yourself a heart attack," he said, and although his eyes were on the same level as mine, they were as inscrutable as ever. Actually, now that I thought about it, his eyes looked even more sore and red in the morning light, and he was still shockingly pale, his hunched stance distant and his lips pressed into thin white muscle.

"I didn't mean to," I protested, my voice barely audible. "I just haven't completely figured out the...method to my abilities yet. But now I know that—you know—I'll be more careful." I smiled weakly. "Hey, I totally still saved you first, didn't I?"

Jason kept his oddly brittle gaze shunted, mouth tight. "You did."

"Well...I wasn't exactly expecting a thank you; wait, yes I was. Come on, at least some gratitude. I came back and got you out even though we failed the first time!"

"Brace yourself," was all he said, and before I could ask why, he lifted me up in his arms and rose to his feet. I cried out at the pain of the movement, and bit down on my lip hard to hold back sudden tears. He was being careful not to touch the painful parts of my shoulders, but it still hurt.

"I can walk!"

"Don't be stupid. We need to get out of this place."

"I said *I can walk.*" My voice just sounded childish, which didn't improve my mood.

"Be quiet, Marilyn."

I gritted my teeth and he carried me out of the wooded area on a path we hadn't been on before. Soon we came out onto another tiny deserted backwater road, where a plain blue Ford Escort was parked in the cold sunshine.

"How – ?"

"I said I'll explain later."

He placed me in the back of the Escort and reached over to tug another blanket from the boot over me. As he steered the car out into the road, I asked, "You can drive?"

"Not legally."

"Then really, I should – "

Jason directed one of his looks at me. "You should sleep."

"Tell me what happened first! What did I miss?"

"You should sleep."

"And you should stop telling me what to do. Where did you find this car?"

Looking supremely irritated, he snapped, "There was a small farmhouse nearby, and I realized the tenants were on holiday. I broke into the house, hid the black car in their barn, stole the Escort, and filled the boot up with clothes, food, and money."

"That was convenient," I said, and he shot me another look in the rearview mirror. This time it was I who looked away first, thinking hard. Jason had just lied, I was sure of it. Jason rarely lied – he never bothered – and he had no skill at it. And it wasn't Jason's nature to take things from other people like that. Already then, it was starting up again. He was trying to control me for some reason; he was going to betray me to whoever he got the car from. What was I going to do? I leaned over into the car boot to see the bags he'd mentioned, and found a dark oversized shirt and a huge pair of dark sweatpants from the nearest duffel bag, full of plain dark clothing. The only footwear was two pairs of trainers, about five sizes too big. Dressed, I then closed my eyes. I heard Jason expel his breath sharply in front when he thought I'd fallen asleep, and I was even more convinced I was being driven into one more trap. Well, he'd have to stop for petrol soon. I lay back.

When I opened my eyes much later, it was dark outside again and we were still driving, now down a main road busy with traffic. Jason didn't realize I was watching him; he was focused on driving the car into the petrol station and listening to the radio without enjoyment but with attention. In the strips of light from surrounding street lamps, his eyes glowed unnaturally, the whites looked dark red, and when he lifted his head briefly to check the mirror, I caught sight of sharper teeth glinting in his mouth.

He finally saw me watching him, his own eyes unblinking. Sweat trickled down his temple. "Do you want anything from the petrol shop?" he asked. "We won't try and find a motel for the night for a couple more hours. You can get cleaned up now. From the blood." His eyes darted away, jaw clenched. "Use the spare clothes while I pay for petrol."

"Yes, that would be nice," I agreed lightly. "Can I have a daily newspaper and some tissues from the shop?"

He nodded once and got out of the car, taking the car keys with him. He was no fool. I waited until he was in the shop and bending over the newspapers, and I ran. I ran across the parking lot and vaulted over the fence into the wide field. There were houses at the other end of the field; I just had to get to there.

"Marilyn, wait!"

I sprinted faster, weeds whipping my feet, but it was no good. I was bone-drained and felt as strong as a rag doll. Jason easily caught up and yanked me back into his arms.

"No!" I cried, twisting in his grip. "No...I know you're lying about everything! I know this is a trap; you're plotting something!"

"Marilyn...no!" He pulled me closer to him. "Marilyn, I *promise*, it's not like that. I lied to you about the car because...because I didn't want to burden you with what happened. It's not your problem, it's mine. I was...ashamed. That's all there was...I'm not plotting anything, I promise. I'm not lying to you."

I stilled and looked up warily. There was deep unhappiness in his wan plain face, for all his features were as harshly controlled as usual.

"You didn't want to *burden* me?" I said scathingly.

"I know; how unlike me," he replied tightly.

"Jason...just tell me how you found the car and the clothes."

"It's too cold out here; come back into the car and I'll tell you."

But he already knew I'd refuse; his lips were twisted as I shook my head.

"Fine. You'd just collapsed, you weren't moving. I tried to resuscitate you, but I was panicking badly, and...I could smell the blood everywhere. It was all over you, and it was on my hands and my lips, and my brain was reacting strangely. Not like me. I knew I wasn't in control of what my brain was telling me to do...attack. I tried to stop, to back off, but the blood was everywhere. I...I was going to.... But then two people—a man and a woman—found us, walked in. They must've tracked us down. They weren't with Redstone, but they had guns, and they saw us and...." He paused, having trouble getting the words out. "Before I saw them, I heard them. One of them said, 'Another walking fortune hits the bucket; people gonna be pissed.' But I couldn't stop. It was...I just...I killed them. I didn't even realize...but it was easy. Then I buried their bodies and tracked down their car. They had the blueprints to the Arden House there, and maps and guns, rope, the duffel bags with money, clothes, food...and an adrenaline shot in the medical kit, which I used on you. There was no trace of their identity, just army-regulation guns with the serial numbers erased."

"Bounty hunters?" I asked numbly, and he jerked his shoulders.

"They were working against Redstone; they had created a false trail away from us before tracking us down."

"So in other words, it's not just Arden and a bunch of mercenaries that are after us, but also bounty hunters, and whoever torched Arden in the first place."

He didn't say anything. He was still waiting for my reaction.

"Let's get back in the car. It's freezing," I said.

"Marilyn, I killed two people."

"It was a necessary, logical move, because otherwise they would've harmed you and me, right?" I said, thinking fast. "You were protecting yourself, and it's stupid to see it any other way. Only those who couldn't survive such an encounter would see it differently. Besides, we've both killed a man before."

"Is that really what you think?" he asked slowly.

I started to shiver and scrubbed my face with my hands. "Yes, that's what I think," I whispered fiercely. "I think that if I want to be free and I want to be *me*, then that's what I think.

We have to be the strongest. Not controllable. That's all I know."

Jason was still as he looked over my head into the night and appeared to think my words over. Then he nodded and quietly took hold of my hand. We walked back to the car, Jason glaring forbiddingly at the other drivers staring at me, covered in blood still. I was exhausted, yet, as I curled up in the passenger seat, sleep still eluded me.

***

It was deep in the middle of the night when Jason found a rundown motel next to a shabby looking retail area located between several main roads.

"I'll drive tomorrow," I promised him tiredly as we stepped out into the tiny graffitied parking area. Equally tired, he just snorted before directing me to use the blanket to hide the blood-stains. He brought out the two duffel bags stuffed with money and clothes from the boot, hoisted them onto his shoulder, and wrapped his other arm around my shoulders. I leaned into his steadily burning body warmth and we headed into the motel.

Jason's concern over my state was undeserved, however. The peroxide-haired receptionist handed us a room key without removing her eyes from the Danielle Steel novel she was reading. Jason still kept his careful grip around me until we were in the room. Unsurprisingly, it was a nicotine-stained hovel of a room, but it looked close enough to paradise for now, even with a brown carpet. There were two twin beds in the room; Jason dumped the bags on one bed and crouched to turn the cheap radiator heat up, even though it was already boiling in the room. I stayed rooted to the spot. All I could think was *now what?* I wanted to run again. I'd spent my life cooped up, and now I wanted to run.

In the end, Jason pushed me into the bathroom.

"Check your injuries," he said, and turned me to face the mirror. I quickly looked away, saw him observing, and so looked back to the mirror with an unconcerned expression.

"Get the blood off yourself, Marilyn; I'll go and get the medical kit."

"But what about your own injuries? Don't they need to be looked at too?"

"You're the one who nearly dropped dead earlier."

Once he was gone, I pulled off the t-shirt and trackies, removed the crusty bandaging on my chest, and gingerly stepped into the shower. The water was lukewarm and flecked with rust, but it was still bliss. Careful to keep my back, shoulders, and chest out of the tepid water spray, I soaked my hair and dabbed the rest of myself clean with a wet towel. As the blood came off the effects of the surgery underneath started to become apparent, and I became more and more afraid. In the end, I switched off the shower and stepped in front of the mirror, unable to put it off any longer.

"Oh my god," I uttered. The first thing I saw through the condensation was the long straight strip of puckered red scarring along my chest, stretching down over where my heart would be, and stopping in the middle of my ribcage. The flesh surrounding it was bruised, swollen, and stitched up, and was still leaking slightly. There was more bruising all down my ribs and breasts. It was disgusting. When I gingerly touched the long thick incision over my heart, I could feel the unnatural current of energy humming underneath, contained deep under skin and bone. The scar would be very ugly even when healed. I gazed in the mirror and tried to picture how other people would react to seeing it. But this was what I looked like now.

There was a rap at the door. I hesitated, but I was bone-weary, and part of me challenged Jason to try and use my weak state against me.

"Hold on," I said, knotting one ratty towel around my waist and then holding the other one in front of my breasts. "Come in."

I couldn't help but continue staring at the heart scar in the mirror as Jason walked in behind me, holding a small medical kit. He first started at the sight of my undress, wide eyed, but then his gaze seemed to focus on my upper back, lips whitening and jaw tightening.

"It doesn't look badly infected," was all he said, however, clearly attempting (and failing) to sound encouraging. "We can just clean and—"

I twisted around to the mirror to reveal the rest of the damage. "Oh my GOD."

I had never thought I was a vain person, but I had been bitterly wrong. Horror and shame flooded through me as I looked at the horrific lines of livid, angry wounds, leaking and swollen, that circled around my shoulder blades and covered the length of my spine from the base of my neck to the tailbone. The swollen, bruised skin fought against the neat metal stitches, the red flesh curling up at the edges and seeping. There were clear signs of infection, and the partially formed scar tissue already pulled at the discolored skin around it. In the base of each of my shoulder blades was a metal hole, like a type of electrical port, a sleek foreign engine part buried into the muscle and connected as part of the bone. The skin around the metal leaked as it tried to heal and adapt to its new structure. I reached around and touched one of the holes with outstretched fingers. This was where my wings were supposed to go. Not that I'd ever be able to have my wings now. I wasn't even sure if I'd be able to go invisible again. I closed my burning eyes, teeth together. My body was trying to break me. Like everything else.

"Face the front," Jason said, his eyes still on my back, his face still giving nothing away. "I'm going to clean these cuts. It might hurt."

I hoisted myself onto the counter and sat cross-legged on the sink with my back to Jason. I rested my forehead against the cool surface of the mirror and focused on not crying too obviously as Jason carefully reached around to put clean gauze across my chest. He then moved onto the smaller stitching along my temple and skull, slowly washing and applying Savlon. He moved onto my back last, and it hurt, though I said nothing and kept my eyes tightly shut to hide the tears. He worked efficiently and surely, applying more of the stitches from the kit before sticking down the gauze over my shoulder blades.

"At least the scars won't restrict your movement," said Jason as he packed the kit away. "And scars can be useful; warn people off. I have a burn scar all down my thigh from when I was a little kid. I used to tell people I was secretly a monster, and the burn mark was my natural skin revealing itself under the human skin."

His tentative voice made it clear he was making an effort to communicate with me. Why? Trying to make us both equally vulnerable? I turned round to face him searchingly; his deep blue eyes widened and he looked away again.

"How did you get the burn really?"

And of course, he didn't answer, just looked away.

"Don't pack away the medical kit," I said, putting my top on underneath the towel and hating how I could still feel disappointed. "We need to check up on your surgery now. Wait...did you use up all the Savlon?"

"I'm fine. You need food now."

"What do you mean you're 'fine'? Jason, they said your surgery had complications. Let me see."

"I'm fine!" He began to walk out the bathroom; I grabbed his upper arm. He looked down at my hand slowly, nostrils flaring as he breathed out through his nose.

"You need food," he repeated with difficulty.

"Jason, if you want me to ever eat again in my life, let me check your injuries." I said it sweetly and simply, and he stared at my hand for a few more seconds. I smiled. He wasn't used to people who didn't bend to his will. He certainly wasn't used to people who bent around his will.

"Okay." As I pulled my hand away he stripped off his t-shirt in one motion. "There."

My mouth dropped open.

His body was sheened with sweat and the lost weight made his musculature stark, but he was completely whole. No wounds. No open flesh. No severe injuries or cuts, nothing. There was an older looking purplish scar blemishing the edge of his triceps, and another one clipping his shoulder from where he'd been shot on the fence, and there were other older silvery marks down his stomach and across his chest and collarbone. The only thing that could've been recent was a long red lined cut down the center of his rib cage, but it looked half healed and too old. I turned my gaze to his arms, and for the first time noticed that the insides of his forearms were full of bruised holes and little slits, as if he'd been subjected to many injections and transfusions, like an addict. But I had already seen the worst of the damage...the cuts on his face and around his head.

"What...how?" I whispered, confused.

"Curiosity satisfied?" He asked. His voice was so level it sounded distorted, and his eyes full of strong, strange emotions I couldn't identify for the life of me. He moved to walk out of the bathroom again, and I quickly hopped off the sink and stepped around to stop him. He backed up, muscles tensed, and I placed my hands on either side of his face, my own face as calm as I could make it as his lowered eyes bore into mine.

"You're still wounded, Jason. Let me look at the cuts on your head."

He sat down on the edge of the bath. It felt like a victory. I removed the rest of the gauze from the base of his skull. The cuts there looked deeper than the others on his head, and there were yet more signs of deep injections and tube cuts. There were even incisions behind his ears, matching those on his face.

"I don't understand," I said at last. "Levi, Jaid, and me —"

"I know," he muttered, barely moving his mouth.

"Jason —"

"Don't."

"Does it hurt?"

"No."

Something in the way he said it made me think, and I surreptitiously pinched the sensitive skin on the back of his neck. He didn't react, but a few seconds later, asked "What?"

"You don't feel any pain at all, do you?" I said.

He hesitated, then shook his head. "I don't feel tired either...although I *know* my brain needs to sleep. I don't feel hungry, even though it's been days and days since I last ate. I should be feeling all of these things. The room doesn't feel any hotter than it did before...the temperature is always the same to me, this one continual warmth. They've changed something in my brain, but I don't know what...I can't feel it. I can't feel my body fighting whatever is happening to me."

He stood up abruptly, muscular shoulders even tenser than usual, and walked around me into the other room. I turned to watch his progress and he spun to face me again, struggling to continue the conversation. "But you shouldn't use your abilities because of the damage it does to our bodies."

"So let's get this straight," I said. "You can't feel temperature, pain, hunger, or fatigue...what else is different with you?"

"You never listen to anything I say, do you?"

"You were driving without the headlights on earlier, so you can see in the dark. And somehow you saw me when I was outside the car...heat detection?"

His cheekbones were oddly flushed; he stepped back again, closer to the wall. "Blood. I could smell it before you were anywhere near the car and I knew it was yours. It was wired to my brain, making me...but there was heat detection as well. My eyes are different too. I can see for miles if I need to...it was how I found those people's car."

"You cut my lips when you resuscitated me," I remembered suddenly. Keeping eye contact, he slowly reached up, peeled back his lip, and pressed a pressure point above his gums. Metal knife-like fangs were pushed out over his teeth.

RUN my brain screamed. *RUN*. It was my turn to step backwards. Jason retracted the metal fangs.

"You're the perfect predator," I whispered. His face suggested it was anything but perfect. "This makes you the strongest—"

"I'm *weak*," he shouted, and I jumped. "I don't know what they've done to me! I don't know what's happening to my brain! My head, it keeps telling me to do things I know I don't want to do, and my body isn't *mine* anymore!" Unable to contain his anger, he picked up the duffel bag and flung it savagely into the wall. He kicked over the bedside table with a crash, and then spun back to me. "My mind was the only thing that was ever mine, and they took it from me! And then they left me here, weak and pitiful." He punched the wall and slammed another duffel bag against the floor, breathing hard.

"Jason, calm down," I snapped, stepping closer to him. It appeared to be the wrong thing to do; he turned on me lightning fast, and when his eyes focused onto mine, something cold and inhuman glowed from the back of his eyes. Pure panic flooded my brain and I stumbled back. His eyes never left mine, and I thought he was going to hit me. Hurt me. He stepped forward; then, to my horror, he stopped dead and hit himself squarely in the face. His fist came away torn and bleeding from the metal fangs protracted over his teeth. Breathing raggedly, he gave a cry of furious frustration and sat back down on the bed, head in his hands. Shaken, I pressed myself against the opposite wall and wished myself a thousand miles away.

After a few minutes of silence, Jason said quietly, "You know what the funny thing is? They gave us the abilities they thought would be best utilized by our personalities. They thought I was a predator." He wrenched his eyes to mine. "I was never a predator, Marilyn. I just wanted to be me, and I wanted to be left alone. Whole."

"You looked after me when I was bloody and had a heart attack," I said, my voice starting to rise. "A predator would've killed me."

"It wanted me to. It...I...my brain kept telling me to kill you. I would have if not for...."

Slowly he stood up again and walked closer to me, movements cautious. I could still see the unnatural glow in his eyes, feel the heat radiating from him. I kept completely still, head lowered in a neutral position, careful not to trigger his need to dominate or give him the feeling he was being threatened. That was a gift of mine, wasn't it...being passive? And here I was, being passive yet again. *He* was forcing me to be passive again. Trapped.

And that was when I decided we were going to part company tomorrow.

"Being around you makes it worse, Marilyn," he said stiffly. "You confuse it. Me. Make it harder to control, to separate...the predator doesn't know what you are, or if you are weaker or stronger. It tells me to...but I know...." He seemed to have trouble speaking the words, breathing hard. "Every time you help me, Marilyn, every time I can't understand you, I'm losing Me. I can feel it changing. And I can't stop it...I can't make Me in control when you're around. You twist things. You're helping the predator to kill Me."

I said nothing, just stared at him and refused to look away. I would not be passive any longer. In the end, he walked past me into the bathroom. Bitter tears stung my eyes as I heard the shower being switched on. Quietly, oh so quietly, I climbed into the clean underwear and tracksuit bottoms, cleaned my teeth out the window, turned off the lights, and crept into the bed nearest to the door. There was no point running away now; I needed to sleep, to think. Besides, I could already tell he was planning to get away first. It was in his eyes, and I'd seen that look before in others, such as my father.

I was lying on my stomach in silence when Jason finally came out of the bathroom. I watched him under my eyelashes as he moved through the semi-darkness to his own bed. The glow had left him; he just looked exhausted and lost. The stubble along his hard jaw made him look much older than his actual age. He lay down on his adjacent bed and slowly turned his head towards me. By that point I was no longer looking at him, of course.

I didn't sleep. I watched the silent bromine sunrise peeking through the curtains and creeping across the dingy brown carpet. I imagined having a pair of beautiful glossy wings and flying through a marmalade yellow sky.

CHAPTER EIGHT

I got up before Jason and went to the reception office to snaffle all the maps and local travel guides. I spread them out over the tiny side table in our room and began to memorize them and plan my next route. It was approaching lunchtime when Jason finally sat up in his bed and looked straight at the door. It was how I definitely knew he was planning on sneaking away in secret, without me knowing. Good, it would save me a lot of hassle.

"Good afternoon," was all I said, however, as I scribbled on the side of the map. Jason rubbed his eyes. If anything, they looked even redder today, the dark blue irises being swallowed up by the crimson. He sat down at the table opposite me, stretching out his legs across the limited carpet space.

"I shouldn't have slept," he said to the table.

It was back to no eye contact between us, then.

"Oh, I'm fine thanks, and yourself?"

"I mean it."

"Don't be stupid; how long had you gone without sleep before last night?"

"Three days."

"Then you needed to sleep."

"I could've gone without for longer."

"And that's very admirable, I'm sure. Speaking of which...." I pushed the stale sandwiches and chocolate bar from the bag at him.

He shook his head. "You need to eat more than me."

"Well," I said sweetly. "If you don't eat, you're just going to collapse and die at some point. However, if you *don't* want to die, you could just time your meals so you don't forget to eat. Eat on a schedule...a meal at 8:00, 1:00, and 6:00. And now just happens to be...a bit past one." I pushed the sandwich back at him, and decided to add a dose of guilt along with it. "If I could convince my mother to eat, sleep, and live, I'm sure I can convince you to do the same."

He gazed at me for a second and then started to eat, clearly finding no satisfaction in it or in the situation at all. And it was still evident in the stiff shame of his posture that he was dwelling on his plan to flee. It was liberating that he felt so guilty about it, whereas I...I felt nothing except impatience for him to make his move and leave. Resentment that I was having to help him. That was all.

"What are the maps for?" Jason asked at last.

I indicated the nearest one. "I'm planning the safest travel route to get to my dad's place. Avoiding all towns and preferably travelling without a car." He looked up sharply as I continued. "Ayer and Wrexham knew my dad. I don't know how my dad knew them, but it means he must have some information on them, or can help point...us...in the right direction."

"Which would be what?"

"Track down Ayer, Wrexham, and the Board members."

"Track them down and do what? Kill them? Don't kid yourself, Marilyn; you're not a killer. So you'll call the police on them? Tell the government they've been bad? Chances are, the state already knows all about Arden and was powerless to do a thing about it. Or just as likely, simply didn't give a shite. All the major parties depend on people like Wrexham and the Board for donations and support in Parliament; they probably helped get Arden through the legal loopholes in the first place. No, it could be worse than that. The government could have invested in Arden themselves."

"That is a truly excellent point," I replied, not listening to him in the slightest. I did not intend to get the government involved. I was tracking the Board down for me. For knowledge. For my freedom. When Jason said nothing else, I stood up.

"I'm going for another shower."

He compressed his lips together and nodded. So that was how it would be then. I turned on the shower and started to wait for Jason to run away. I imagined what it would be like when I saw my father again. He was just a means to an end now, of course. He wouldn't be glad to see me, but he'd give me the information I needed, and that was all I cared about.

When I judged enough time had passed, I opened the door again. To my instant chagrin, Jason was still there, hurriedly scribbling a note on the table with one duffel bag over his shoulder. Hoping he hadn't noticed me, I began to close the door again, but he straightened up and turned. So I shut the door behind me and crossed over to my bed.

"No hard feelings," I said, smiling as I sat. "Make sure you take your fair share of the money. You can take the car too, if you want. I won't need it."

His eyes were dark. "You knew I was leaving."

"I'm wonderfully clever like that."

His nostrils flared. "I left a note." I pulled a blandly interested face and he stopped talking immediately, muttering only, "Sorry."

Then he hitched up the bag and walked out the door. And that was it, he was gone.

The room was silent. Overwhelmed with anger, I stood up and punched the wall. Pain exploded in my hand as someone rapped on the front door. Aware it wouldn't be Jason, I yanked it open. The peroxide blonde receptionist looked mildly alarmed.

"You better keep the racket down!" she wittered. "The eskimos in Greenland heard you two arguing last night."

"That won't be a problem anymore," I smiled fiercely. "I'll be out of here by the evening." I shut the door in her face, and had to satisfy myself by punching the wall again.

***

Just before I left the motel, I finally skimmed the note Jason had left. It just said that he'd left enough money so that I could stay on the down low for a while, and he was sorry for leaving me, but I would be better off without him and him without me. I ripped the note up and headed out to the car park with the duffel bag emptied of everything except necessities and money. The Ford Escort was still there. I drove it out to a deserted field and then walked back to catch the bus to the nearest retail park, full of large chain stores and supermarkets. I bought an entirely new outfit and some hair dye, then walked seven miles to another supermarket, where I changed in the store toilets. The outfit consisted of a tight chest-flattening sports bra, a boy's pair of black jeans, a boy's grey t-shirt, and a baggy hooded sweater. I applied the hair dye in the toilet sink, ignoring the disapproving looks other customers were giving me, and the color came out in a reddish-darker brown. I then used the scissors from the medical kit to cut the rest of my hair off and shove it down the tampon bin. I was no hairdresser (as the outcome testified), I just wanted to look unrecognizable and make the shaved patches less prominent. The plain boy watching me in my reflection told me I was successful enough. Certainly I looked different from the girl-GE people would be searching for.

It took another bus ride to get to the train station. At the train station there was far more security than normal, and as I waited for the next train to London, I saw the security men handing out posters with our faces on them. One was crumpled on the ground. It had our five faces emblazoned across the front under the words HAVE YOU SEEN? There was a reward going of £500,000 and a brief description of us as dangerous runaways from a special ward.

I glanced at the photographs again. Clodagh's photo hadn't been included. The photos had also obviously been taken at the beginning of our stay at Arden. I was virtually unrecognizable from the girl in the first photograph, who still had long kinked green hair, an oval face with pink, healthy looking cheeks, a curving smile, and eyes a bright light color. I noted that the posters had been issued by the government, not Arden, then put it in the bin and went to catch my train. No one even gave me a second look.

Even still, I couldn't relax until I was two trains and a bus away, alighting at the contented little suburb borough where my dad lived. The houses there bled old money and upper-middle class elegance, and I immediately felt out of place as I walked down the spacious tree-cloistered street, the evening casting a soft eggshell sheen over the tall, beautiful white housing as men and women drove back from work to the havens of their homes. It took a while to locate my dad's house; I'd only been there a few times in my life, and every visit I had made I had subsequently tried to forget. However, the fifth to last house on the second row had a familiar looking car parked in its driveway, half hidden between the

Mercedes and SUV. It was my Skoda. It had been emptied of all my belongings; my stash of CDs and iPod, the Sudoku and puzzle books, the spare clothes, Adam's Mayfair smokes. They were probably all stashed in an attic somewhere now, along with all my mum's possessions and old camping equipment, leaving this strange, clean, empty car.

Something small and red flashed in the corner of my vision; there was a tiny camera hidden in the flower basket above the main door—the red flash meant it had just been turned off. I walked up to the main door and straight into the peach papered hallway, ignoring the urge to knock; I wasn't there as a daughter, but as an intruder. No point knocking.

The hallway smelled of pine scented air freshener, and the beige carpets were alarmingly clean. The alarm system and intricate key pad beside the door were turned off. I was heading up the stairs to where my dad's office was when a petite, pretty woman with sandy brown hair popped her head out from the kitchen.

"Brendan?" she called, and then stopped dead when she saw me, her mouth dropping in horror.

"Who are y...? *Marilyn*?" She folded her hands protectively over the large swell of her pregnant stomach. "You should not have come here!"

I ignored her and made my way up onto the equally beige landing. My dad was in his study as I'd predicted; he looked up as I walked in, and I knew from his tired expression he'd been expecting me.

"Sit down," he said, wearily indicating the chair opposite his desk, which was littered with framed quotations and family photos. "We have about ten minutes to talk."

I stayed standing. "Until what?"

"Until the M15 realize all my security is disabled and arrive here for you."

I swallowed and sat down. My father didn't seem to know where to look either, and he seemed smaller and older than I remembered. He was going bald, and there were new papery lines around his eyes and mouth.

"You can stay here and go into government protection if you want," my father said. "But I doubt you'd like that. Instead, I've booked six flights to different locations, four in your name, one in my name, and one that goes to Mexico in Fiona's cousin's name. I've got ten grand in cash for you now, and once you're in Mexico, I'll wire you the rest via the Swiss account I made. No time to pack; you need to get to Stanstead Airport now."

"No," I said. As he blinked, I shut the door behind him, back in balance again. "I'm not going anywhere until you tell me what the hell is going on. You knew about this Arden project? You knew I was in there?"

He cleared his throat, his startlingly open eyes frozen on mine. "I swear I had no idea you were in there, or involved with them. I found out they had you five days ago, and I immediately got into contact with everybody I could think of to help search for you. But then you disappeared again—"

"But you knew about Arden."

He cleared his throat again. "Yes, but...but rumors only. I only found out for sure five days ago, when a Redstone PMC insider sold information to the M15...and as soon as I found out Wrexham was involved with the Arden Project, I started to dig. I found out that an independent contractor had a mole inside Arden, and she owed me a favor and confirmed you were inside."

"But you knew that Arden was creating genetically enhanced mercenaries and you did nothing?"

He blinked rapidly, continuing in a strained voice. "I offered funding to the group of assassins who were planning on destroying the Arden Project. I offered it to Redstone, Genetech, GM Inc, the Firm, and I tried to make the government intervene early. However, they wanted to wait until the end result, and I couldn't change their mind."

I was thinking rapidly, trying to sort out my brain. I didn't have long; I had to ask the important questions.

"But you knew a mole who was inside Arden, and you already knew Ayer and Wrexham—or they knew you. How?"

He appeared to be stressed; he kept on blinking as if something was caught in his eye. "You need to leave."

"Just tell me."

"I used to work with Wrexham. He introduced me to Ayer while I was working on a job. Arden Project was nothing more than Ayer's dream at that point, but Wrexham—"

"You worked for Wrexham? And that's why he singled me out?"

"I didn't work *for* anybody," he said defensively. "He hired my exclusive service. You see, Wrexham used to own a brilliant company, Skybound Inc., which had a monopoly over virtually every sector it entered. And I...I was different back then, you understand. I helped him keep deals sweet, prevented the business underworld from muscling in and interfering. Industrial sabotage, corporate eliminations, that was me. I was with him for thirteen years and his stranglehold only deepened; he had a finger in every pie. But then I met Fiona, and she got pregnant, and I wanted out. I wanted to live her life, the kind of peaceful life I'd had as a child. So I turned government witness and screwed everyone over, Wrexham included. It ruined his company; he only went in the clink for a few years, but Skybound got nationalized and went bankrupt soon after."

"You called yourself 'Gatsby,'" I said, remembering the name. He sat back in his chair as far away from me as possible.

"I was arrogant," he said.

"You screwed up." I couldn't keep the anger from my voice.

"I never thought Wrexham would be able to find me, or any of my family. Marilyn—"

"So essentially, you work for the government now?"

"Somewhat."

"Good. I'm here because I need all the information, or files or whatever, that you have on the members of the Arden Board and Ayer and Wrexham, any contact details you have, and information on where they were last seen."

"Mara, I don't even know—"

I cut in ruthlessly. "I've got about five minutes before your MI5 people surround this place, right? So let me tell you this: I will destroy any mutual relationship you have with them, and I will destroy the life you have with your new family—unless you give me what I need. Once you tell me how to find the Arden Board, I will get out of your life for good."

"Unless you go to Mexico you'll either be captured and exploited as a killing machine or you'll be killed," he said. "You won't last five minutes. Don't you understand what's happening here? Every power in the world wants possession of the five of you, every hit-man and merc sees you as the new competition or game, and don't even get me started on what will happen if the independent scientific organizations or the media find out about you."

"Sounds lively, at least."

"Don't you dare joke about this, Mara, don't you dare. Look, I don't have any files or information on any of them. I don't have any power like that...I just tell my handlers what they ask me, and that's it. So please, I'm begging you, just take my money and leave for Mexico."

"Who was the contact you had working as a mole inside Arden for a private contractor?"

He knuckled his eyes. "No! Enough! I can't in good conscience let you be a part of that world!"

"Dad," I said, walking forward and leaning on the desk. "I'm now a genetically enhanced killer. Stop with the bullshit, because your good conscience can piss—"

I abruptly stopped speaking. The street outside the window was far too quiet. I swore and backed up again.

"I don't even know why I thought coming here would help," I said bitterly, turning to leave.

"Wait." He wordlessly pulled out an address book from his drawer, his hand shaking and throat swallowing silently. "The contact I had. She's a low-tier vigilante who goes by the *nom de guerre* Zola. I knew her when she was the protégé of a bounty hunter called Crescent, but now they are both under the thumb of a hit man named White Knight; it was him she was working there for. Whatever you do, don't get in contact with him. He delights in owning vigilantes, and I'm sure he'd delight in a GE even more. I doubt you'll find Zola now that she's lying low. But here...her various work numbers. Try these...and if not, try this address as a last resort." He ripped out some paper and handed it to me. His hand was shaking slightly and his eyes redder than normal, but still too crystalline to ever read. "Mara...."

He didn't complete the sentence. I pocketed the paper, slung my duffel bag back over my shoulder, shouldered past Fiona, who was waiting outside the door, and went back into the hallway. I could smell a roast dinner cooking from downstairs, and heard my brothers watching cartoons in the living room. I remembered that the window in the spare room was easy to climb out of, so I made my way there. Then I realized Fiona was trailing behind me, hands over her stomach again.

"Don't hold it against him," Fiona said. "He tries to do the right thing, but he is lost too."

"I don't hold anything against him," I said, cracking open the window and peering out into the silent night. "And I'm not lost." I climbed out the window. "Probably for the first time in my life. Funny, that. Congratulations on the pregnancy."

Fiona looked close to tears. Even still, she was much prettier than my mum was. The perfect wife. I twisted my body and leapt out onto the neighbor's opposite window.

Below me, two cars had pulled up and I saw men sneaking up through the garden as I hoisted myself up onto the roof and stole over into the garden opposite. I then hopped over the fence and started running. There was no pursuit.

The address I'd been given was one in central London. I caught the train there and slept at the deserted station. And I spent the night dreaming of wings.

CHAPTER NINE

The next day I found an overpriced dump of a hostel near Kings Cross and paid for one night. I spent the morning procrastinating by buying a cheap mobile phone and trying to hunt down the blue Porsche number plate. I called the automotive regulation office, the Porsche listings, and the nearest GPS office I could find. As expected, what little information was accessible told me there was no record of that blue car existing anywhere. So it wasn't until lunchtime that I finally got out the piece of paper Dad had given me and dialed the first number on the list.

It was picked up on the second ring.

"I want to speak to Zola," I said without preamble.

"Well congratulations, Miss Aske," replied a surprisingly low, smooth male voice. "Your call has been upgraded to me instead. I've been waiting for you to get in touch."

"I'm only interested in speaking to Zola, thank you."

"Don't be foolish, Miss Aske. Zola will tell you only what I permit her to tell; why not cut out the middleman and talk to me directly instead? Besides, ah, I'm afraid that if you're trying to find the Arden Board, no matter which path you take you will end up with my name in your hand. I'm the person who has been collecting the answers that you need."

"Who are you?"

"I've got quite a few names, but as for the best known, I think the quote goes, 'I am become a Knight for the kingdom of dreams and their shadows.'"

"You're a pretentious prick then."

There was barely a hitch before the White Knight started to laugh. "The very definition. But let's be civil; you intend to find Ayer and Wrexham and all the others who wronged you, and although you have already judged my character to be sadly lacking, I believe we will deal well together. So, name a convenient time and place and I will do my best to be amenable and help you on your little journey."

Spooked, I held the phone away from me. What was his reason for being so accommodating? I did not believe for a second he genuinely wanted to help me.

"Hold on," I said. "In the interest of clear communication and so on, let me break all social etiquette and make something clear to you. All I want from you is information, and I will deal fair and square for it. I will pay, with both currency and reciprocal information concerning Arden. But that's all I want and all that will happen between us; a trade of information. Don't try and pull anything else on me; you've probably heard the rumors about what I am. Well, you have no idea what I'm capable of. And I have answers of my own that you'll want if you care about Arden. So if you want to deal, you'll cooperate without any stunts or sneaky crap." I marveled at my own idiotic bravery.

"If I had any morals, I'd be offended at the very assumption," replied the man, sounding increasingly amused. "As it is, I'm much obliged for the elucidation."

I gritted my teeth, but just said, "Good. I'll meet you at the entrance to the...British History Museum, under the columns at noon tomorrow," and hung up, throwing the sim card in the bin.

The only other thing I did that day was spend some time memorizing the map of the British History museum and its local area. I had only been there three times before, but it was still the area I knew best in London. I spent the rest of the day sleeping. When I finally was able to get myself out of bed, it was only to clean my wounds and redo the stained bandaging. A brief attempt to turn invisible was quickly abandoned; the pain was too immediate and it was clear my body wouldn't be able to handle it. I had to become stronger first. Which I would do. I was becoming stronger all the time.

***

The next day came with the first appearance of sunshine. I bought a different boy's jumper, a rucksack to replace the duffel bag, and a pocket knife, then shoved the remaining wad of money into my bram and headed to the British Museum. The sunny weather felt new and vulnerable, with the fresh tentativeness of having recently unfurled from winter slumber. The wide entrance to the museum was full of mothers with shrieking children, and groups of students sat on the steps leading up to the marble columns, all chatting, reading, revising, or eating.

I sat down at the top of the steps beside the farthest column and scrutinized the crowds. After a few minutes, someone caught my attention. A man was striding towards the steps, the men around him subconsciously getting out of his way and the women turning to stare at him. He looked like every Hollywood cliché of an assassin, complete with dark Aviators, slicked back hair, and black clothing.

As he walked up the steps, I had a sudden suspicion; I turned to my left just as another lone man took a seat about a meter away from me, on the same step. He raised a questioning eyebrow at me, looking rather entertained by my reaction, and I knew that this was the White Knight. He was a good few inches over six feet, trimly muscular, yet didn't look especially threatening. He was dressed in a pair of quiet jeans with a tucked in long-sleeved shirt, scarf, and wireless glasses. He looked like an intellectual academic or a young househusband. And as he leisurely rolled up to his feet and came to sit right beside me, I saw that he had charmingly leonine, refined features, with high hard cheekbones and a pair of dark hazel eyes softened by his glasses. His coffee-gold skin and thick close-cut hair suggested biracial black heritage. He watched the Hollywood assassin look-a-like walk past us with a manner of unassuming interest on his pleasant face.

"Damn…you're an anticlimax," I commented.

"Something every man likes to be told by a pretty young woman." He smiled in a self-depreciating way and lit a cigarette. Sobranie Whites.

"I see we've already started with the mind games, though."

"What can I say? Some things are just habit." He offered me a smoke which I ignored, then stubbed his own out on the steps after only two puffs. "Pleasure to meet you, Miss Aske. You'll forgive a weary old man his little tricks, won't you?"

I eyed him. Nothing about him was old or weary; everything about him, from the way he sat to the way he pronounced his words, was languid, gallant, and well mannered. He was acting the gentleman. Of course he was; what could be more appealing to a stray teenage girl on the run than a princely rescuer coming to her aid? He was a good predator making himself as appealing as possible. A different sort of predator to the one Jason would have made.

"Can we just get down to what we're both here for?" I asked, suddenly cold. "Information."

He gave me a vaguely amused look. "You are seriously going to keep pretending that's all you want? How boring. Why don't you just offer to pay me to kill the entire Board up front? I would, you know. And it would be in the name of ethics, of course, which is always an advantage."

"As if you have any interest in ethics."

"Only in the name, I assure you!"

"Droll. I know you're not a vigilante, despite the name, *Knight*. I don't want anything from you except answers to questions; you tell me how to find who I want to find, but then I take it from there."

His eyebrows rose. "Well, it sounds like it shall be a wonderfully simple meeting then."

"That's up to you, Knight."

"Of course. But please, call me George; I find colloquial names are rather more appropriate when two people aren't meeting by moonlight. Now, where would you like to go for lunch? All these vague utterings are working up my appetite."

I scanned the crowd around us. "We are sticking to a public place. And I'm not hungry."

"Miss Aske, give me license to say you clearly haven't eaten well in some time. It's far more proper to do distasteful business over a good meal, and I happen to know there are some excellent restaurants around here where you can ask questions to your heart's content." He got to his feet in one elegant motion, and the corners of his mouth twitched as I got to my own feet, trying to copy his grace but probably failing. Jason's quellingly stony expression would've come in handy.

"May I pick the restaurant?" He asked.

"I'll pick. Come on." I swung my bag back over my shoulder and walked down into the street.

"You won't make us go to McDonalds, will you?" he asked, effortlessly keeping at my side.

"Of course not," I said. "Burger King is far classier."

He groaned dramatically and I guided us both to a French restaurant I'd checked out earlier. It had lots of dark corners, private tables, and several back entrances, and an accessible window in the toilet. It looked fairly expensive, but it was safe to say he would pay.

"Here," I said brightly as George raised both his eyebrows at me. I smiled as if I'd never seen the place before.

"One of my favorite places," said George as the waitress directed us to the table I was making eyes at; the one next to the bathroom door in case I needed a speedy getaway. George, after an abstract survey of the restaurant, pulled out my chair for me in a practiced manner and asked for menus and water with a charming smile.

"I'd recommend the crème brûlée here," he said, leaning back in his chair with the same challenge still in his uplifted eyebrows. He hadn't glanced at the menus. "I don't know how they make it so creamy and light, but it's just wonderful, and they use some cinnamon to wonderful effect."

"So it said on the Chef's Specials board when we walked in," I agreed.

He grinned, showing white teeth, and poured us both a glass of water. "You sound so sure of yourself, Miss Aske."

"I am," I replied, sipping the cold water. "You are charming enough, but I've seen your type before. So please just leave out the bullshit and start driving your end of the deal. You know what was done to me and what I want from you, but what is it you want from me? What information? Because I highly doubt a man like yourself is just here for the potential cash."

He sipped at his own iced water, mirroring my own actions. "You've seen my type before, eh? How impressively arrogant you are."

Heart hammering, I made myself just give a careless shrug.

He sighed. "Very well, Miss Aske, as you ask...let's conduct business."

As he spoke, his educated English accent changed seamlessly into a South African one, the vowels changing shape and throwing me off balance as I realized I had no idea which accent was his real one, if either was. He was playing games, then. And I would be out of my depth if I tried to reciprocate.

"You are quite correct, Miss Aske, I do not need your money. I don't need any answers from you, either, and I'm not here to give Orphan Annie the other half of the locket. As I have told you, I kept a close eye on the Arden Board throughout all its adventures, and it was I who sold its location and security details to Redstone, after their government leak got hit. I have all the fiscally relevant information I need concerning Arden, though you are welcome to try and convince me otherwise. However, I am still prepared to give you the answers you ask for, and at a much cheaper rate than normal. Each question you ask me will cost three hundred pounds, plus an additional guarantee that once you have your answers, you will stay here and listen to my own proposition for you. Over dessert, of course, because we're not barbarians."

I swallowed, calculated how much money I had left in my bra, and took a risk. "A hundred pounds per question, with a two hundred pound bonus at the end, and I'll agree to consider your proposition properly and fairly, without walking out."

He shrugged, eyes gleaming with relaxed enjoyment. "You drive a hard bargain, but what choice do I have?" he said lightly. "Ah, and here's our waitress, come to save me from your merciless bargaining skills. What would you like to order?" His voice was now back to deep unaccented English. I picked the most expensive item off the menu, not bothering to use the meek, gentle voice that always made strangers like me. There was no way I could compete with George in the manipulative department; I'd look lesser if I tried.

"I'll have the braised veal," said George, handing over our menus, "and a large glass of Merlot."

"First question," I said as soon as the waitress left. "Tell me what happened to the Arden Compound and its employees after the GE's escaped from the lorries."

George smiled and placed one hand palm up on the tablecloth. I peeled out some notes and placed them in his hand as he smoothly said, "Once all the GE's were out, my informer reported back to Redstone PMC and they all entered the compound. In the resulting fire, all technology, equipment, and information was either destroyed or confiscated by Redstone. All the scientists and workers either fled or were executed on the spot. Two of the leading scientists have been taken into government custody and are being pumped for information they don't have. All fourteen members of the Board, including Ayer and Wrexham and the seven main doctors involved, are on the run. They are all ruined, of course, and in hiding from various debtors, competition, governmental vultures, ethicists, and people wanting their knowledge. As far as I know, three of the doctors and two of the Board members have already been hunted down by private contractors, one Board member committed suicide, one doctor died in a car crash, and the rest are still running for the rest of their lives. Proof of the deaths so far."

He took from his pocket three photographs and passed them over. I clamped down on my jaw as I looked at the dead bodies of Drs. Gauk, Luo, and Robertson, bound in wire and motionless in the crumpled grass. I didn't recognize the other two photographed men in their suits. But it wasn't enough...Ayer and Wrexham were still somewhere, with their knowing smiles. George pocketed the photographs.

"Give me information on the whereabouts of Wrexham and Ayer. Tell me where I can find them."

He leant forwards onto his forearms mockingly. "A poorly phrased question. I don't have that information, not quite yet...though I'm sure you could help me rectify that. I have all the other Board members pinned like bugs, but not those two. But you couldn't afford the answer to *that* information anyway, unless we came to another beneficial arrangement."

"Such as?"

His lips curved back into a slow laugh as he drank from the wine. "We are getting ahead of ourselves," he said. "You haven't touched your food."

Willing myself not to throw up, I took a bite, and then returned to the water as George sampled the veal.

"I admit, I thought the first question you'd ask would be about what happened to the three other GEs who didn't escape with you."

I said nothing. He bit into the steak and rubbed his fingertips neatly on the napkin.

"Obviously Zola was wrong when she mentioned any kinship between you and the other GEs." He paused meaningfully. "I tell you what; I'll give you this answer for free as part of a new client bargain. So, the other GE's...let me see. First there was the...how did Wrexham present the six of you again? Oh yes, the Black Widow was first; no doubt Ayer made up these ridiculous names whilst masturbating to his dastardly plans. She was the Northern Irish girl. She was already dead when Redstone recovered her body. It was sold to the Chinese government for medical experimentation. The Intelligence—the small black boy—escaped with Harold Wrexham and was last seen in a Mexican airport. There was a rumor that The Predator, after escaping from Redstone, became entangled with those dull American contract killers, Jefferson and Demeter, but this is unconfirmed and highly improbable. There was also a rumor that he'd been taken into MI5 custody. The Phoenix and The Robot ended up being re-captured, this time by the private security team of a Russian oil tycoon who has been trying to muscle to the foreground of his national politics for a while now. Like the majority of people, he'd foreseen the ruin of Arden and simply waited it out until the project was finished before swooping in. Unfortunately, Solovyov has been boasting to the world about his current ownership of two GEs, and his intentions to use them to find out how the genetic modification worked and to create his own personal team. He and the two GE's are as good as dead already. The only one left is The Angel, who escaped Redstone PMC and disappeared. You."

I knotted my hands tightly in my lap, my nails digging into my palms as I processed the information. I focused every inch of my being into not feeling anything, not remembering anything, not allowing George to control me. "Thank you. Now tell me what you know about finding Ayer and Wrexham." I barely recognized my own voice.

"Of course. But you see, that particular answer ties in with my own proposition for you."

"Which is what?"

He took another sip from his wine. "Bluntly put, I do not believe you are capable of tracking down and killing Wrexham, Ayer, or any of the nine remaining Board members, as I know is your intention. Even if I do give you the information, you will be unable to use it to any good effect."

"You don't know what I'm capable of."

"I have a rough estimate, thanks to Arden's wonderful business pitch. And you are valuable beyond belief, only your value hinges on being alive, and preferably allied with me. But I'm digressing; let me explain. It's a specialty of mine, finding people, and in fact, I've created quite the tidy network over the years, which enables me to keep track of people rather efficiently. I help people out, and in return they help me out. I am already being inundated with clients demanding similar information to what you're asking for. However, I am going to offer something special to you. I will work with you to track down Ayer and Wrexham — and all surviving Board members, if that's what you want — and I will help you exact whatever sort of justice you want on them. Kill, maim, or threaten, as you like. My only term is this; we work together as temporary business partners for as long as it takes to kill the Board. The length of the contract is contingent on their deaths. I don't require any other sort of partnership or for you to do anything other than focus on the Arden Board, but we work together."

I stared at him. "I don't want to work with you. I just want — "

"If you want to find and kill them, then you need to accept partnership with me. You'll be dead and useless to the world in seconds without me. I can teach you everything you need to exist independently and survive on your own with everyone gunning for you." His tone was too persuasive. "I can house you—you have nowhere else to go—and give you protection and the skills to defend yourself for the rest of your life. Once Ayer and Wrexham are dead you can go your separate way, as agreed, and you won't have to rely on anyone else ever again."

"And you gain from this arrangement how?"

My head instinctively started screaming *No, no, run, get out of here! He's trapping you! You're going backwards.* I felt the tell-tale electrical juddering start up in my chest as my heart began to speed up, already getting painful. I clamped down and forced my body and blood back to normal. He hadn't appeared to notice anything.

"Numerous ways. I gain from the death of Wrexham. From the personal benefits and prestige I will receive when it is known you are my associate and business partner. From the prestige that will come from being your mentor and inducting you to the ways of what I like to call the *Otherworld*. The momentary entertainment it will bring." He looked into my eyes, his smile as thoughtful as a cat's. "You'd be free to leave at any time, of course; just don't expect me to continue the contract on my own. Equally, if you do complete the contract, I will give you the money and new identification documentation to set up your own new life."

"And you're so likely to keep your word," I retorted.

"As likely as you are to keep yours," he replied languidly, leaning back in his chair. "I suppose you'll have to trust me. Or research previous customer feedback, though that might be somewhat trickier."

"I need the loo," I said.

"A non sequitur," was his reply, and I made my way to the bathroom, where I promptly climbed up onto the window sill. I was just about to wriggle through when I stopped. Why was I running away from this? Hadn't I said I'd never run away again? I wouldn't be trapped this time anyway; I'd be free to leave any time. It wasn't a step back, it was a method to finally get to Ayer and Wrexham and gain complete freedom. Start anew. Be whatever I wanted, separate from everything else. George would have tricks up his sleeve; of course, there was no way it was as simple as he claimed. He'd try and make me dependent on him. But I could deal with his tricks...I could be tricky too. And this was my chance to finally be free, to be powerful. He was offering me an opportunity, and it was my illogical fear that was holding me down now. I had to be more like George in order to escape. But I could be like that.

George was waiting at the table as I slid back into my seat.

"Your food is cold now," he remarked. I looked up at him with the pent up anger inside of me finally turning to ice, and I knew it was naked in my eyes and couldn't control it. George looked back at me from under the lowlights, and something greeted me from the depths of his own eyes. Something malicious and amoral shifted into his expression, and in his curved mouth, a loving refusal to feel ashamed of it. He reveled in it. He reeked of power.

"I'm in," I said.

"I'm glad," he replied silkily, taking the last bite of his veal. "I'll get the bill."

CHAPTER TEN

George guided us both through the crowds of shoppers and traffic with a light hand on the small of my back.

"Come back to the hotel where I'm staying," he said. "We will just waste time if you go back to wherever you were. This way we can pool information and get you caught up on the files tonight, and catch a flight for America in the morning. It's my suspicion that Ayer went back there; that's the place to start the hunt."

I was about to refuse when he added, "Obviously you'll have your own room, and I'll be out for most of the night anyway."

I agreed, distrusting him intently, and he opened the door to a parked silver Jaguar. As he steered the Jaguar out and down the road, one of the many expensive mobile phones in his ashtray started to ring over the uncommonly loud engine. He picked it up and laughed down the line as a female started demanding something,

"She didn't go back to her pretty blond boy, did she?" he taunted. His voice had changed yet again, with a subtle French-American international lilt. "You owe me ten grand, my dear!" He hung up and tossed the mobile into the back with a smile. "Zola has been staked out at some club in the middle of nowhere waiting for you," he informed me. "She's feeling rather...possessive. Females are rather rare in our line of work, let alone females with abilities such as yours, and she's showing hints of vaguely interesting feminine righteousness."

"You're showing hints of vaguely uninteresting misogyny," I replied indistinctly. He laughed again, and I stared out the window. Adam. I thought I'd forgotten about him. They'd tried to use him against me. Good job I hadn't let them.

We arrived outside an expensive stone and gold gild hotel surrounded by elegant white designer shops and fancy restaurants. George tossed the keys to a porter and we walked into a sweeping marble reception foyer. I looked painfully out of place amongst the beautifully dressed people lounging around conversing in hushed voices, their hair and faces all perfectly groomed. My unwashed boy-chav-cancer patient look was attracting a bit of notice, but George only seemed to find it quietly amusing as we headed to the elevator and pressed the button for the penthouse suite.

"If you ever need to find me in the future, this is as good a place as any to ask," said George as we stepped out. "I usually stay here when in London under the alias of Knightley Gatura." He opened the door to his suite. My mouth nearly dropped open. I had thought I was accustomed to luxurious hotels—back from when I was a kid and my dad had taken me on holidays—but this was in another league entirely. It was a vast apartment with white minimalist decor, the kind of lounge and adjoining stainless steel kitchen found straight out of a high-end catalogue, complete with impressive flat screen TV, Xbox, Wii and DVD combo, and sound system. The bathroom was all gold and marble, and easily twice the size necessary for a bathroom. There was nothing personal in the apartment, just modern art and bare necessities, although there was a pile of folded newspapers on the glass coffee table.

"You have that room," George said, placing the keys on the counter and going into his room, clearly inured to the apartment's beauty. I peered into the spare bedroom. It wasn't exactly what I thought he'd meant when he said I'd have a room to myself.

"I hate to be rude," said George through the open door, "but I have some previously arranged business I have to attend to now. I'll be gone for a few hours, so don't wait up. Until then, enjoy this place. I have excellent taste in choosing my abode, do I not? There's food in the kitchen, CDs and DVDs in the compartment, and you'll find my compiled dossier on Arden on the kitchen table. Take a look, add anything you deem important, let me know what you think." As he spoke, he carelessly stripped off his shirt and flung it onto the bed without regards to modesty, replacing it with a dark green silken designer shirt and the jeans with immaculately tailored charcoal trousers. I turned away, and a few minutes later he emerged, fastening the expensive cufflinks into place and having exchanged his cheap wireless glasses for gold-rimmed ones, and the battered watch for a Cartier. He looked completely different. I hadn't realized it before, but he was...beautiful. The type of striking, refined beauty that would cause people to stop and stare in the street. He now walked differently too, his shoulders up, head high and arrogant, his height more noticeable.

"I'll leave the door open," he added, seeing me still standing in the middle of the room clutching my bag. "I'm also expecting a certain shared acquaintance to get into contact before we leave tomorrow morning, so we'll have to wait for that."

"What business is so important that you have to rush off?" I asked.

He smiled charmingly. "You should know better than to ask me that, Miss Aske! Besides, we're on a schedule, I'm afraid. If you're lonely without my company, I keep a photograph of myself under my pillow. Feel free to borrow it."

"The day I'm lonely without your company is the day I stop looking both ways before crossing the road," I replied, and he raised an eyebrow.

"That's hurtful," he said. "When the idea of keeping your docile company for the foreseeable future brings nothing but happiness to *my* heart. And other parts." His eyes travelled up and down my body with such exaggeration that I knew he was just playing games, and I couldn't feel alarmed. Not that I ever thought my current appearance could inspire any sort of desire in others.

"I warn you, don't go there," I said, finally moving to dump my bag in my room. "It's tempting, but try not to fall in love with me. I'm a woman of mystery. I'll only break your heart."

"As long as you take care of *your* heart," he replied, smiling as he headed to the door. "We don't want any damage done to that genetically modified piece of scientific glory. Especially before we've had a chance to see the full range of your unique supernatural ability."

I spun around. He didn't lock the door behind him.

As soon as he was gone, I moved the dossier to the lounge area and sat with it on one of the large white leather sofas. The dossier was overflowing with compiled papers, pieces of scrap, and clipped in photographs, numbers, and sheets. At first it appeared illogical and without order, but slowly I began to figure out the structure belying its initial appearance. Equally, it was clear after closely thumbing through it that sections had been removed in preparation for my viewing, and many of the pages which appeared to be nonsense or benign were in fact written in code. I decided to try deciphering it later and found the section trailing Ayer. George had less information than he'd pretended; the last trace of Ayer was at JFK airport in America four days ago. Wrexham hadn't even been mentioned since seen fleeing the Arden Fire with several men, all of whom had turned up dead in various rivers. I was tempted to walk out on George, but realized I had no chance of getting to America without him. So instead I tried to think of where to go from here. I had lived in close proximity to Ayer for months in Arden. What did I know about him? *The snow globe from his mother...*the image of the stenciled white and blue lion symbol flashed in my mind. I scribbled a rough drawing of it onto a piece of paper and, cursing the fact that George didn't have a computer in the suite, made my way back down to the reception area. The long-suffering receptionist allowed me to use her Internet, but it was to no avail. In the end, I asked her if she recognized the sign.

"Why would I?" she replied, affronted.

"Looks like you're searching for the Nittany Lion," commented one of the tourist businessmen, leaning over as he waited for his documentation to be returned. "It's Penn State's symbol."

"Penn State?" I asked, barely daring to hope.

"Sure, the Pennsylvania State University," he said. "Went to UPenn myself; not all of us were born with a rich daddy."

"Thank you," I breathed, and Googled Penn State with the name "Ayer."

Bingo. There was a Professor Benjamin Ayer in the biochemistry department, and a Professor Susan Ayer in the economics department. It took a few more minutes before I found a picture of Susan Ayer, but when I did I knew they must be Ayer's family all right. Ayer had kept the snow globe on his desk; he clearly loved his mother and the university very much. A plan began to form in my mind, and I headed back to George's suite, tense with success. The parallels of using Ayer's family to track him down and capture him had not escaped me.

Back in the suite, I was unable to relax and I had no desire to watch TV or listen to music, and the dossier code was proving harder than I'd thought. The fridge was only stocked with Sipsmith London dry gin and a few out-of-date cheap microwave meals (a puzzling choice of food considering George's obvious enjoyment of his wealth). So I began to look through his room. Scattered everywhere were fancy colognes, shaving products, and watches, and the wardrobe was full of Italian and French designer suits. The only thing of interest in the room was a closed suitcase placed on top of an unmade bed. I noted the two hairs carefully caught in the zip and extracted them before opening the case. Disappointingly, there were yet more clothes inside; only these were cheaper and plainer. There was also an army uniform and a porter outfit, and a bag full of colored contact lenses. Under the false bottom I found another bag full of passports and IDs, several police badges for different countries, five boxes of different types of ammunition, a Zippo, and a penknife. I couldn't find a gun, a private mobile, or anything else. He had to store the truly private stuff somewhere else. However, despite my attempts I couldn't find it. Did he have a house to keep his things, somewhere he could escape to when he wasn't "working"? If I could find out the location....

I replaced the two hairs into the case zip, retreated back to the lounge, and flipped through the code of the partial-dossier. Frustrated, I put it aside and began to riffle through the newspapers on the table. At the bottom of the pile was a regional paper from a town in Warwickshire, dated that morning. It seemed like a curious paper to have, especially as all the others were national. Then I found the reason he had it on page seven. A tiny article mentioned that two bodies had been found in a burned down agricultural warehouse, the men identified as Dr. Grigori Novikov and Tito Delaney, the retired CEO of the world famous First Institute. A witness had come forward and said he'd seen the men being dragged there earlier by a young male in his early twenties. The male was described as around 5 foot 10, pale with dark hair, and being in poor health with a severe wound to head, chest, and left hand. He was last seen talking to a tall black man before disappearing through the wooded area behind the warehouse. Police were urging any witnesses to step forward.

The door opened and I jumped to my feet as George walked in, carrying a plastic bag. There was a ring of bloody fingerprints around one of his biceps, barely noticeable, but I had no doubt he'd left it there deliberately. He took one look at me and his eyebrows rose languidly as he placed the bag on the table.

"Find out anything new?" he asked.

I pushed back my hair and told him that Ayer's parents worked at Penn State University. We could track down Ayer's family, and no doubt find Ayer and then Wrexham from there.

George fixed me with a rather sardonic look, but simply nodded. "Good work, my dear Miss Aske. I'll call up and rearrange our flight to Philadelphia."

He picked up the hotel phone and I went into the kitchen to look for something to eat. But something else was diverting my attention; the plastic bag left on the table. Inside, I could see an oblong gift box. Did he have a loved one nearby?

I darted out and picked up the box. My name had been written along the top in blunt handwriting that I instantly recognized. Jason's writing.

Nestled in the cotton inside were two severed fingers. Sickness curled in my stomach as I forced myself to look closer. I inspected the shape of the nail, the battered knuckles...but I already knew they were Jason's.

George appeared, taking the box from me and smiling silkily. "It's alarming the rate these GEs are dying off or being captured, isn't it? It's almost as if there is something defective with you all. Something wrong with your alleged abilities."

Had he killed Jason? No, Jason was far too valuable. Did he have Jason captured? Had he forced Jason to kill those other Board members in the paper?

"So another GE is gone...I don't care," I said, shrugging. "It just increases my own value, right?" I tried to return to my own room, and his hand shot out and grabbed my shoulder, his fingers digging into the sensitive bruising on my shoulders. He tilted his head and his gleaming eyes were mocking on mine.

"You're a quick learner," he said. "Or a quick imitator, at least. Your monosyllabic boyfriend isn't dead, Miss Aske, I'm just trying to provide you with some motivation. I have a lot of investment in you, and I really can't afford for you to disappoint. So let's just call Jason a guarantor bond to ensure this partnership plays by the rules."

"Which means what?"

"You misbehave, and Jason loses more appendages. And I've got to admit, having now met the boy, the thought is appealing. If he has any charms, they somehow escaped me."

"You won't harm Jason badly; he's valuable like me."

He smiled quietly. "Incorrect. He's all but useless to me, dying a little every day. And disappointingly easy to catch; I merely told him I had you and he turned into a dear little lamb. But as a sign of good faith between you and me, he'll remain unharmed for the time being, and I won't sell him on to various clients as I would have normally done. You see how this partnership works?"

"I do."

"I hope so, Miss Aske, but I doubt it."

I kept a kitchen knife under my pillow that night and lay awake for hours, arms hugged around me and fingertips stretched out over the empty scarred holes in my shoulder blades. I refused to think of Jason. Instead, I repeated the same old mantras; that once I killed Ayer and Wrexham, I'd have freedom. I repeated the word "free" in my head so often that it began to blur and distort against my lips.

***

I woke up to the sound of faint voices from the other side of the closed door. The deep, drawling voice was clearly George's, but the female voice he was speaking to seemed equally familiar although I couldn't quite place it.

"Wrexham has completely disappeared from the map, Knight, and most of the others are backing off from finding Ayer since it's been circulated that he's yours."

"Good. But remind me again, Zola, why are you here? I have a flight to catch." George sounded idle, his voice blandly English.

There was a slight pause before the woman said, "I'm here because I'm concerned about Marilyn, George."

I hauled myself out of the bed, smoothed back my short hair, dragged on the jeans under the crumpled t-shirt, and walked into the main room. Immediately the female went quiet. George, looking as affable and clean as ever, looked up, and his eyes passed over my unkempt assemble.

"Next time," he advised, "replace the two hairs in the zip a centimeter further to the right; you were slightly off."

He sat on the sofa with one leg crossed over the other, dressed in a light grey suit and blue shirt with a diamond pin in the lapel, and his glasses were gone. He dangled a half empty wine glass in his hand. A slender middle-aged woman sat on the sofa opposite George, her body language uncomfortable and prim. She had soft brown hair and looked like an upper-class society wife, but as she said my name and looked up at me with anxious relief, I knew who she was.

"Mrs. Shäfer," I whispered numbly. She got to her feet and gave me a bird-like hug. I wasn't entirely sure why I jumped at the contact, but I let her draw me down to the sofa beside her as I attempted to hide my exhausted disbelief. Without the grey hair, she looked about a decade younger, and her eyes were now a pastel blue. She had been my father's source all along? Zola the vigilante, feeding information to everyone? But...but why was she working for George? Why hadn't she helped me when I was in Arden?

"No, not Mrs. Shäfer; she was just a cover identity, Marilyn," said Mrs. Shäfer, smiling at me. "I go by the name of Zola in these circles."

"I'm one of the privileged few who know Zola's true name and identity, naturally," commented George. "However, it's not a particularly exciting name, so I won't bother having any fun teasing you with it. Zola here is one of those whatyoucallthem...one of those saintly sacrificing things. You know; er...vigilante. Luckily for her, however, she's got a rich aristocratic husband, so her morals are quite free to dictate the terms of her paycheck."

Zola flinched and cleared her throat. "Even if I was dirt poor, I would still see the social and legal injustices of this world!"

"Of course you would," said George, without the remotest bit of sincerity.

"You must excuse George," I said to her. "His own lack of morality stems from the great financial hardship he struggles to overcome daily. Oh wait...." I cast a pointed eye over the splendor of the room around us.

George laughed and drank from his wine glass before saying, "It grieves me to correct you, but I'm the *other* type. I'm a free man. My lack of financial hardship gives me freedom from the tyranny of morality. Inadequate people will always band together and use morality to justify their mundanity. Slave morality, as Nietzsche would say."

"This isn't a matter of philosophy!" shot back Zola, looking as if she was chewing on a wasp. "It's a simple matter of what is right and wrong, following what my heart believes."

George all but rolled his eyes. He turned to me and said with a bored smile, "What about you, Miss Aske? What do you believe in?"

"Like most people, I believe in whatever makes me feel good about myself."

George burst out laughing. "And that brings us nicely onto the subject of why Zola insisted on coming here this morning," he said. "Rather than just call to say she had finally paid off the last debt she owed to me with the execution of Kaminev, she decided to grant us with one last corporeal visitation before she had permission to disappear from our lives forever. Now let us bask in her presence, and hope she hurries up and goes before we catch our plane."

"I came to check up on Marilyn's health, as I am one of the few experts left alive who knows first-hand what Arden did to those youths," said Zola defensively. "I was worried and came to answer any medical questions you might have about yourself. I also brought you clothes." I noticed for the first time the small bag on the floor beside her. "In fact, I'm the best qualified person to stay with you, Marilyn, as you recover...help you adapt, teach you how to use your ability properly. You aren't experiencing any chest pains, or bleeding, or electric shocks? I see you removed your casts early, which is exactly why I need to stay with you both as you hunt down Ayer—"

"I cannot express how much horror that idea gives me," interjected George,

"And I'm fine," I added. "You're not needed."

Zola's expression confused me; her eyes kept darting toward George, who was smiling serenely to himself. In contrast, she looked increasingly nervous.

"Okay," she said. "Okay, then just let me check you over, Marilyn. Let's go over what I've brought you in your room—feminine talk—and then you can go and catch the flight."

George was still smiling into his wine as I walked into my room with Zola closely behind. She closed the door behind us, opened up the duffel bag she'd brought, and placed the new clothes on the bed. She then brought out a medical kit, along with a blood pressure kit, heart monitor, pills, and other instruments I didn't recognize.

"No," I said, stepping nearer to the door.

"Marilyn," she said, straightening up and facing me. "I know you can't want to be here with him."

"You mean this *isn't* heaven on earth I'm living in?"

"You were supposed to be captured by Demeter, me, or at least Redstone. You can't stay here with George; you need to leave him and come with me. He's planning on flying to Philadelphia, right? That's what the front desk...that's not the point. Don't go with him to Philadelphia; let him go alone. My husband has money; he will protect us both and we can —"

"You *worked* for George! You let everything happen to us because you were serving his invested interest in Arden! And now suddenly you're telling me —"

"No one works for that bastard by choice!" She was standing too close to me, her voice barely more than a hiss and her eyes wide and pleading. "He has a way of making people owe him favors, of finding people and getting them to acquiesce to him. George has so much shit on me he could screw my life up like origami if he wanted. I went into Arden as he ordered so that I could be the top source of information. I had no power...I couldn't remove you, but I can now. And this is the worst place you could be."

"Out of all the places I've been recently, this is not the worst."

"Don't kid yourself, Marilyn. You're about to fall so deeply into his world, you'll never untangle yourself. George wants Wrexham, Wrexham wants you. George wants every GE, George wants everything, and he knows how to lure you in. Oh, he'll take you out for a fancy meal. He'll buy you jewelry that matches your eyes, and discuss avant-garde art with you. He'll sleep with you, if he thinks it will be beneficial. But once you've lost all use to him, he won't think twice before disposing of you. He isn't in this game because he wants to kill or he wants money. He's creating some kind of network, some plan. He's got his own game, and he is dangerous. Once people discover he's been working with you, you'll be even more likely to be killed."

I turned to walk back out and she slammed the door shut with her hand. "Marilyn, if you don't come with me, I will have to work against you. My debt to George is paid. He can't track me anymore, and my conscience can't let George have you within his grasp. Ayer and Wrexham were human, at least."

I wanted to hit her. Instead, I looked her straight in the eyes, our faces inches away from each other. "Thank you for the suitcase, but I don't need your help. I know what I'm doing, and I'm working for myself. And if I've learned anything, it's that if I'm getting out of this situation, I'm doing it on my own. Otherwise, it's not an escape, it's a transfer."

"Please, Marilyn," she breathed. "I always cared for you, tried to help you. You're trying to become what Ayer wanted, but you won't succeed. You'll just self-destruct, because you're not like them. You're like me, you're good."

I yanked open the door, not caring if I hit Zola, and walked out past George and into the bathroom. I cleaned my face and brushed my teeth, shaking with anger, and when I came back out, George was still sitting in the room, watching BBC News with a paper bag of food on the coffee table, and ignoring Zola. When she saw me, she looked away and went into the bathroom after me.

"I lent Zola use of the toilet to change outfits before she left," George said with his eyes on the TV. "Breakfast is in the paper bag if you're hungry."

I sat next to him and picked out a croissant. Left inside the bag were apples and a massive bag of Skittles. George caught my look.

"I thought young women liked Skittles?" he said. "Lots of pretty colors."

"I prefer candy canes and unicorns."

"I'll make a note. It was sensible of you to turn Zola's proposal down, by the way. Useful, too."

"Why?"

He smiled at me. "Aren't you going to ask how I knew you refused?"

"Because people like me are boring and predictable, etcetera?"

"Because as we speak, she is fixing one of her trademark little explosives under the bathroom sink."

"She WHAT?" I leapt to my feet as he gave me an amused warning look, and placed his finger to his lips, shushing me.

"She can't know we know," he said. "I'm afraid we have to let her leave first."

He shut up as Zola walked out of the bathroom, wiping her hands on her pantsuit. "You win, George, and no doubt you'll track down Ayer, kill him, and win again, too. But I'm gone, I'm out of your game."

George's lips twitched and Zola left without a second glance at me. As soon as the door shut, I ran into the bathroom and found the small electronic bundle of wires taped up under the sink. George followed at a more leisurely pace and said, "Ah yes, in this position it will be the car park that will be obscured with the smoke, and I won't be able to track where she goes. I taught her well, did I not?"

I peered helplessly at the device and ripped it off the sink. Three minutes. 2:59.

"What will you do with it, Miss Aske?" asked George. "Throw it out the window? That would certainly hinder her escape, and the car park will be mainly empty at this time of the morning."

It was a test. I gave the bomb one last look, focusing on figuring out the wiring, but it was no good. George was quietly laughing to himself. I grabbed the device and ran out into the corridor, slamming on the fire alarm as I went. Loud wails screeched out, and people began to spill out into the corridors and run down the fire escapes. I waited about half a minute and then pressed for the elevator. It came immediately along and as it pinged open, I threw the bomb inside and sent it up to the very top floor.

"Very shrewd," said George behind me. He stood in the middle of the corridor with our bags in each hand as people jostled and ran past him. "Very humanitarian."

"Zola won't know you figured her bomb out this way," I corrected, and we both headed down the fire escape. We had reached the bottom floor and were out in the car park when a loud BANG shook through the hotel and sent vibrations across the concrete outside. Smoke and dust billowed out over the walls and windows and through the stairs after us as people screamed and panicked and hotel staff yelled directions. The car park was hemmed in with confused guests, and there was a fire engine in the distance. George and I coolly walked around the back to where a lone porter was having a cigarette with trembling hands. George tossed him his car keys, with the instructions to take the Jag to its registered house address, and led us out onto the road to hail a taxi.

"It was only a small explosive," said George thoughtfully as he gave directions to the driver. "Clearly she only wanted to hinder us so she could get a head start on however she's planning to stop us. Hopefully she'll be out of the way for a while now with her schemes, though we mustn't get ahead of ourselves."

"I thought we were supposed to be going to the airport now?"

"We are, just making a small stop on the way to get you some last minute identification and whatnot. You'll enjoy the experience, I'm sure, though you'll have to get used to wearing contacts for a while; as exquisite as your eyes are, they are really too distinctive for someone playing our game."

Still on the edge of my seat, I sneered at him and aimed for the same cool arrogance. "*Exquisite*? There's a fine line between international gentleman of the world and YMCA sugar daddy, and you just crossed it."

He laughed and sat back in the seat without a worry in the world. "I find that rather galling to my masculinity."

"Buy a sports car," I advised, turning to face the window.

"I already have several," he said. "And don't you dare tell me what I'm overcompensating for."

***

I was still watching out the window as the cab pulled up outside a small side street full of run-down electrical shops and travel agencies. George told the driver to wait and ushered me into the tiny photograph developing shop sandwiched between the other two. Inside, a fed up looking man with a ponytail and a crucifix necklace lounged behind the counter. As soon as he saw George heading towards him, he leapt up and murmured a greeting. George smiled with pleasure and the man spoke quickly. "You want Asif; he's around the back."

George thanked him and, touching the back of my arm lightly, steered me into the back rooms behind the desk. Amid the junk and mess of the back rooms was a table, boxes of storage, three big whirling machines, another locked door, and an overweight man chain smoking as he worked on something. He looked up and I saw he was busy tweaking the photograph in what looked to be some type of official document.

"Who's the bird this time, Jean-Etienne?" he asked testily. "Sure you can trust her?"

George shuddered distastefully and said to me, "You wouldn't believe this is the best place to go for fake identification, would you?" His accent was Swiss-French now. He turned back to Asif. "She's not remotely trustworthy, but she looks as innocent as a newborn lamb and lies like a snake, so she'll be fine. She needs one passport and national security number." He glanced at me. "Go chose a new look, darling. For the passport picture."

Asif unlocked the other door and pointed me to the small mirrored cubicle, full of bags and bags of clothes, wigs, makeup, pads to make me look fatter, and so on. I exchanged my jeans and t-shirt for a thin, blue-flowered knee-length dress and a pale cardigan over the top. It was so completely not my style that there was a novelty in it. It also hid my scars well. I chose the coppery short bob wig over the blonde one and fixed it in place, then put on a layer of old make up by the mirror. I shaded my face to make my eyes look wider spaced, my nose less hard and angular, and so on...all basic tricks. Back when I was younger, I'd watched with fascination for ages as my mum would apply her makeup with similar skill. The contact lenses I ended up choosing were a dark brown. I poked myself in the eye several times before I managed to put the lenses in. After the final touches of makeup blusher and bronzer to make sure I looked less washed out, I walked back to the others, where George was frowning restlessly into another mirror on the window sill. He scanned my appearance as I sat down at the table beside him.

"Good," he said. As I stuffed the left over clothes and spare contact lenses into my bag, George changed into his own outfit, still staring into the mirror, obsessed with the possibility of the slightest mistake. Or he was insanely vain. Probably both. As Asif directed me to stand in front of the wall and took the passport pictures, I watched George changing his own appearance. He applied a sort of cream across his face, neck, and hands, which darkened the color of his skin to pure black ethnicity rather than mixed. He took out his contacts, (it surprised me he'd do this in front of me, but perhaps he simply didn't care that much) to reveal that his eyes were pure onyx, shocking in their darkness. He placed in some lighter brown contacts, and brushed some grey color at the temples of his hair. He still looked very handsome, even though with the new outfit of a cheaper suit and sweater, he began to look older and heftier.

"You're vain!" I said when he saw me trying not to smile at his new, less suave disguise. He pulled a face at me and went back to checking his hair.

At last, Asif had developed the photos and brought them over to us to get the rest of the identification papers together. "All right, mate, you'll be Lynn Adams, travelling to Philadelphia with her uncle Jack Knollys," he told me, sliding the photo into the passport and handing it over.

"Wasn't that simple?" said George, now sitting back down at the table and picking up one of the many open packs of Gauloises smokes overflowing the ashtray.

"Alarmingly so."

"The trick when choosing alias names is to choose ones you know you'll respond to. So normally, similar names you'll naturally react to." He ran his long fingers along the side of the smoke packet. "I hate Gauloises. Hmm." By putting on a jumper under his suit, he looked far more muscular and heavy-set than before, and the stubble starting across his jaw made it look broader. For some reason, when I saw the stubble, I immediately thought of Jason. I quickly forced myself away from that train of thought. George sighed ruefully and brushed a hand over his face.

"My only consolation when I look like *this*," he said, "is that no one ever knows it's me."

"Except me. And I'm judging you, man...oh, I'm judging."

He smiled absently, rolled one of the burnt cigarette stubs between his fingers as if he wanted to smoke it, then placed it back down on the table.

"I'm bored now," he said.

"We're finished," said Asif, handing over the rest of the documents to George. "And don't worry, it's all top stuff, practically legit and untraceable. Just make sure you give my name to the White Knight, yeah? He considers me a friend, knows he can send his people to me, yeah?"

George's smile took on a dangerous edge as he purred, "Last I heard, anyone calling himself a friend of his knew better than to call him the *White* Knight. It has this rather unfortunate effect of irritating him. Between you and me, of course."

"Oh right, yeah, of course, mate."

George smiled. He was still smiling when we returned to the taxi and made our way to the airport.

"Your *people*?" I asked from inside. "Who are you, Don Corleone?"

"I am as of yet undecided on the long term picture I'm working for," he said mildly. "I could end up as an overweight Italian mobster with a peculiar jaw, though."

***

Normally I would have been hyper on edge booking in for a flight with a fake ID. But with George, it was hard to be nervous about it; he was so supernaturally confident, he had the air of having done this so many times he barely noticed it any more. Once we were through customs, he handed me the daily newspaper and left me to find a seat as he went to check out the airport shops. Uneasy with the being left alone part, I just trailed after him, not caring if he knew (which he did). In the end, he just bought some paperbacks and sweets, and without mentioning my not letting him out my sight, he led us both back to the seats, then handed me a book of Su Do Ku and some wine gums.

"You look far away, Miss Aske," he commented, folding out his long legs. "I'll trade you wine gums for your thoughts."

"I don't think you understand; I'm nearly nineteen," I told him mock-patiently. "Sweets aren't the way to bribe me. Nor is *Twilight*, for future reference."

He shrugged airily. "Fine, I'll just have the sweets myself then. Besides, how am I supposed to know what young ladies like these days?"

"Well, they *love* being patronized; that's pretty much universal," I said. He laughed, and question deflected, we settled down to wait. As George started to read some American political autobiography with a faint look of distaste, I sprawled out and watched the other people listening to music and having their private conversations. Yet after so much adrenaline and travelling, it felt strangely restful to just sit there in the middle of the airport with George. I had to keep reminding myself that George was manipulating me to feel like this, that his game plan relied on my becoming attached to him. But it was hard as he kept passing over selected sweets, and dryly reading aloud bits of his book that he found more amusing.

I was leaning next to him, smiling slightly, when a figure in the corner of my eye made me quickly sit up. A black haired male was retreating through the crowds, his back to me. But I could've sworn there had been a small red glint just before he turned.

"Toilet," I said quickly, then followed the man around the corner. But the area was empty, a faint smell of metallic electricity in the air. I kept walking through the terminals and seating, searching all around me until I reached the final exits. Whoever it had been, they were gone.

I turned back and saw George waiting for me a few meters away, his pose as deceptively lazy as ever.

"Did you see someone you recognized?" he asked.

Had Jason managed to escape? Was he following us?

"Thought I saw an old school friend," I said. "It's time we boarded the plane now."

As we queued up to board, George began to point out in undertones how one lady ahead of us was clearly going abroad with her secret lover, who was the man in the blue shirt further down the line. The man behind us was newly divorced, newly rich. Cold reading; something he excelled at. It was all obvious to him, tiny little sparks of ammunition for him to feed off; marriage rings, clothing labels, how a person was standing, what color they dyed their hair, the food they ate. He could use it all against them. Stuff I had always sort of thought about, but never used so consciously or precisely. Most of it was common sense, but I enjoyed it as he then selected people in the crowd and told me to analyze them for him. He listened to my more hesitant suggestions, occasionally extending an idea, approving, suggesting further as I gained confidence. The game carried on as we took our places on the plane…how people revealed certain things, how weaknesses were revealed, and how you could use them against someone to get what you wanted. As he played the perception games with me, quietly destroying those around us, I got a guilty thrill. I enjoyed it, and I didn't even consider the moral aspect until later, when I mulled over it. More proof to me that this life was what I was made for. I felt that for once I wasn't the vulnerable, overly obvious one that everyone else was able to use.

In the end, the lessons died down as we both grew tired, and George signaled for a bourbon from the heavily made up stewardess. She took the opportunity to flirt with him, and he flirted back until she reluctantly left to see to the other passengers.

"I thought you liked to drink gin?" I commented from beside the window.

"Habits have a tendency to get you killed," was all he said, his trademark smile in place.

I watched out the window as we took off into the atmosphere. The sky was turning to the smudged deep purple of evening, and lights were dotting on across the darkening buildings, roads, and city, creating a delicate glowing cobweb underneath us. I was leaving.

Stars shining bright above you,
Night breezes seem to whisper "I love you."

I quickly jerked myself upright, shook my head, and plugged in the airplane radio earphones. Ah, Duran Duran; '80s perfection. I settled back down next to George, who appeared to be toying with the bottle of bourbon rather than drinking it, and for the first time since I'd left Arden, I tried to sleep. It was probably illogical that I still felt safe here, in this confined space, more safe than I had felt for a long, long time. I could sleep here, tucked up in this thrumming cramped container flying through darkness, surrounded by strangers and smiling predators.

I only woke up at one point in the long flight, several hours later. I was curled up in my seat, my shoulder slumped against George's arm and my knees pressed up against my chest. Only one of my earphones was in. I twisted my head to the side and saw George had taken the other earphone and put it in his own ear, still reading under the single overhead light. He looked down briefly from the book...Albert Camus. Shadows ran down his face; the light was trapped in his dyed hair and the airplane engines rattled around us.

"Go back to sleep," he murmured, "or are you scared you will get nightmares?"

"I'm scared because I won't."

He softly ran his thumb over my bare ankle. I repressed a small shiver as his warm hand gently cradled the arch of my foot. "If sleep offers you a reprieve, enjoy it. You're lucky."

I slept. And I did not dream.

***

Philadelphia International was humid, warm, and overcrowded. We got our luggage and I tiredly followed George to the car rental, unable to do much other than just sit wherever was most convenient and watch as he sorted out all the details. He didn't appear to be tired, as effortlessly neat and charmingly relaxed as ever. However, he did smell more strongly of bourbon, and a part of me suspected he'd been using more than alcohol on the flight. But surely that was stupidly reckless for a man in his position? Not that he seemed to be overly cautious; we ended up with a Cadillac about as inconspicuous as a shovel to the head, and began to make our way to State College. I dozed in the passenger seat as we drove through the day and finally stopped at a motel. While I woke up, George stood outside the car making some calls. And when I got out into the warm night air, he glanced at me and hung up.

That night, George gave me the motel bed and took the armchair. Yet when I woke up in the middle of the night, I found that George was lying fully dressed on top of the covers next to me, reading.

"I was uncomfortable," he explained with a shrug.

I instantly moved to the bathroom and slept there instead. I didn't bother explaining to him the reason I was most humiliated and perturbed; when I'd stirred, the first person I thought I'd seen lying beside me hadn't been George. It had been an angry youth with inflexible cobalt-blue eyes and dark hair.

Like I said...humiliating.

The next day was spent sitting in an expensively decorated pseudo-rustic hotel we'd found in State College, searching through the records of all Penn State alumni and the open public records. As I did this, George called up the university, enquiring after a Benjamin and Susan Ayer.

"Too simple," said George, hanging up. "They didn't even check my police identification number, just handed over the Ayer's address. They still live there."

"Obadiah attended the same university roughly thirty-six years ago," I responded with my own info. "But he left for England shortly after, and only comes back to visit his parents twice a year."

George blew me a kiss.

I smiled. "So let's get going," I said. "Let's pay a visit to Mother dear."

"I don't think I've ever been more proud of you," he said sardonically as we packed our things away. "You've already taken on board the classic principles of blackmail and the criminally favored method of using ones' parents and loved ones against them, either as bait, for a message, or as information." He glanced sideways at me. "But I'm sure you already knew all about that."

"Indeed. Though I'd feel sorry for anyone who'd ever try to use *your* parents against you."

"I think I'm to be considered lucky that my parents are long gone."

The only thing left to do was to call up the address' nearest estate agents and find the closest house for sale. Luckily, there was one just down the road from Obadiah's parents' house. I listened to her description of it, thanked her, and then hung up.

"And we're in," I said, and without further delay we loaded up the car and left the hotel. The elderly receptionist watched us leaving with the same eagle eye she'd had in place ever since George had made some joke to her about being named "Humbert Humbert." Apparently she hadn't found it funny.

I basked in the sun in the passenger seat (on the wrong side of the road) of the Cadillac and watched the beautiful mountain scenery winding around us under the crisp sunlight as George made me play memory games with him. First he made me memorize as many number plates as possible, then recite them all back to him, then tell him what you could learn about a person by their car. In turn, I would say a long sequence of numbers or words, or just simply talk for a timed amount, and then George would repeat everything I had just said back to me, word perfect. It was pretty impressive, as I learned when I attempted to do the same thing.

I could feel something changing within me as we drove further into the cocooning world of unfurling mountains and greenery, the heat and the sunshine. Soon Arden would be fully gone. That had to be what I was feeling.

When on the outskirts of the suburbs, George parked the car off the side of the winding mountain road next to a small petrol station, and we began to formalize the plans. It went without saying that George wasn't telling me everything, that he was keeping things hidden. But that was okay, because an idea had been unfurling in my head as well, brought on by the beautiful clear sunshine skies expanding around us. So I listened charmingly, talked enthusiastically, and then popped into the station with George's money to pay for the petrol, a bottle of cheap Gordon's gin, and a lighter, which I hid in my bra. I came out in time to see George washing down a number of small pills with the last of the bourbon while he flicked through his mobile.

He straightened up off the car bonnet when he saw me and tossed the bottle onto the ground. "We'll be playing Mr. and Mrs. Knowles, the house-hunting couple from Ohio," he said in a thick Midwestern American accent. "That will raise less questions than if we try and pass off as relatives, not least because of the racial issue."

"I don't think my American accent is good enough to pass native inspection," I said, handing him the loose change, which he also flicked into the bin. "But I've always wanted to be an English mail-order bride." I shoved the alcohol in the boot; I saw him eye it, his eyes rather jewel-like, before looking me over slowly.

"A gift for you," I said sweetly.

"Go and get changed in the toilets, Mrs. Knowles; you're about to be introduced to the house of your dreams."

Although I enjoyed applying disguises and make-up, I did not enjoy looking at my reflection any more. I changed in the middle of the dank outdoors toilet without the lights on, but as I stripped off, I still caught a glimpse of the ridged red scars across my shoulders, chest, and spine in the mirror, and the metal that glinted out from my shoulder blades. It was fine, I told myself; I simply would never ever get naked in front of anyone again. I hurriedly changed into a pair of mumsy jeans coupled with high heeled Gucci knockoffs and a pastel pink blouse, all provided by George. The suburban estate we were going to was nice, middle TV America, so we were going for the standard *nouveau riche* husband and young secretarial wife look. I switched the contacts for hazel ones.

When I stepped out of the toilet, someone had jammed a piece of paper under the door. Looking around, I picked it up and unfolded it. Inside was a small photograph of me, the one from my file in Arden, with the green hair. Underneath was scribbled in erratic handwriting, *Possibility of GE Angel surviving if enters Ayer House – 13%. Possibility of GE Angel surviving if escapes now – 38%.*

I looked up, and for a second could've sworn I saw a red flash somewhere amongst the trees.

Who would send me such a thing? It wasn't Jason's handwriting. Who was following us, and if they wanted to help me, why didn't they just reveal themselves?

Did they know I would be walking into a trap at Ayer's?

Sweating slightly, I pocketed the paper and headed back out to the car as George replaced the false bottom of the boot back in, hiding the selection of powerful looking guns, ammo, revolvers, and a set of knives. There was casual admiration in his eyes as he looked my outfit over. He now wore chinos with a cheap buttoned shirt that gave him the look of a social climber who'd gained money so quickly, he was still unsure of his position in society.

"You look more like a Republican kindergarten teacher than a secretary," he said, grinning. "I want to hand all my newborn children over to your care."

"Do I get one of the guns?"

He shook his head, mock-disapprovingly. "Afraid not, Miss Aske. You'll be playing another role in this covert operation."

I looked around me again before I got back into the car. The feeling of being watched was stronger. Yet it wouldn't matter soon. I was ready now, my plan was formalized in my brain and it was all mine. Across the car, George smiled at me, apparently content in my obedience, and we set off for the last time.

CHAPTER ELEVEN

Obadiah Ayer's family home was a large stone house situated at the end of a beautiful suburban street and down a sloping drive, and was surrounded by acres of fields for horses, with a backdrop of the mountains. As we parked at the top of the estate's street, I could sense a new mood had come over George; he seemed quieter, less quick to talk about nothing. He cut the engine.

"Remember, we are just investigating the house at first, making sure there are no traps. We circle and gather information about who's inside, and only then—"

I interrupted. "You've said all this already. Getting nervy, are we?"

He leaned across and flicked me on the cheek. "I'm never nervy, Aske."

I smiled back, and we both got out the car.

George had parked in a spot shaded by an oak tree, next to an actual white picket fence. The hot butter sun was overpowering the rinsed out blue sky, and I could hear the sounds of children squealing and running along the parched front gardens, along with the sounds of garden hose pipes.

"This is surreal," I muttered, as George put on some Aviator sunglasses and looked around the neighborhood, putting his car keys in his pocket.

"Ahs afraid ah sticks out raadah badly wid aw deese white folk," he drawled. "Maybe this isn't the best place for me to go incognito?"

I gawped, shocked, which was probably his intention.

"Nonsense!" A perky tall brunette with her hands full of PTA leaflets was just walking out of the fenced garden; she stopped beside our car. "Our neighborhood is really just lovely! We already have an African-American couple living around the corner, and Obadiah and his partner are often in residence with his parents at the end of the road. So you see, we welcome all ethnicities and sexual orientations! You're looking at the house for sale?"

"Well, looking at the area in general," I said. "We really love it here; perfect for raising a family."

"Oh yes, it certainly is! And we welcome all nationalities here too. Where are you from? Australia, with that accent? Not that I know my geography, but does it matter? Actually, if you're looking at the property next to the Ayer's and you need a guide, you could always ask them for the spare key. Of course, Dr. Benjamin and his wife are away at the moment, visiting their eldest son in Washington, but Obadiah and his partner have just come back home, and I'm sure they'd be happy to help. This place is just so accepting of everyone, because in the eyes of God...we're all the same!"

I looked across at George in disbelief — *Ayer is here* — but he was just smiling and nodding in an exaggeratedly interested manner as he hauled his suitcase out of the boot.

"Aw shucks, ah thanks you mightily, ma'am," he said with definite venom, and the woman blinked, unsure what to do about this sort of passive hostility.

"Thank you for your help," I interrupted breezily. "I may take you up on that advice."

"You're right; places like this do tend to wind me up somewhat," George murmured as we walked down the slope towards the drive of the last house, his hand on my back. "Apologies. Still, first we do a surveillance of the house and then we meet back and plan our next move."

We passed the For Sale sign on the house, and walked down the path towards the solitary end house, which was hidden from the rest of the neighborhood by the hush of the trees. We stopped at the foot of the drive and George said in a low voice, "This is all strangely convenient, isn't it?"

The Ayers' stone house appeared undefended. Adrenaline began to tighten up my muscles as we kept to the shadowed path beside the drive and walked closer into the clearing around the house. The sun reflected off the top of a dark blue Porsche parked next to the front door. It was eerily similar to the rental that had stalked me all those months ago

"What is it?" George asked, removing his hand as I let out a deep breath, trying to control myself. "Aske?"

"It's nothing," I uttered. "Nothing at all."

Everything had come down to this moment. Dr. Ayer had been responsible for the Showman breaking into my home and killing my mum. He was the one who had controlled everything I had turned into. Although I knew I was better off now than I had ever been before, I still wanted to kill him.

"Okay, let's split up and survey," I said.

George breathed slowly into a smile and said, "Isn't it time to get out your powers then, little Aske?"

The adrenaline was spiking and fizzing down my spine now. I said, "Turn around," and as he did so, I stripped, tossing my clothes and bandages into a bush. With my lighter hidden in my palm, I started to control my heart and switch into invisibility. My skin cells shifted, my blood churned, but the pain was cleaner, chemicals, blood, and tissues bound together by electricity and veins and my own body's power.

"I'm ready."

George turned around, eyebrows raised, paused, then shook his head admiringly. "It actually works," he stated. "I was starting to wonder if there weren't...glitches."

"No glitches," I said. "I'll check around the back of the house first, you go left."

"Wait." George was circling me, eyes darting, hands out ever so gently as he tried to sense where I was. "This is light-bending, correct? So if there was no light, or if someone used smoke, would they see you?"

I hadn't considered that. "Not sure. But my blood is visible when it's separate from me," I said.

"Can you turn a specific part of you invisible while the rest remains seen?"

I looked at him, not that he saw. He didn't even seem to be trying to.

"Not sure."

He just smiled. "We have lots of discoveries to make, once this is over. I wonder...," he mused, but then straightened silently. For the first time I could see a hint of indecision in his smooth, leonine face.

"Meet back here in twenty minutes," he said. "Remember, this is just surveillance; you look around, you try *nothing*, touch *nothing*. You don't go *near* anyone or anything."

He turned and took off to look at the previous house, all grace. I quickly made my way around the house, noting there were no cameras outside, not even a basic alarm system on the doors and windows. There were no dogs or signs of anybody, except upstairs, where there was a single room light on, even in daylight. The entire place stunk of a trap.

I was about to head back when I noticed someone had taken out the trash and left it heaped up in black bags by the fencing a little past the house. It seemed newly moved; instinct made me go and open up the bags, kneeling on the gravel to search through the cereal boxes and decomposing fruit.

Finally, at the bottom I found something; grey sweatpants and a crumpled t-shirt, both stained with blood...the clothes Jason had taken from the car. He'd been wearing them the last time I saw him; they even faintly smelled of him still.

Was Jason here, with Ayer? How? George had captured Jason...unless George had been working with Ayer all along, both of them luring me here.

A movement made me glance up; a red flash through the lit window, a shadow across the curtain.

It was time to act.

I returned in time to see George walk into the shadows of the barn house, murmuring on his phone. I followed him in as he said, "Yes, we're here. Of course it will work. Zola was too predictable; she kidnapped the male GE from my car and took him straight to Ayer, hoping to cut herself and the girl a deal. Wrexham's been following us since the airport; he'll arrive too late though."

He hung up and began to unbutton his shirt, revealing several knives and a gun with an attached silencer strapped to his chest and under his shoulders. Not giving him a chance, I stepped up to him and drew back my fist. Almost instantly, he whipped around and placed the revolver against my forehead, his glittering eyes looking past me as he held the gun in place. I nearly pissed myself.

Thinking panic-fast, I let the fear go into my voice. "What are you doing?"

His eyelids flickered but he kept the gun in place. "Precautions, Miss Aske."

I let out a deep, distressed sigh and whimpered, "George, I think they know we're coming for them…and I think they have my friend Jason. I think…I think they killed him." I let sobs choke my voice. "I don't know what to do now, George."

He drew back, slight aversion on his face as I upped the act. "I know I have to go in there and kill them, George, but I don't want to die." Heart hammering, I leaned past the gun, wrapped my arms around his waist, and buried my face against his chest. He tensed up with surprise for a second before cautiously sliding one arm around my shoulders.

"You must be brave," he murmured. "You are more than a match for these men."

I didn't give him time to process what I was doing as I leaned up and kissed him on the lips. What I didn't expect, however, was his instant reaction as he lowered his head fully into the kiss and deepened it, forcing my mouth wider open as his gun dug painfully into my wounded spine.

"I just need you to be on my side, I need you to help me," I whispered tearfully against his mouth, and he kissed me harder, lips almost bruising, hands possessively gripping.

I drew back slightly, breathing hard, and saw the quick flash of triumph through his calm eyes before they were hidden in the customary fey amusement. He was no longer suspicious.

"I'm with you, Aske," he said.

I leaned back up and tugged him down for another kiss. He obediently lowered his face, and I suddenly changed the angle of my head and head butted him, hard. Stunned, he staggered back as I wrenched the gun out of his hand and brought my knee up into his groin, then his head, stomping on him as he fell down onto the floor with a crash. He started to his feet again, eyes cold beacons of fury in a bloody face, but when I pointed the revolver at him, he stopped dead still, his breathing ragged. He touched his bloody mouth and nose, looked at the blood on his fingertips, then back at me, breathing hard.

"You have a problem with the sight of blood?" I asked mockingly.

"It's more the sight of my own blood I have a problem with," he drawled back. "You know I'll have to kill you for this?"

"I don't care. You were on Ayer's side all along. You gave him Jason."

His lip curled scornfully. "I am not on Ayer's side, though I'm an admirer of his work. You *heard* my phone conversation; I'm here to kill Obadiah Ayer and Harold Wrexham, and then take all three of the GEs for myself. The only way to find Ayer was through that idiot Zola, and the only way to lure Wrexham here was by promising him two more GEs to take for himself... particularly the daughter of his petty nemesis, Gatsby. Now, let me —"

He shot upwards and I shot him in the shoulder. Despite the silencer, the gun made a shockingly loud WHOOSH sound as he jerked back and hit the floor. Incredibly, he started to laugh before suddenly groaning, clutching his shoulder as he crumpled back down.

"No more games," I snapped. "I'm ending this and getting out." I hit him on the head with the gun again and he was finally out cold. After stripping him of a knife to accompany the gun, and keeping my lighter in my hand, I grabbed the vodka from the car then headed back for the house. My veins felt alive with action and decision and culmination as I slipped inside the door, locking it behind me.

I was inside. I didn't have long before Wrexham would be there, but I had long enough.

Looking around, I found I was in a warm, wooden paneled kitchen that led out into an equally beautiful oak hallway. The place had a contented, complete atmosphere, and I saw a child's drawings and photographs hanging on the walls, and pen markings of a child's height next to the fireplace. Fruit piled up on the kitchen counter along with endless knickknacks, all indicating peaceful childhoods and peaceful lives.

I turned on the oven gas and gas stove, then found the water heater in the small utility room next to the kitchen and undid the pipe links. I then began my slow ascent of the stairs onto the landing, pouring out the vodka in a line behind me.

I could hear something from the furthest room and warm artificial light spilled out from under the slightly ajar double doors. My heart was painful with electricity as I looked through the crack into the room. Immediately, I saw Dr. Ayer and another man seated at a wooden table overflowing with fruit bowls, desserts, platters of meat, roast potatoes, popcorn, spaghetti, vegetables, and wine. Dr. Ayer, his brushed hair softly shining in the light, quietly ate at the head of the table, his companion to his left, and they both wore clean pressed black suits and white shirts.

A soft groan rent the air, and I noticed the bed and the bedroom furniture that were pushed back behind the table, and the figure lying on the neat white bed...Jason. His body twitched, then stilled. There was an ugly leather mask strapped over his mouth.

Next to him, laid out on the bedside table top, were six syringes, a bottle of clear liquid, a rope, a razor, and two knives.

Ayer's companion raised his head to look at the grandfather clock beside the bed. "You know they'll be here soon. There is no doubt Marilyn will try and kill you tonight, now you have Jason as prisoner and Zola's dead body in the next room. The Knight intends to betray us both as well; he will kill us to win Marilyn even more deeply onto his side"

Obadiah delicately bit into an apple. "Many people are planning my death tonight."

"And yet you remain so goddamned calm!"

I recognized the other man; the chief surgeon from Arden.

"She'll be here soon, Richard. You should leave."

"I told you," said the other man heavily. "I can escape from the bathroom window exit when I need to; I'm not leaving you. After all we've been through, how you even thought I *would* leave is beyond me."

With my face pressed up to the crack in the door, I watched as Obadiah looked at Richard, his face as refined as I remembered, but his eyes like soft green liquid. "I didn't think you would leave; I hoped. If I die tonight, which is the most likely outcome, I want to die knowing that you are alive and safe."

Richard made a strangled noise and wiped his mouth. "I love you," he said into his fingers. "You know I do; why isn't that enough for you? Why can't you just turn your back on Arden and leave with me? What can you hope to achieve now with this suicidal dream of yours?"

"Suicidal or not, it's still achievable. You knew that it would come to this if Arden was destroyed, Richard. That I would choose this route. Respect my decision; this is my dream, and it will finally be complete, and everything will be worth it. Whether Marilyn kills me, or whether she hears my offer and chooses to kill the other men and GEs instead, it will be worth it. The final stage, the rebirth."

"Yes, I know. I understand you," said the surgeon shakily, returning to his meal. "It was just my foolish dream that one day you'd turn your back on all that and choose me and this life instead."

Obadiah got out of his seat and placed his hands on Richard's shoulders. "You know I love you, Richard. But that means nothing and it conquers nothing. It's just a consolation prize for those who can take nothing else from this world."

"Something I will always disagree with, even if you scorn me for it. For me, love is the only prize worth conquering. Why else would I do all this?" Richard turned up his head to be kissed. As Obadiah bent and gently kissed him, I quietly pushed the door aside and walked in, gun in one hand, dagger and lighter in the other. By the time Obadiah withdrew his head, my knife was pressing against Richard's vulnerable throat. The effect was instantaneous; Richard gasped and jolted back against his seat, and Obadiah backed up, his slender hands raised in the air.

"Marilyn," he breathed. "Marilyn, you don't understand, listen to me."

"No!" I spun and kicked over the table; the table and food went crashing to the floor. I backed up and pointed the gun at Obadiah's head while keeping the dagger at Richard's throat.

"I deserve to die," said Obadiah unflinchingly as he stared at where he thought my eyes were. "I failed you and myself. Wrong investors, wrong choices, flawed scientists."

"No," I snarled, abandoning Richard and striding up closer to Obadiah as he moved back against the bed. "No, you deserve to die because of what you did to the others, to me and the others, and all for the sake of what? Money? Business? Some insane idea you cooked up one day?"

He said nothing.

"Say something!" I brandished the lighter, knowing one flick....

Ayer cleared his throat and closed his eyes. "What I did is nothing I'm ashamed of. I helped others who were special, like myself, who should be able to overcome all the entrapments of this unfair, pathetically mundane world and achieve greatness. Morality, loyalty, money, family, society, it's all designed to keep you entrapped, and I was freeing you. Now Marilyn, put away your emotions and make your final decision. Either kill me now and submit to the Knight's entrapment of you, or else listen to what I have to say and let me completely free you...the final stage. Become the Angel of Vengeance, winged, perfect, and finally as I created you...free."

"You're not God!"

"Says who? You? Who are you? God?"

I didn't move; he'd taken control from me again. I could feel my heart rate increasing, a tightness in my chest as it struggled, locked into its electrical pattern. Surging up in my mind's eye were my mum's emerald eyes, lifeless, Jason tied up on the bed, Levi and Jaid gone, Clodagh dead, me trapped in the white room. But in the corner of my vision I could see Richard, watching us with tear-stained cheeks, and in front of me, I could see the madman who had been controlling me all this time, whey-faced as he backed closer and closer to the bed and the unconscious prickly dark head of Jason.

"No." I said simply, and I let the gun and dagger drop to the ground. "You can be a god of nothing; I withdraw. I'm taking Jason and getting out of here. Fuck you."

"Ref-ffusal Affirmative," said Teddy Goldberg behind me, and as I turned he emptied the gun twice into both my shoulders. I hit the wall, falling down amid spirals of pain and crimson blood apparently appearing from nowhere. "Affirmative: I-I-I am the strong-gggest GE."

I stared up in dizzy horror at the thin youth who had once been Teddy as he kept his gun trained on me. His hair had nearly all fallen out since I last saw him, and what was left of it was baby-fine and white. His once baby-shaped face was skeletal and lopsided, half frozen, while his wide, protruding flashing red eyes were filthy with irises of grey metal and electronic sparks running around the corneas. One eyelid was drooped, spasming, the other open too wide. A sheen of ashen sweat covered his face, and the entire back and side of his skull was metal. His hands were covered in wiring where the veins should've been. The way he stood, he appeared to have a tic in one side of his head; he couldn't keep it from moving. His spine was unnaturally straight, one leg awkwardly placed before the other like a puppet...or a robot.

"Timetime of arrivallll was ten min-minutes ahead of pred-preddd-d-diction," Teddy said, his jerky voice piercingly high and metallic, and I could hear his head whistling and humming. His inhuman eyes locked onto mine as he lowered the gun to exactly where my right knee was. Half his top lip stretched up, but the bottom failed to follow the movement.

"Ddddidn't I t-tell you the per-percenttages?" he grinded out. "Nowww it is to-oo late."

I prepared to die.

CHAPTER TWELVE

"Intelligence, wait" said Harold Wrexham as he stepped through the door behind Teddy. He peered sideways at Obadiah Ayer, motionless beside the bed, and started to chuckle. "Intelligence was brilliant, of course, so congratulations," he said to Obadiah. "Works perfectly, despite a few emotional glitches that had to be taken care of. Still, it managed to locate the Avenging Angel, even without Shäfer's help. Good work, Diah! Unfortunately, your role is now over, partner. Any last words?"

"What?" asked Ayer.

"No!" I screamed from the ground as Teddy shot Obadiah in the head. Blood splattered back over the bed and the sleeping figure of Jason as Obadiah crumpled to the floor, dead. Barely a second later, there was another BANG as Richard collapsed onto the floor a few feet away, blood seeping out onto the carpet.

There was silence as Teddy swung the gun back to me and I lay still. His eyes were going frantic, the pupils vibrating, and I couldn't tell if he was looking at me or not. Wrexham swept his eyes over where I was lying against my warm blood.

"Now, Marilyn, if you wouldn't mind finding out where Ayer has hidden your wings, we can get to the business of collecting the needed genetic and electronic parts from you and leave before George recovers and starts causing trouble."

"Wh-what?" It was hard to hear with both my arms burning in murky pain.

"You heard me."

"Why do you need me to find the wings?"

Wrexham looked impatient. "There is a device in your spine to make sure you can always trace your wings. Intelligence, activate."

I cried out as Teddy bent down and with his metal hand, jerked my head down and stuck his finger in the side of the metal hole in my shoulder blade, switching something. Instantly I could hear a faint beeping noise in my ear, and it seemed to be emitting from the bathroom.

"Can you hear it?" Wrexham asked.

My immediate reaction was to lie, but instead, I said, "Yes...it hurts my head."

"Get up and lead us to them."

Unsteadily I rose to my feet, my arms hanging painfully at my side, muscles screaming, but managed to keep the lighter clutched in my fist. "I think they are downstairs."

"Bodily symptommms indic-dicate lie."

"It's through the door! I'll prove it to you!"

Teddy's eyes and gun were fixed on me, the pupils juddering as I crossed painfully slowly over to the door. There was a trail of blood behind me as I walked onto the landing, the beeping in my ear getting higher-pitched as I walked in the wrong direction. Teddy's eyes flickered between me and the blood as he walked out behind me, as he saw everything and processed and calculated.

"Ddddo not try an-dd fight or ffff-flee," he ordered. "Based on a-llllocation of heat, air move-m-ment, blood, room layout, per-personal profilllling, history, and physical —

needs, I can call-calculllate every every move you m-ake second-ds before you've maddde it."

Wrexham and Teddy followed me out into the hallway. The beeping noise in my head was getting fainter and fainter.

In the hallway, I could smell the gas laced in with the air. I carried on, walking past the stairs, and then as Wrexham followed me, I darted to the side and heaved him down the stairs. Inhumanely quickly, Teddy stepped to the side and allowed Wrexham to flail and fall, and he fired the gun at where I was standing. However, I had already flung myself down the stairs after Wrexham, to hit the bottom on top of him with a crunch. There was a slight delay as Teddy processed this strange movement before he started down the stairs, shooting. I yanked at the carpet rug and Teddy tumbled down to the bottom on top of Wrexham as I scrambled back up the stairs. He easily grabbed my leg and pulled me back to the ground, where I landed flat on my face. As I tried to get away, he dragged me back off my feet and, ducking my head butt, side-stepping the knee to the groin, blocked my escape and hit me hard in the solar plexus. I fell to the ground and he methodically stamped on my head. Blood blinded my eyes.

"Teddy," I groaned as he kicked me in the chest and I nearly blacked out in pain.

In the end, it was George who saved my life. Both of us heard the window in the kitchen smash as George heaved himself through, and for a second Teddy's reactions were delayed as he paused to process the unpredicted force entering. In that second, I kicked up into Teddy's face, leapt up, and ran up the stairs. As Teddy started up after me, I grabbed the lighter from the floor, flicked it into life, and flung it down at Teddy and Wrexham.

BOOM

I raced into the bedroom, slamming the door against the blossoming flames.

"Jason!" I yelled. Something gave me strength as I heaved Jason into my arms, the pain immense as I dragged him into the en suite bathroom, locking the door behind us. He was stirring as I looked for the escape route Richard had mentioned. The window was surrounded by black corrugated metal; outside on the wall was an attached electrical pole to climb down. I would never be able to climb down with Jason. I could barely support my own weight now, all my energy gone. I pushed Jason against the toilet as I despairingly tried to figure out what to do.

My wings, find my wings.

The bathroom door burst open and Teddy stood in the doorway, twisting red flames behind him, and his face a bloody, burnt mess, red eyes flickering and whirling and head ticking frantically. Some of the wiring and metal from his head and hands had come loose, hanging down his neck with flesh and thick gloopy blood. His eyes travelled past mine, and for the first time I saw the pair of folded glossy black feathers and dull metal spilling out of the cabinet to my side. My wings.

"Explllosion to occ-occur in 1:02:41 ti-me," said Teddy, and he stepped forward. But something was wrong; only one of his eyes was on me, the other was turned inwards. His other leg moved in a separate direction, halting him. He tried again to walk, but turned left and hit the wall, then turned to face the other side. "Ide-dentified M-M-Marilyn Aske," he juddered. "Iden - IdM-M-Marilyn Dentify Dent Marilyn Marilyn, friennnd. Teddy. Teddy?" He attempted to move and instead his hands shot out into the wall. I heard both wrists snap; he wheeled around to face me. I looked into

Teddy's eyes, searching for the boy I'd known in Arden. Trying to find a trace of him left inside that metal skull.

"Teddy?" I whispered.

"I-I-I am 87% still Teddy." His voice caught on the last word, and began to vibrate, "Teddy Teddy Teddy Teddy." His eyes searched around the bathroom for me. His broken hand shot out into the bathroom, and he spun and hit the other wall.

Sensing my opportunity, I clutched the feathers and pulled them out of the cabinet to me. Feathers spilt down my invisible forearms in an intricate design, and the metal wiring and fasteners stuck out like knifes to fit into my shoulders and spine. I twisted, found the metal in my shoulders, and pushed the wing electronics towards it. The metal retracted up into the bone, making me groan with pain, and as the wire entered the prepared slots in my skin, electricity and shock coursed through my vertebrae, my veins being scraped, the blood lit up from within. I jammed them deep into my central nervous system, feeling it all link up, and heard some grinding and whirring as the metal clicked and twisted within me, until suddenly it was connected properly. I had wings. I flexed my shoulder blades and the wings spread out behind me, though they were invisible in the mirror. Elated, I turned to Teddy, moving my wings, and muscle, sinew, metal, and mechanics moving in tandem. There was another bang, and I heard furniture and roofing collapsing outside.

"Teddy, how do we all get out of here?" I yelled. "I can't fly carrying Jason!"

"Essssscape ess-ecape Teddy helllp me me me me," Teddy told the broken, blood smeared wall as he walked into it again and again, turned around, and walked into the bath. I began to haul Jason to the window, slapping his face to try and wake him.

"Teddy, you can get through the window, too," I cried through the heat and smoke, not sure why I was delaying as the house collapsed around us. I leaned out for Teddy's hand and he shifted, placing my hand on the wiring at the back of his head. He was still moving back and forth.

"Help me." There was no fear in his eyes as they searched for me, grinding my hand into his wired skull.

"Teddy," I cried over the sounds of shattering glasses, the crash of the stairs caving in below us.

"Plllllease," he grated, keeping my hand on the back of his head. "Plllllease memememe essss-escape. Hellllp Mar-Marilyn."

I started to cry, rocking from foot to foot, letting Jason drop fully to the floor. "I can't, Teddy. I'm not like they wanted me to be; this is destroying me. I'm not strong, I'm weak. I can't see one more person die. I can't take any of this."

"I'm not a-a-a person anymore." One of his eyes found me. "Help me."

Sobbing, I pulled the wires in his head free, just as Jason staggered upright, supporting himself against the wall. We both watched as the light sputtered out from Teddy's eyes, and his mouth attempted to form words that would never be heard.

Smoke was filling the bathroom and wrapping itself up over Teddy's body. I turned to Jason. His eyes were dull and confused as he looked around, and I all but pushed him out the window. As he instinctively held onto the iron and half slid, half fell down, I clambered out after him and hurtled myself into the air.

For a second I thought I was falling, but then my wings beat upwards, and I was going higher.

When the explosion came, billowing up all around me in a furious wave of hot anger, it buffeted me higher several meters, my skin electrified and insulated with the heat.

Circling up higher and higher until I felt safe, I at last looked down at the house. Gritty fire streamed out of the top floor windows, orange ribbon flames dancing around inside the bathroom, oddly muted under the overpowering sun-washed sky. I looked down at the front of the house as a figure burst out of the ground floor window, glittering shards of glass pouring out around his body and sticking in his skin like diamonds. George rolled along the ground, coughing, before surging to his feet and running around to the back of the house. Blood streaked his filthy clothes as he appeared to be searching for something, yelling, looking upwards at the fire and smoke everywhere. Jason had already disappeared. As I lay suspended in the pure air, like a dream from above, I watched George, still coughing from the flames and smoke, dodging the roofing and stone falling from the house as he scaled up the pole to the bathroom window, trying to get to me. Another explosion made him fall back down to the ground. But there was too much smoky fire for anyone to get in or out, and he just stood on the ground, staring upwards for a long time.

I was glad he'd survived.

In the end, freedom called me like a faint breeze of fresh air, and I beat my wings, propelling myself higher, out away from the blood and smoke and fire and endless death. I was invincible, bathing in beautiful clear, clean streams of crystal and gold sky. I didn't look at the world below as I glided through the atmosphere, alone and complete.

CHAPTER THIRTEEN

"The four victims who died in the savage arson attack in State College, Pennsylvania have been identified as British citizens Marilyn Aske, Edward Stanley Goldberg, Richard Flannigan, and American citizen Obadiah Ayer. All bodies were buried at their respective local churches in small private ceremonies."

***

I flew for hours before returning to the ground world. I landed in a softly lush garden, overgrown with rosemary, lilac, hollyhock, and thyme. It was only then that I realized my cut feet were still dripping garnet blood onto the green grass. I had left a small trail falling behind me as I flew away, like Hansel and Gretel's breadcrumbs.

But would he follow?

I forced my heart to switch back until I could see my bare toes again, pallid flesh against the rich earth. In front of me a beautiful garden fountain softly gurgled, its cold water trickling over smooth stones and white marble to spill over the edges of the stone to the crystal clear pool below. I walked across to the small water monument, clean grass crunching under my feet and wings brushing down my bare back, and regarded the water.

Sweet dreams till sunbeams find you,
Sweet dreams that leave all worries far behind you.

I dipped my feet into the bubbling cool water, and found I was smiling to myself as the frothing water washed away all the blood and dirt.

But in your dreams, whatever they be,
Dream a little dream of me.

Soon I was too weak to stand, so I sat in the fountain, and then I lay down, the water smoothing away all pain and tears and immersing me in its beautiful watery cradle. I was free. I had nothing, I belonged to no one, I could choose anything. I could be anything. I wasn't sure if it was freedom or failure I could taste sweet on my lips, and I didn't care. I only knew that the fire had been the end of Marilyn Aske, and that I was smiling still, but also sobbing. What now?

"Marilyn?"

I looked up. Jason stood a few feet away from the fountain, his face grey and blank, a wounded soldier as he watched me cry.

He'd followed my breadcrumbs.

He faltered. "Please," he asked. "Marilyn, I...I'm sorry. I need...can we start again? Differently?" He broke off painfully and just stared at me, desperate longing in his eyes.

I stepped out of the fountain, water sluicing down my body onto the grass, and opened my arms. He inhaled raggedly and something came loose within him as he stumbled forward and pulled me tightly against him, bringing his arms around me. As I burrowed into his warmth, arms clenched around his waist, he started to cry silently into my neck. I stroked his bloody hair and ran my clean fingers across his grimy cheeks, then kissed his temple and watched the sky overhead as the pomegranate-stained sun sunk below the moon.

"Come on," I said at last. "We need to find a home."

***

"Stephan Knightley, who identified himself to our reporter as a close friend of Marilyn's, said, 'Marilyn was greatly valued during her life, and her death is an immeasurable loss to the world. But I still feel her presence alive and laughing at us all. I'll see her again one day, I have no doubt.'"

End.

ABOUT THE AUTHOR

R.S. Gardner is a twenty-something year old from England, currently living in New Zealand and backpacking around the world rather than face cold rainy reality. More often than not she can be found with her head in a book at a random train station somewhere.

She has worked in various traumatic jobs, such as law firms, on fishing vessels and doing motel maintenance in the middle of the Australian desert. Hopefully these experiences gave her creative inspiration, if nothing else.

Printed in Great Britain
by Amazon.co.uk, Ltd.,
Marston Gate.